LUCIFERS SWORD
CORRUPTISSIMA REPUBLICA PLURIMAE LEGES
MC
-SAN JOSE-

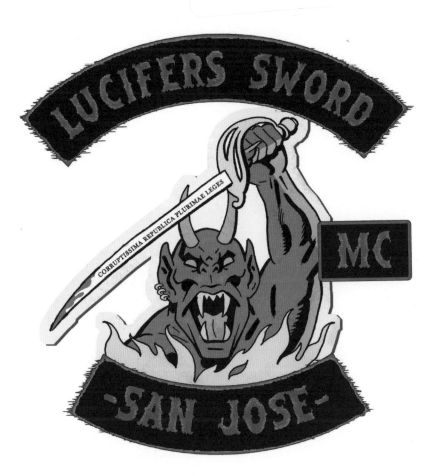

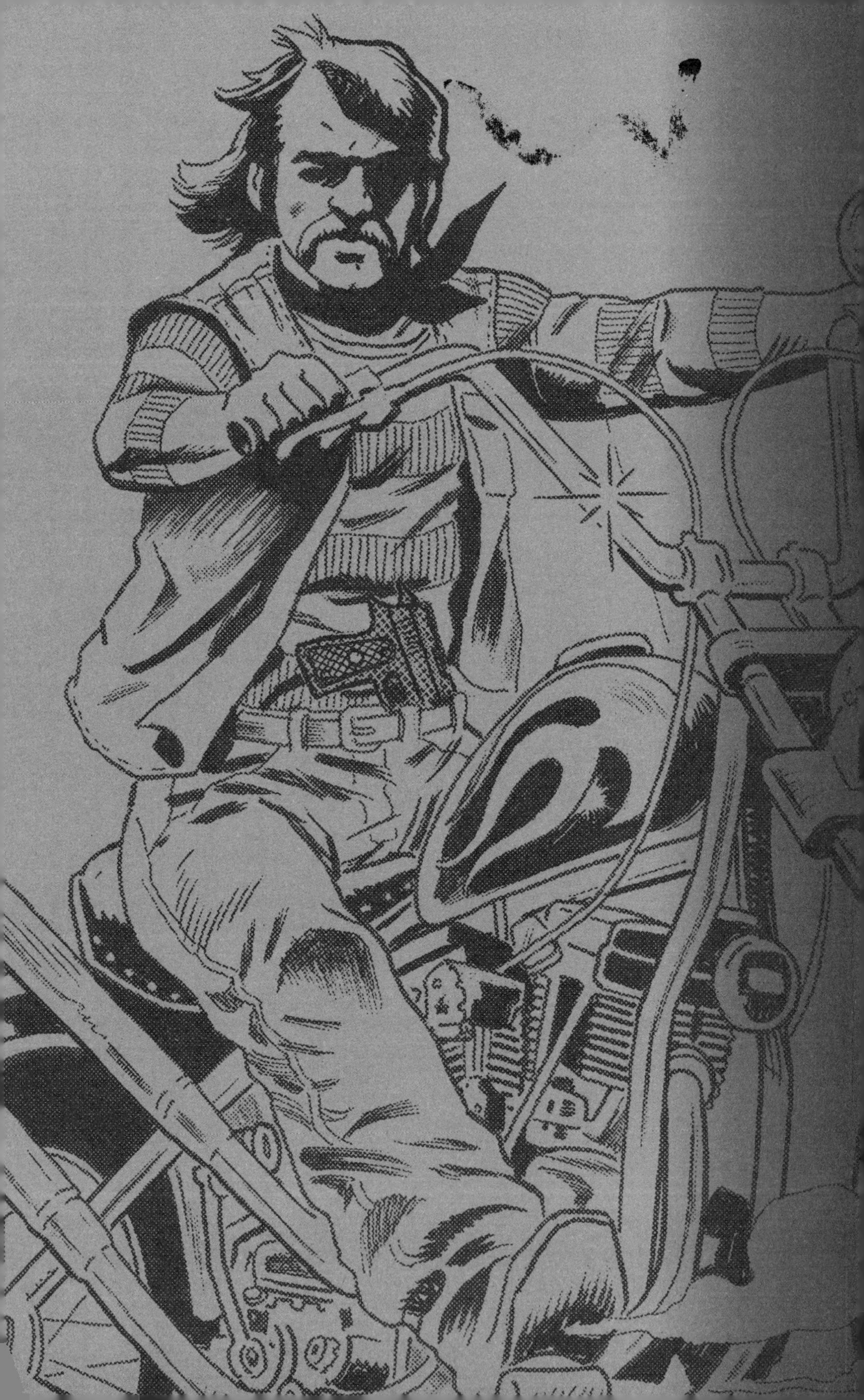

LUCIFERS
SWORD

LIFE AND DEATH
IN AN OUTLAW
MOTORCYCLE CLUB

PHIL CROSS
with Darwin Holmstrom

illustrated by
RONN SUTTON

motorbooks

First published in 2014 by Motorbooks, an imprint of Quarto
Publishing Group USA Inc., 400 First Avenue North, Suite 400,
Minneapolis, MN 55401 USA

Motorbooks titles are also available at discounts in bulk quantity for
industrial or sales-promotional use. For details write to Special Sales
Manager at Quarto Publishing Group USA Inc., 400 First Avenue
North, Suite 400, Minneapolis, MN 55401 USA.

To find out more about our books, visit us online
at www.motorbooks.com.

ISBN: 978-0-7603-4658-7

Senior Editor: Darwin Holmstrom
Project Manager: Jordan Wiklund
Art Director: James Kegley
Layout Designer: Kim Winscher

Printed in China

10 9 8 7 6 5 4 3 2 1

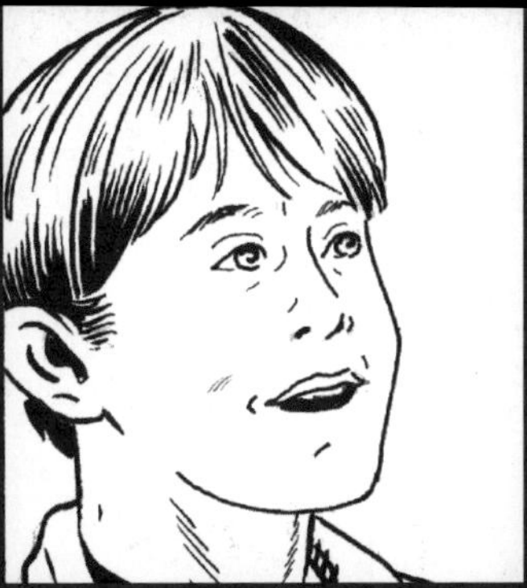

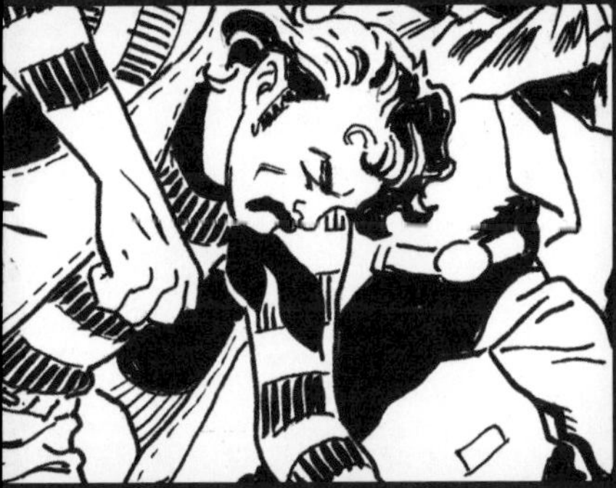

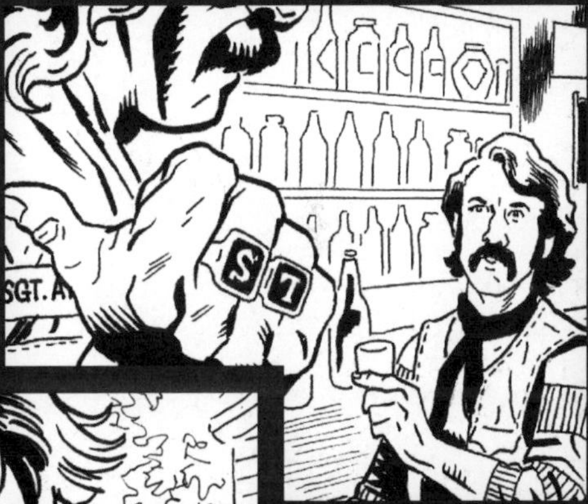

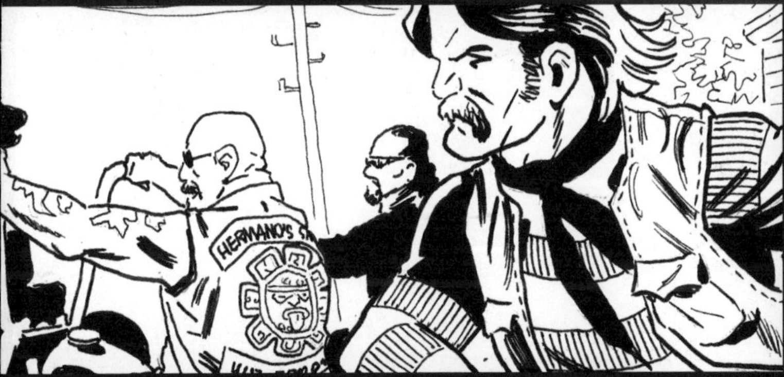

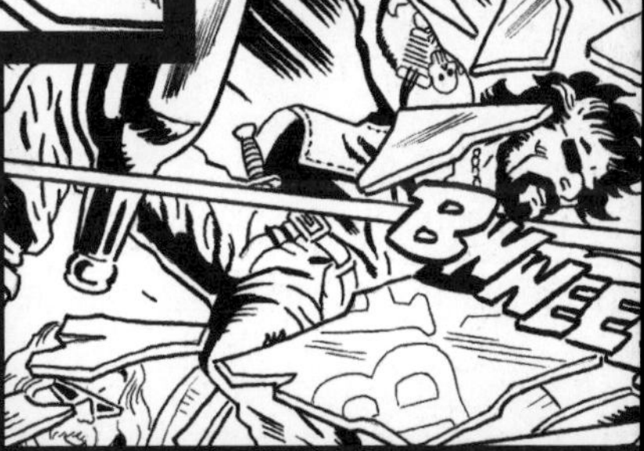

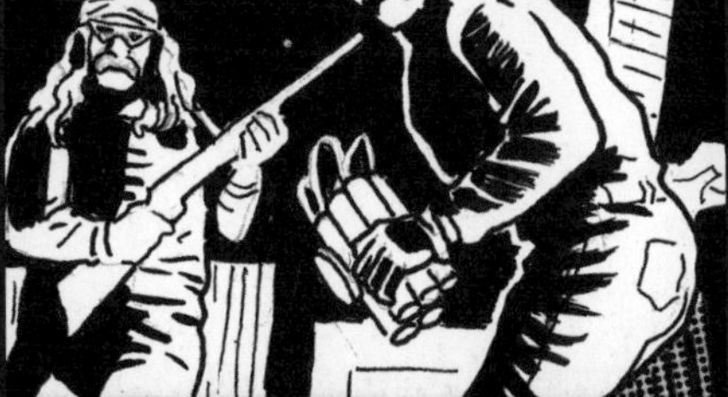

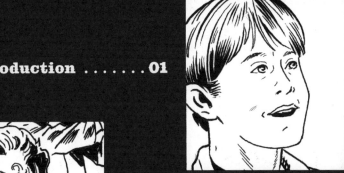

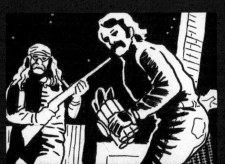

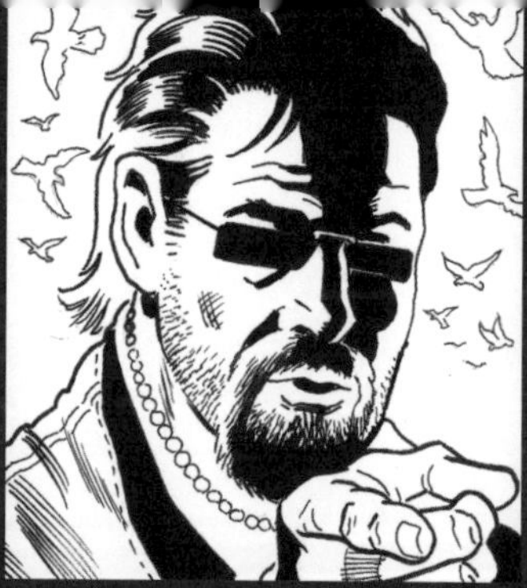

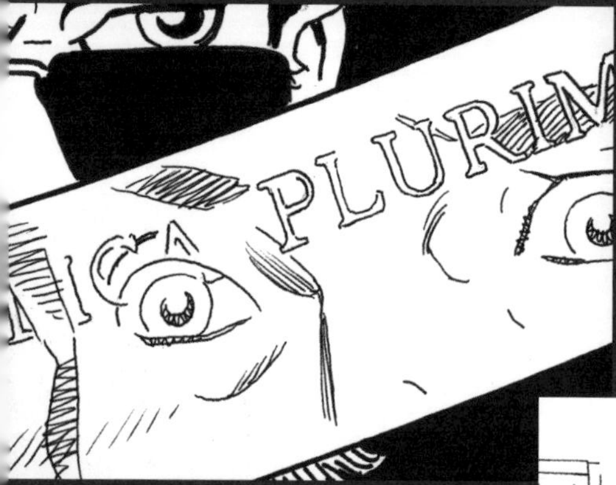

ICA PLURIM

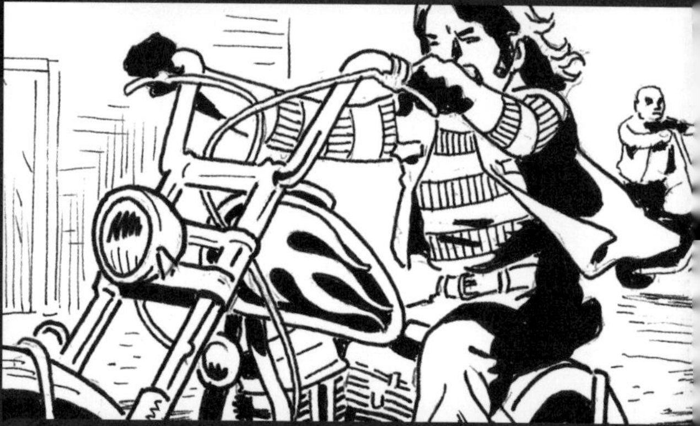

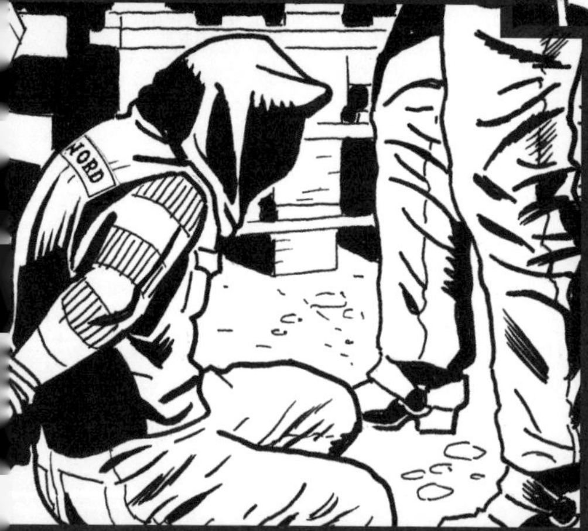

WORD

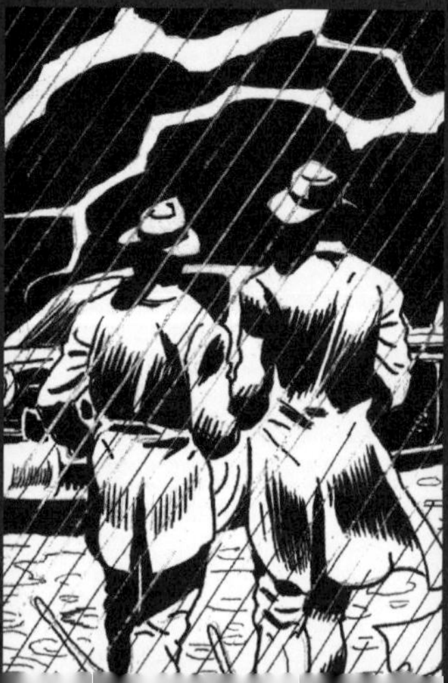

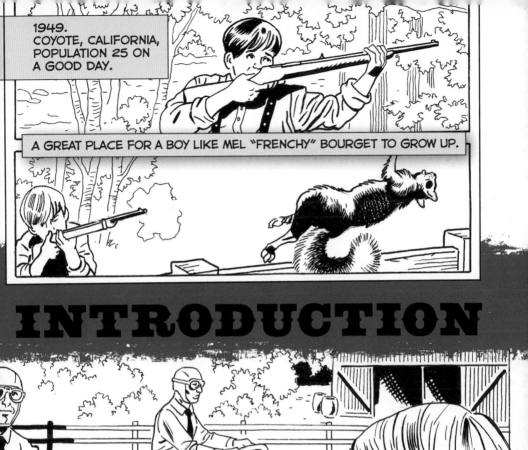

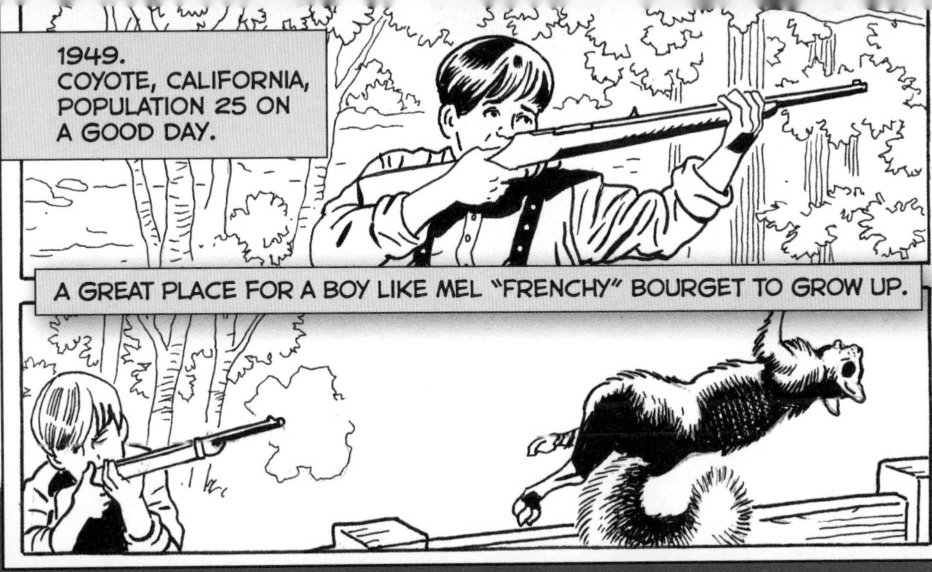
1949.
COYOTE, CALIFORNIA, POPULATION 25 ON A GOOD DAY.
A GREAT PLACE FOR A BOY LIKE MEL "FRENCHY" BOURGET TO GROW UP.

INTRODUCTION

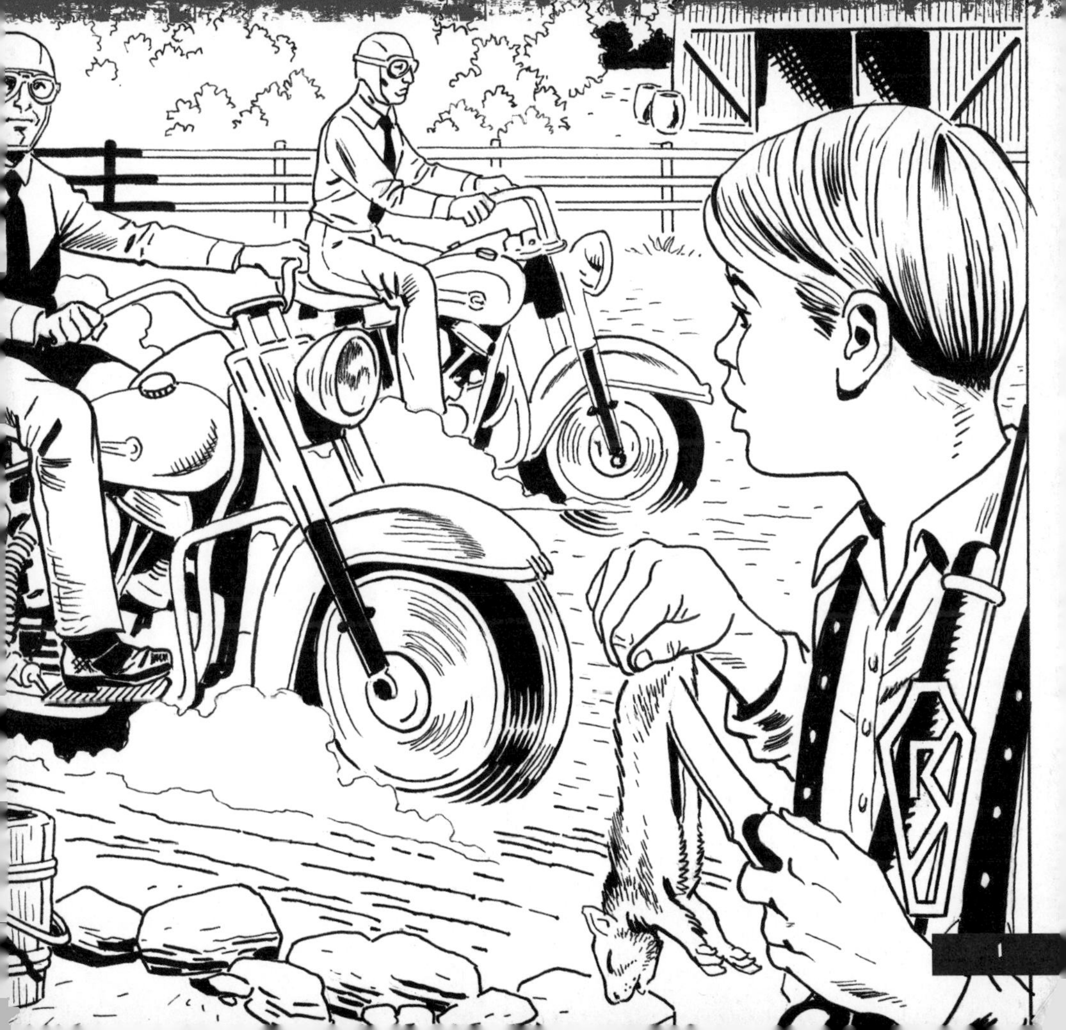

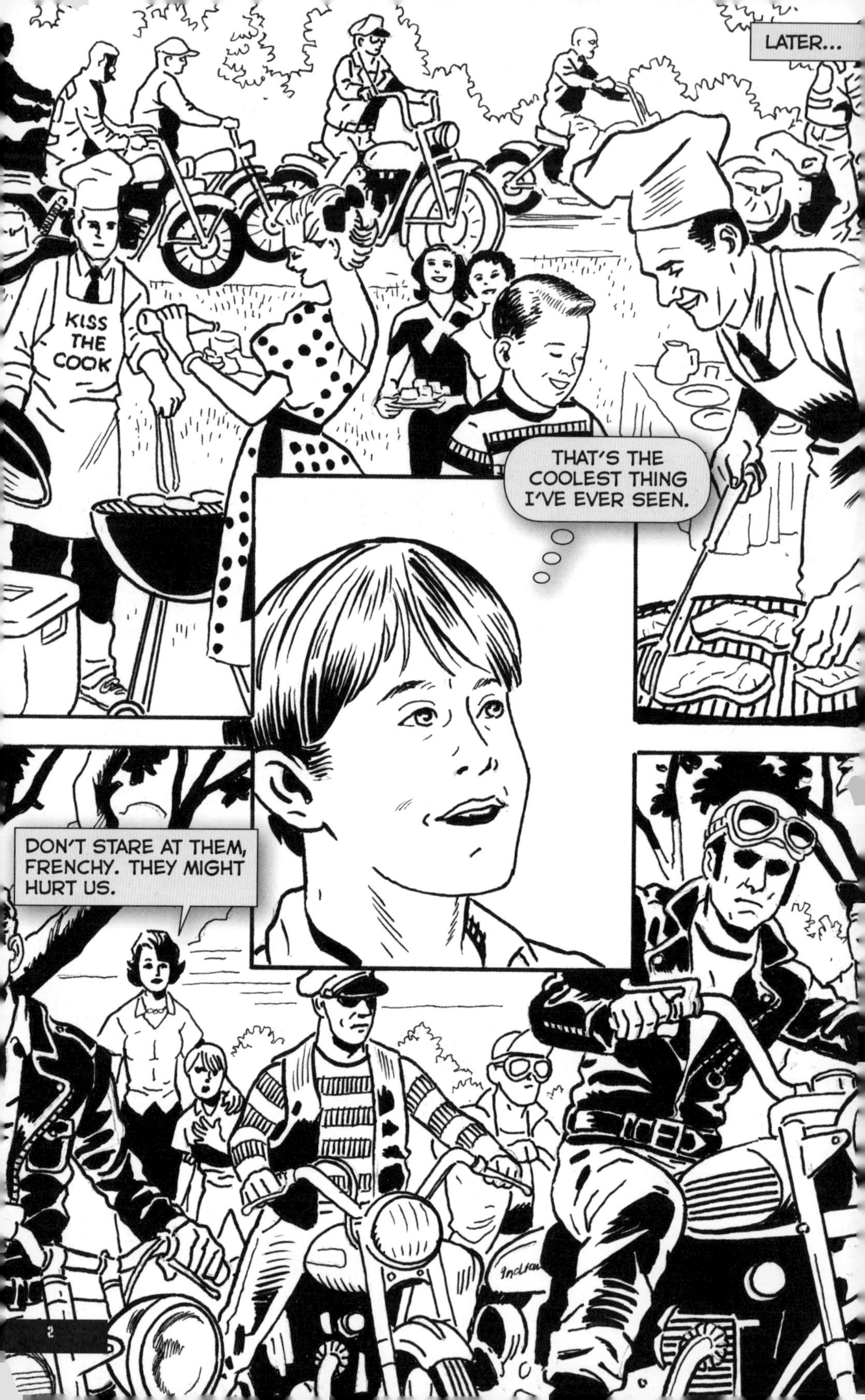
LATER...
KISS THE COOK
THAT'S THE COOLEST THING I'VE EVER SEEN.
DON'T STARE AT THEM, FRENCHY. THEY MIGHT HURT US.

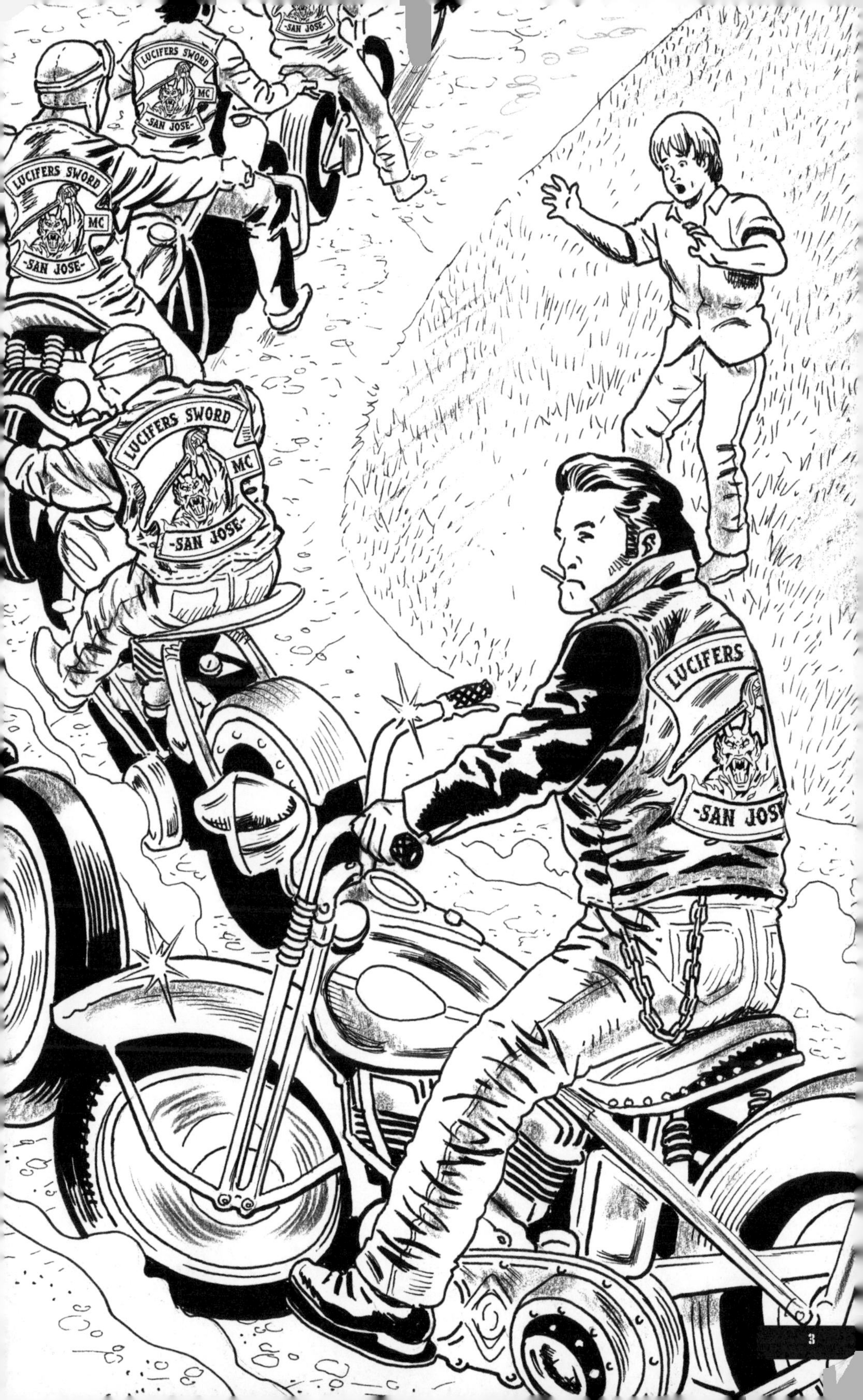

-SAN JOSE-
LUCIFERS SWORD
MC
-SAN JOSE-
LUCIFERS SWORD
MC
-SAN JOSE-
LUCIFERS SWORD
MC
-SAN JOSE-
LUCIFERS
-SAN JOSE

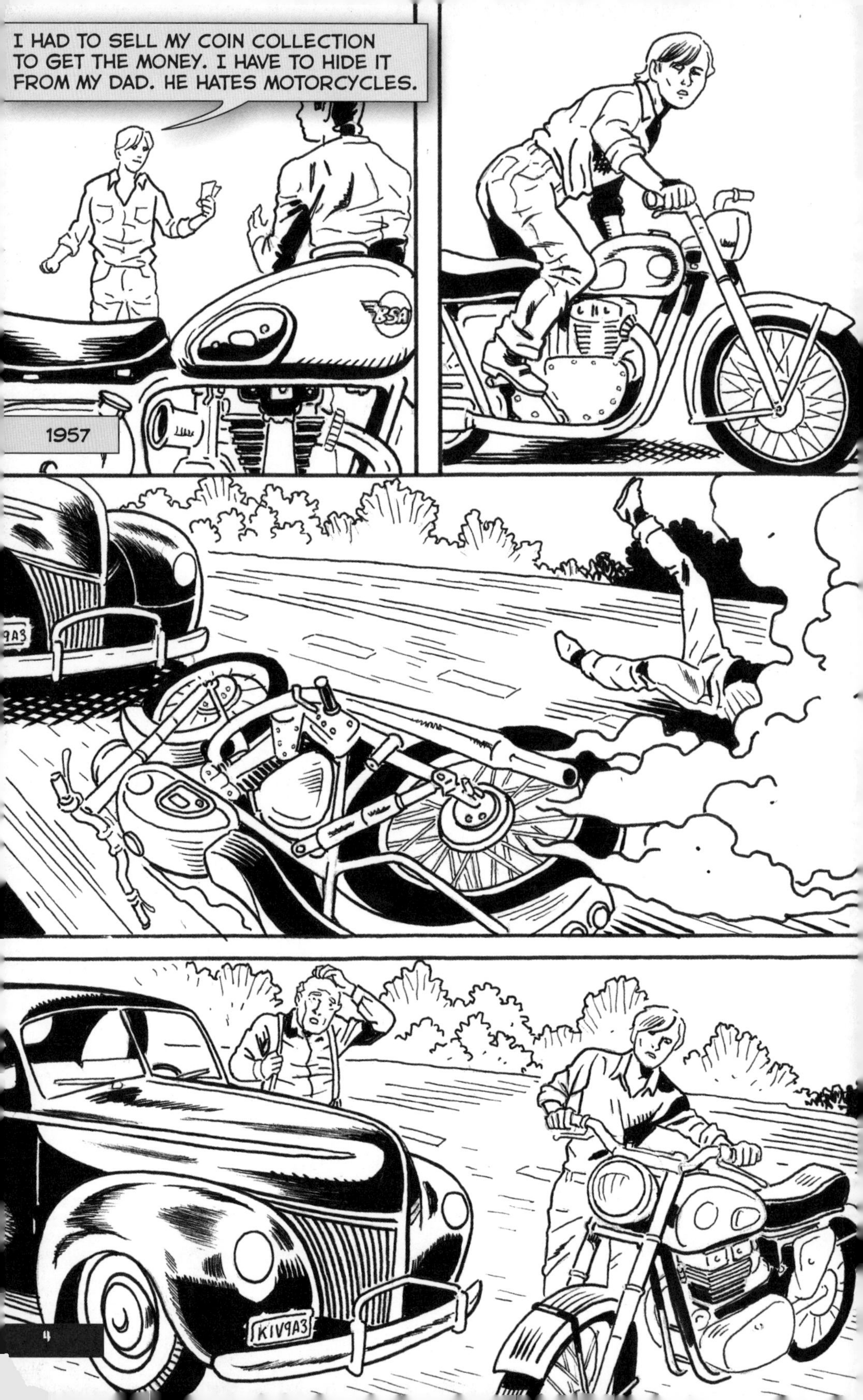
I HAD TO SELL MY COIN COLLECTION TO GET THE MONEY. I HAVE TO HIDE IT FROM MY DAD. HE HATES MOTORCYCLES.
1957
BSA
KIV9A3

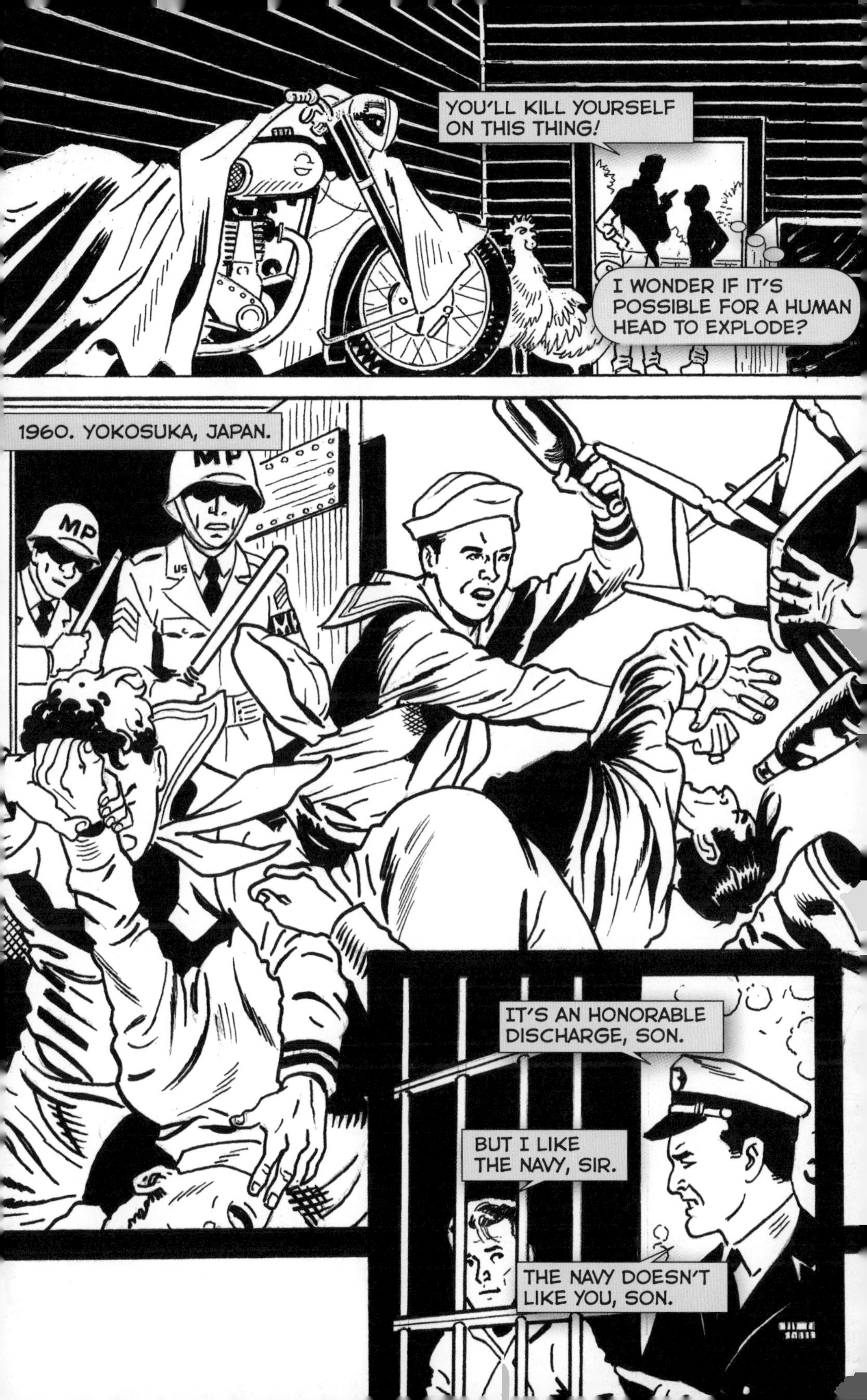
YOU'LL KILL YOURSELF ON THIS THING!
I WONDER IF IT'S POSSIBLE FOR A HUMAN HEAD TO EXPLODE?
1960. YOKOSUKA, JAPAN.
MP
MP
US
IT'S AN HONORABLE DISCHARGE, SON.
BUT I LIKE THE NAVY, SIR.
THE NAVY DOESN'T LIKE YOU, SON.

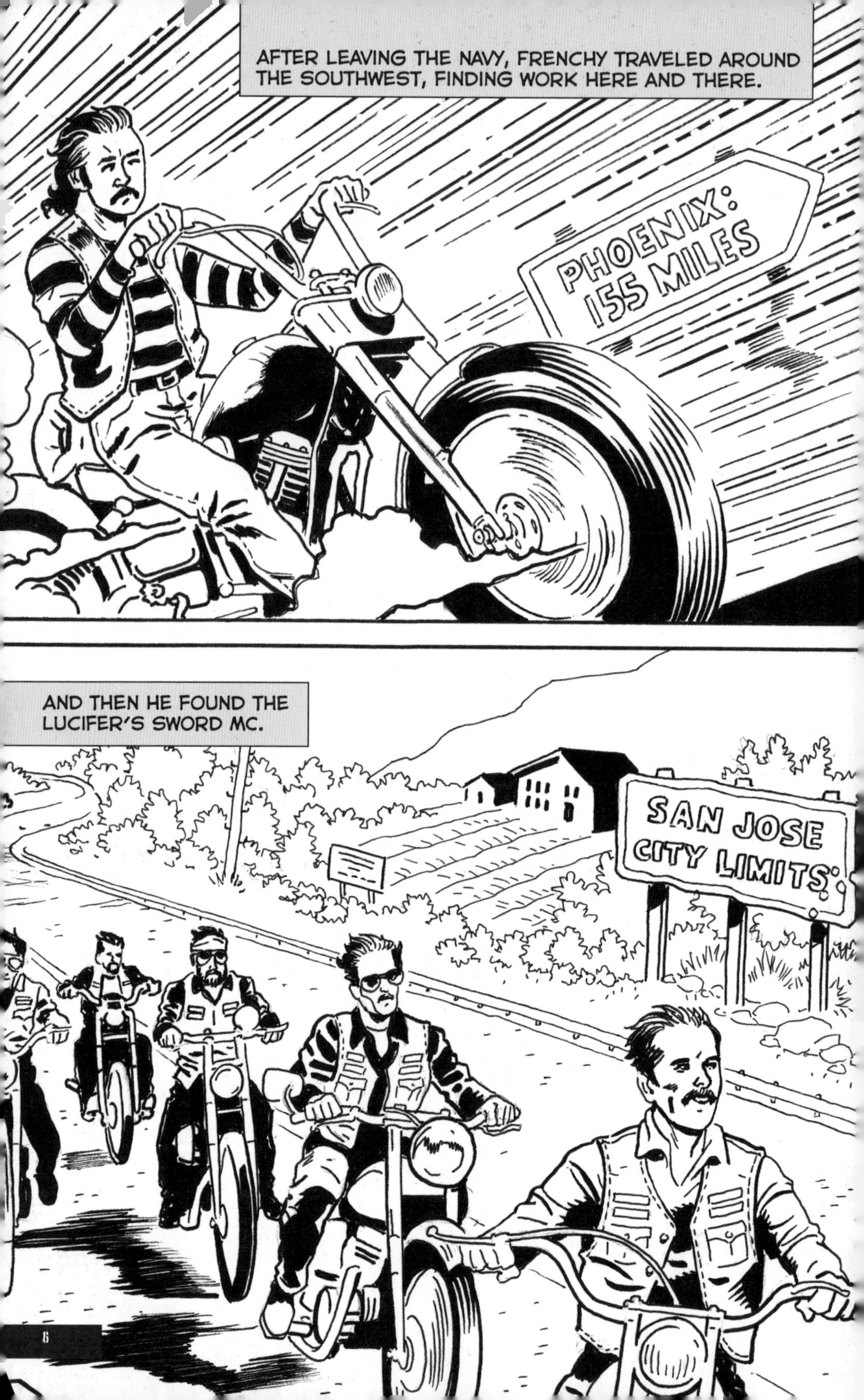
AFTER LEAVING THE NAVY, FRENCHY TRAVELED AROUND THE SOUTHWEST, FINDING WORK HERE AND THERE.
PHOENIX: 155 MILES
AND THEN HE FOUND THE LUCIFER'S SWORD MC.
SAN JOSE CITY LIMITS

LUCIFER'S SWORD MC #1

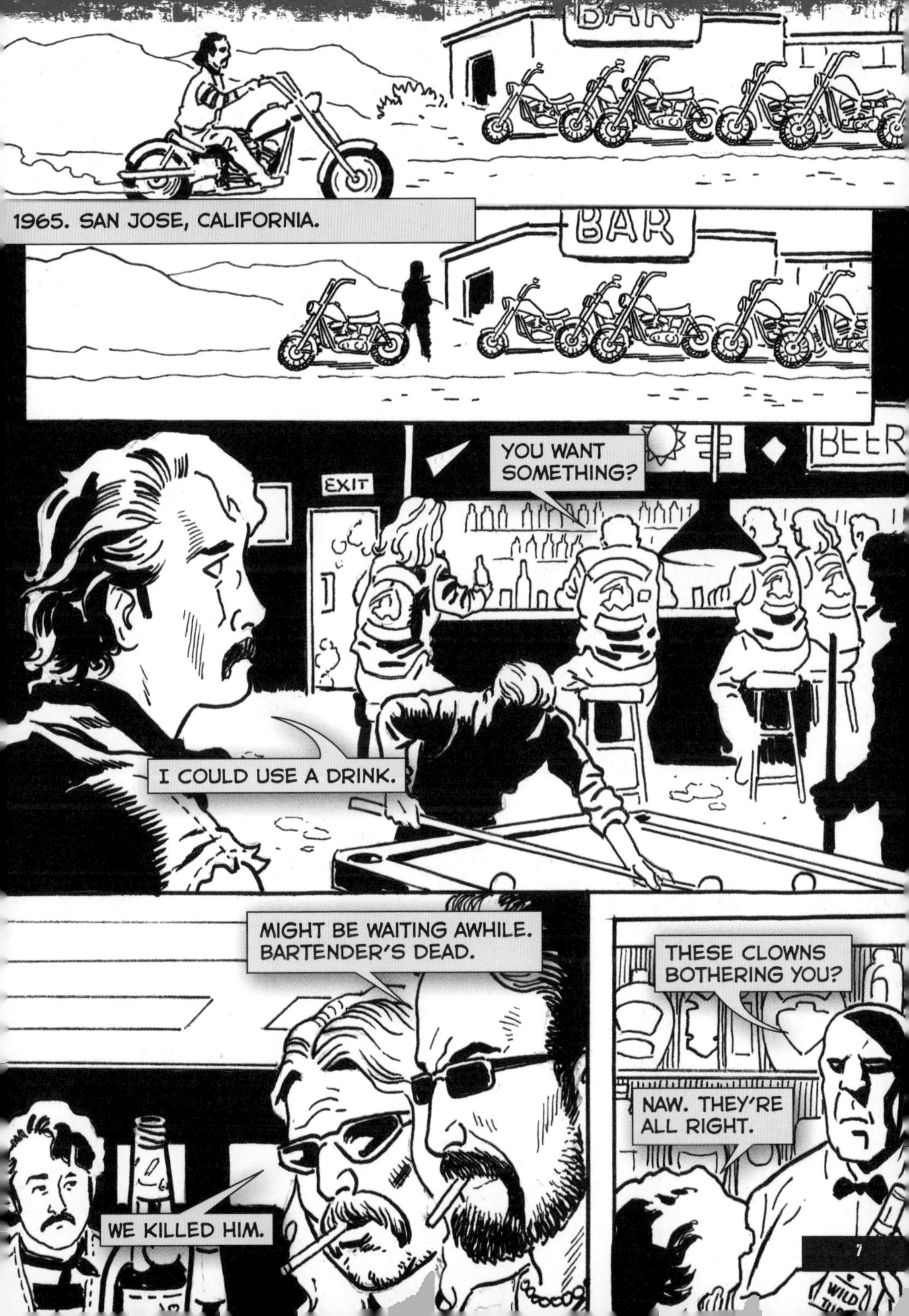
BAR
1965. SAN JOSE, CALIFORNIA.
BAR
EXIT
BEER
YOU WANT SOMETHING?
I COULD USE A DRINK.
MIGHT BE WAITING AWHILE. BARTENDER'S DEAD.
WE KILLED HIM.
THESE CLOWNS BOTHERING YOU?
NAW. THEY'RE ALL RIGHT.

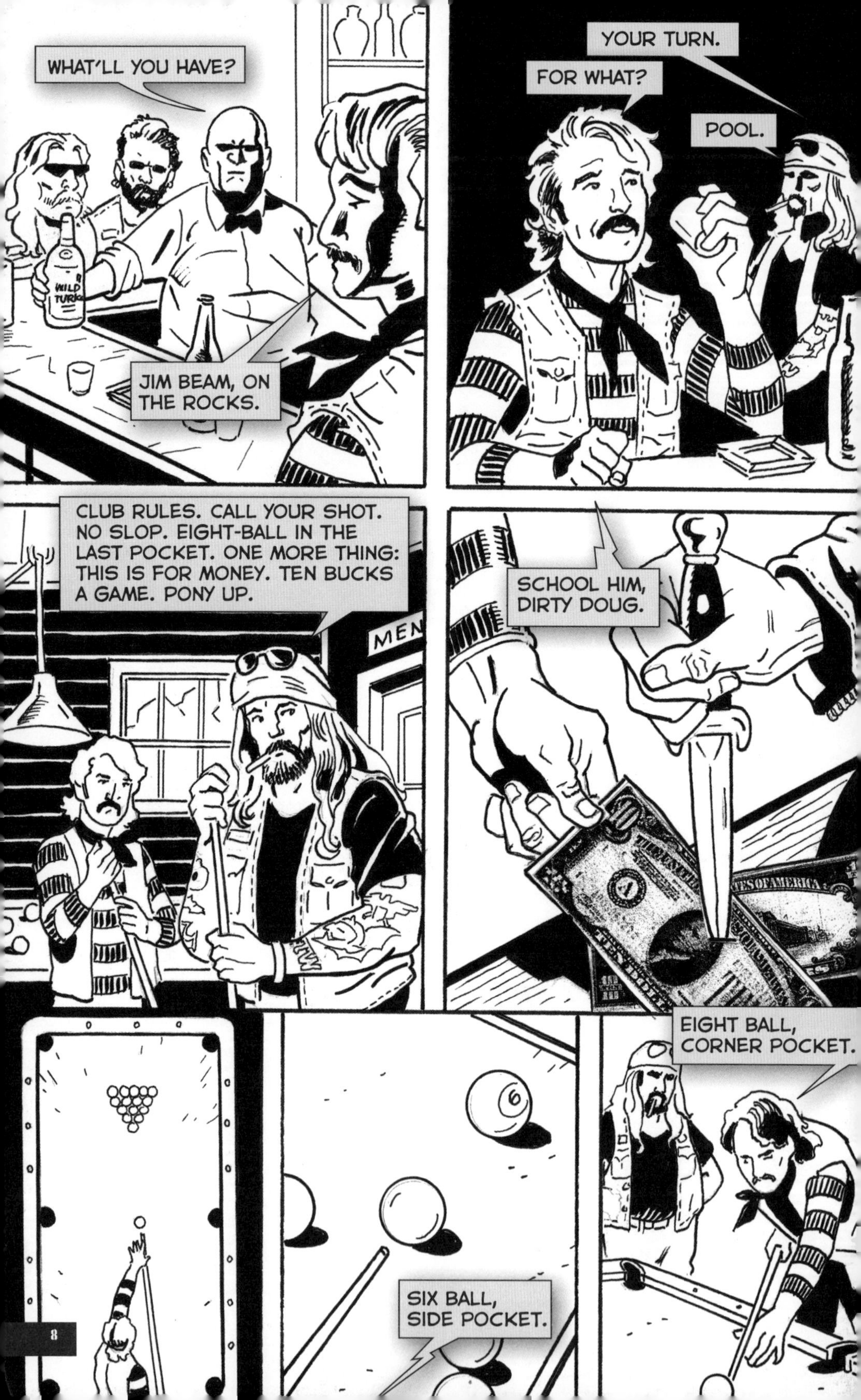
WHAT'LL YOU HAVE?
JIM BEAM, ON THE ROCKS.
YOUR TURN.
FOR WHAT?
POOL.
CLUB RULES. CALL YOUR SHOT. NO SLOP. EIGHT-BALL IN THE LAST POCKET. ONE MORE THING: THIS IS FOR MONEY. TEN BUCKS A GAME. PONY UP.
MEN
SCHOOL HIM, DIRTY DOUG.
SIX BALL, SIDE POCKET.
EIGHT BALL, CORNER POCKET.

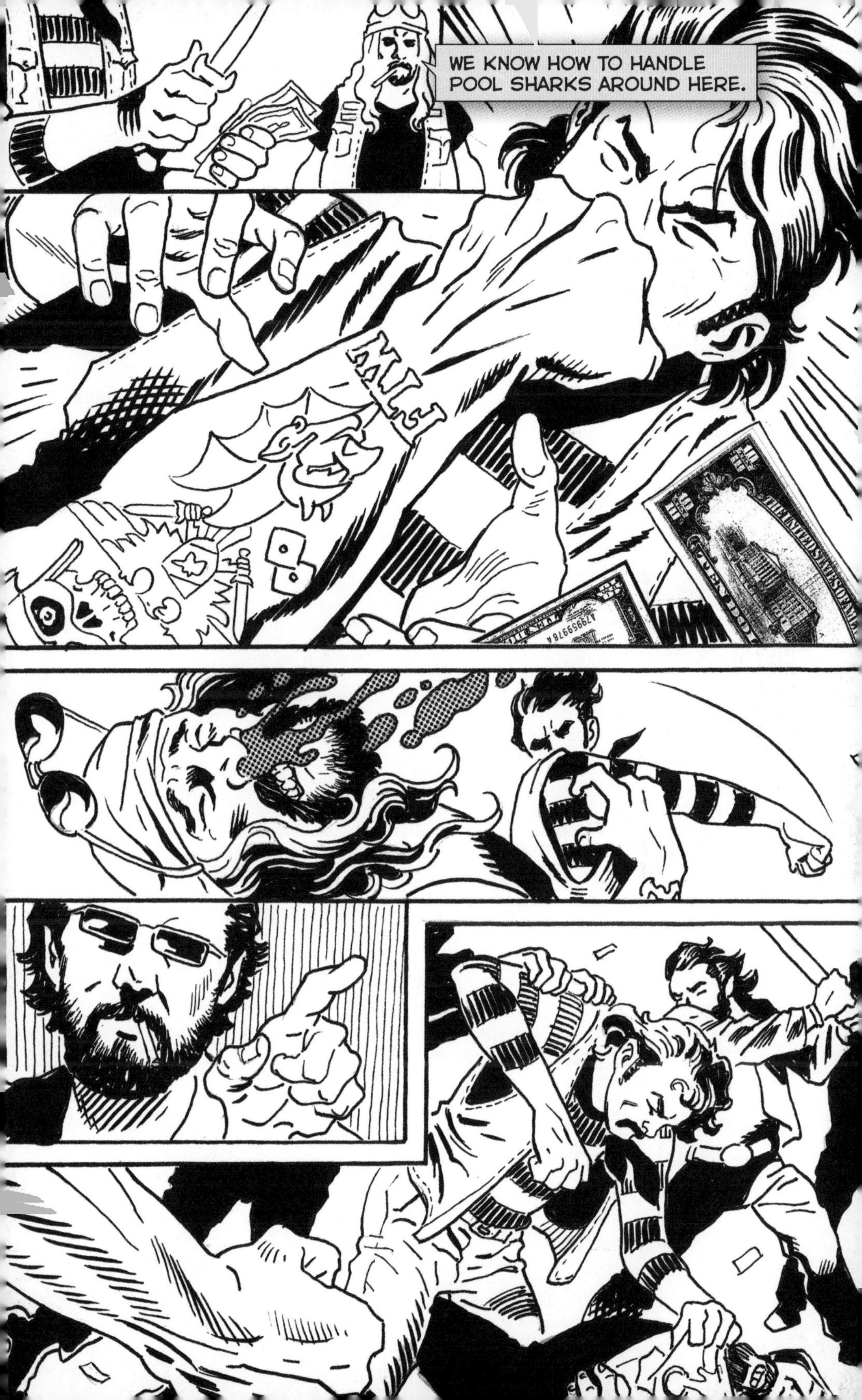
WE KNOW HOW TO HANDLE POOL SHARKS AROUND HERE.

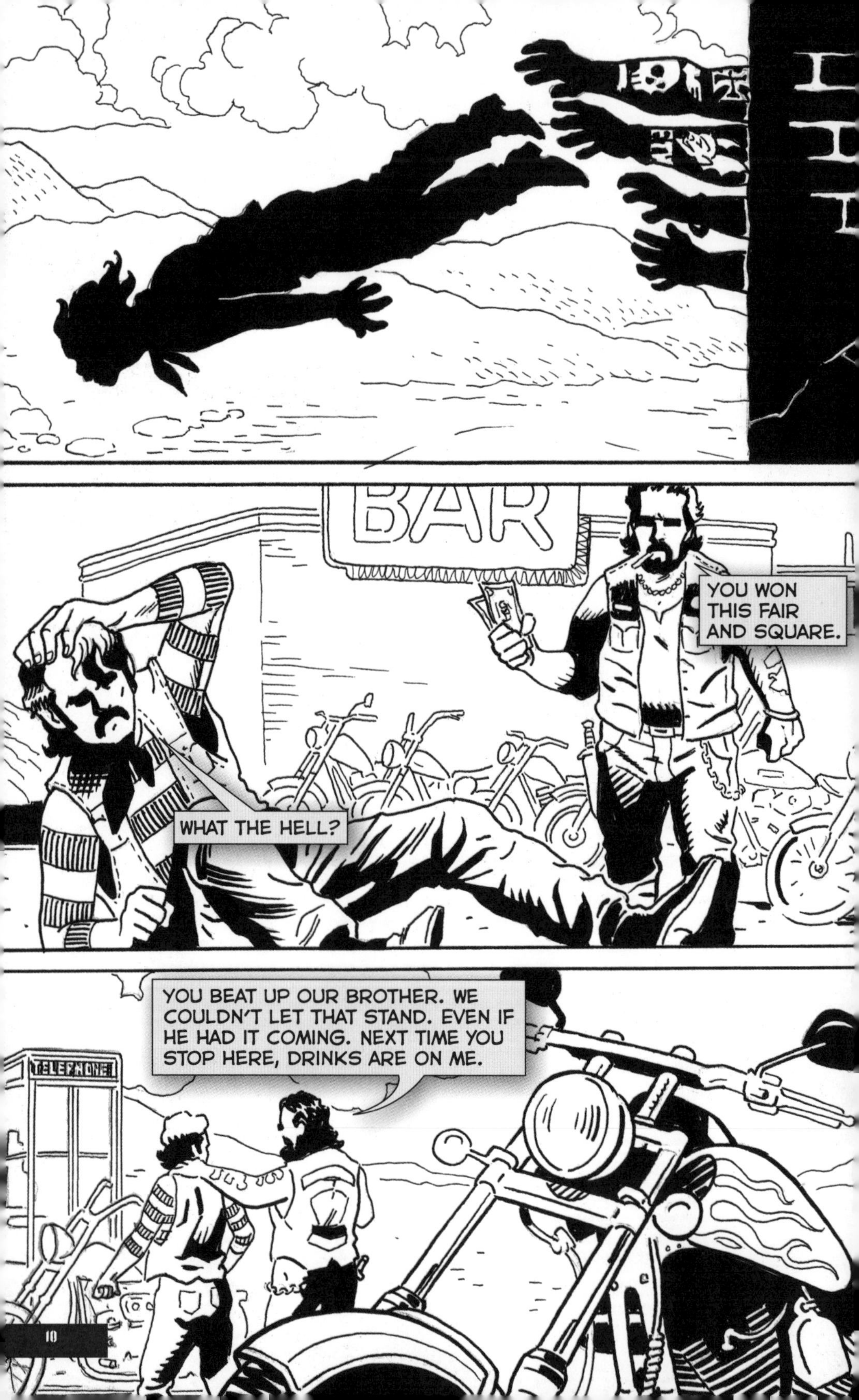
BAR
YOU WON THIS FAIR AND SQUARE.
WHAT THE HELL?
YOU BEAT UP OUR BROTHER. WE COULDN'T LET THAT STAND. EVEN IF HE HAD IT COMING. NEXT TIME YOU STOP HERE, DRINKS ARE ON ME.
TELEPHONE

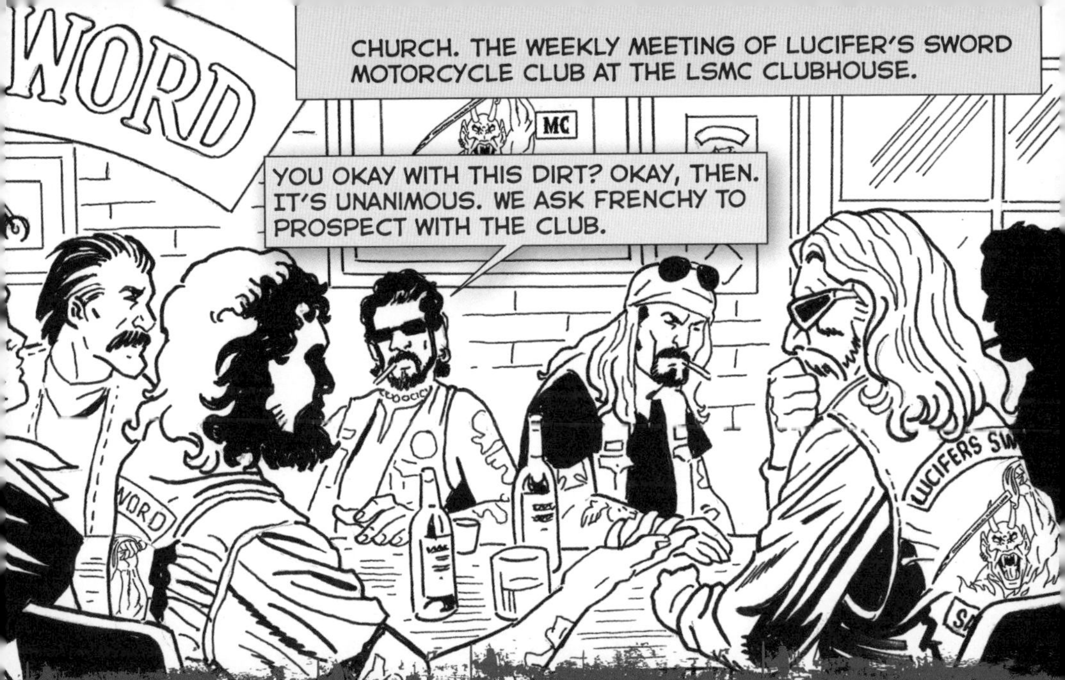
CHURCH. THE WEEKLY MEETING OF LUCIFER'S SWORD MOTORCYCLE CLUB AT THE LSMC CLUBHOUSE.
YOU OKAY WITH THIS DIRT? OKAY, THEN. IT'S UNANIMOUS. WE ASK FRENCHY TO PROSPECT WITH THE CLUB.

THE PROSPECT #2

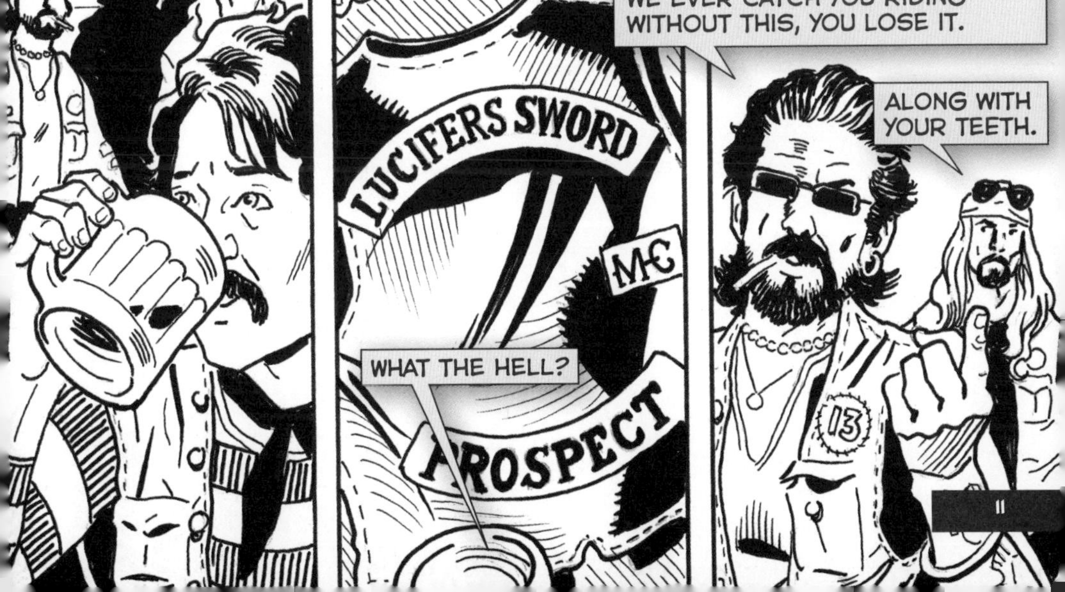
LUCIFERS SWORD
MC
PROSPECT
WHAT THE HELL?
YOU ARE NOW THE LOWEST FORM OF LIFE THAT WE RECOGNIZE: A PROSPECT WITH LUCIFER'S SWORD MOTORCYCLE CLUB. IF WE EVER CATCH YOU RIDING WITHOUT THIS, YOU LOSE IT.
ALONG WITH YOUR TEETH.
13

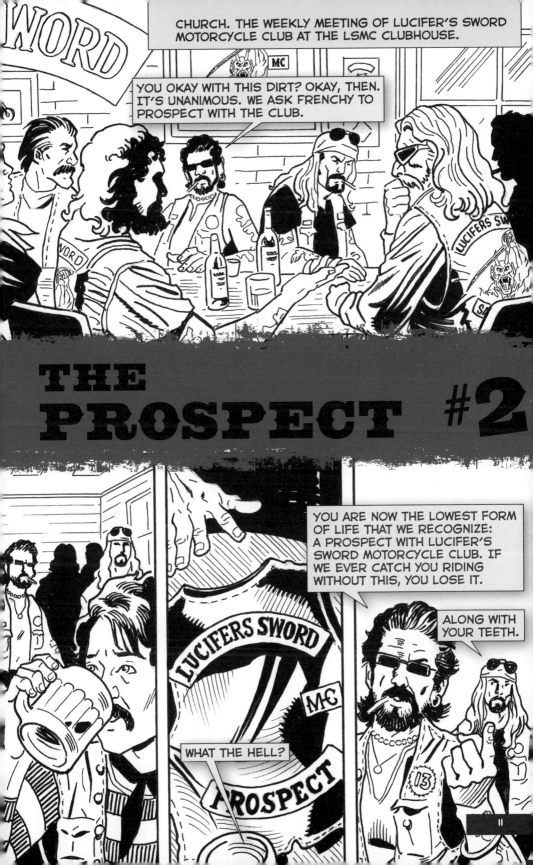

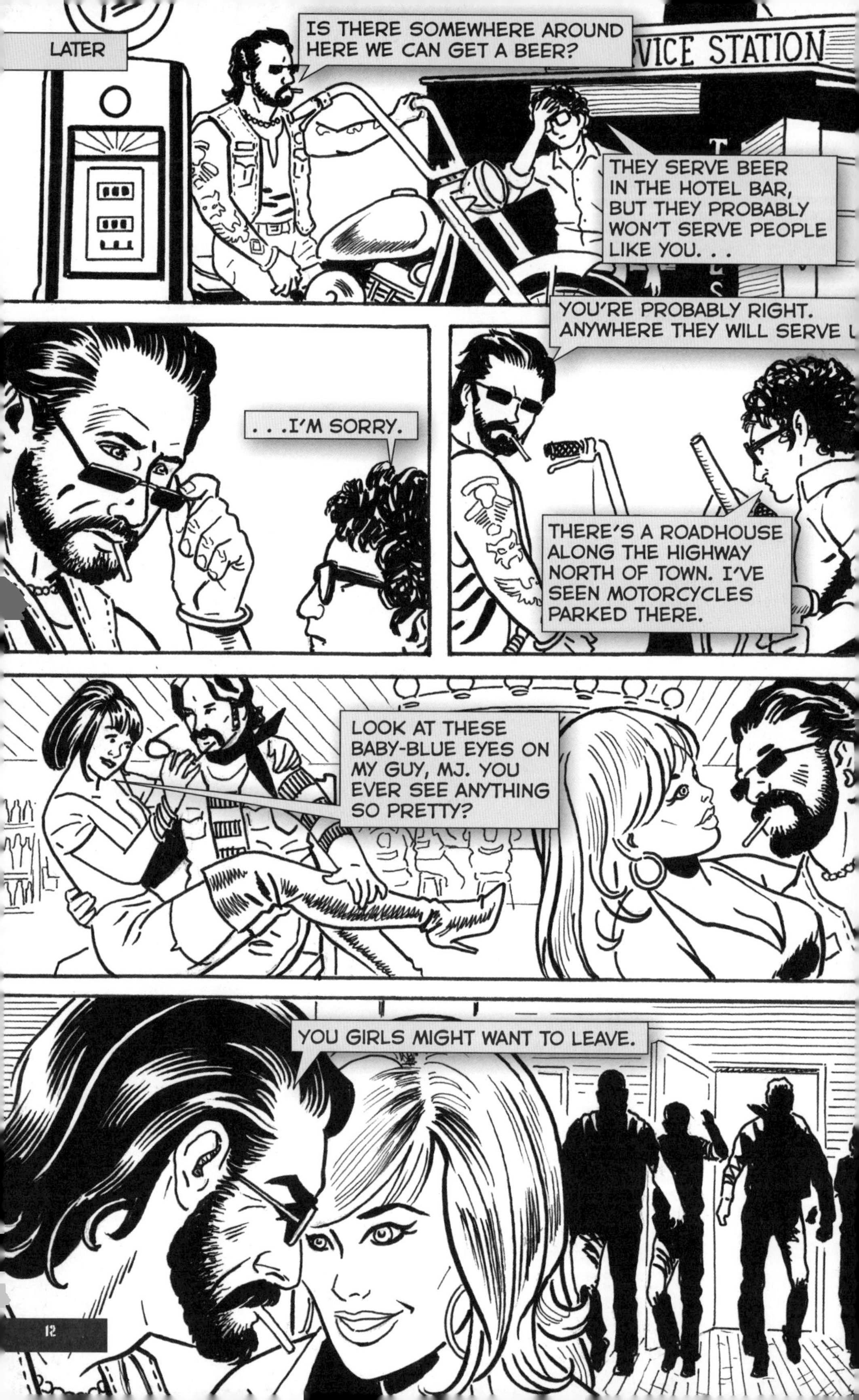
LATER
IS THERE SOMEWHERE AROUND HERE WE CAN GET A BEER?
VICE STATION
THEY SERVE BEER IN THE HOTEL BAR, BUT THEY PROBABLY WON'T SERVE PEOPLE LIKE YOU. . .
. . .I'M SORRY.
YOU'RE PROBABLY RIGHT. ANYWHERE THEY WILL SERVE
THERE'S A ROADHOUSE ALONG THE HIGHWAY NORTH OF TOWN. I'VE SEEN MOTORCYCLES PARKED THERE.
LOOK AT THESE BABY-BLUE EYES ON MY GUY, MJ. YOU EVER SEE ANYTHING SO PRETTY?
YOU GIRLS MIGHT WANT TO LEAVE.

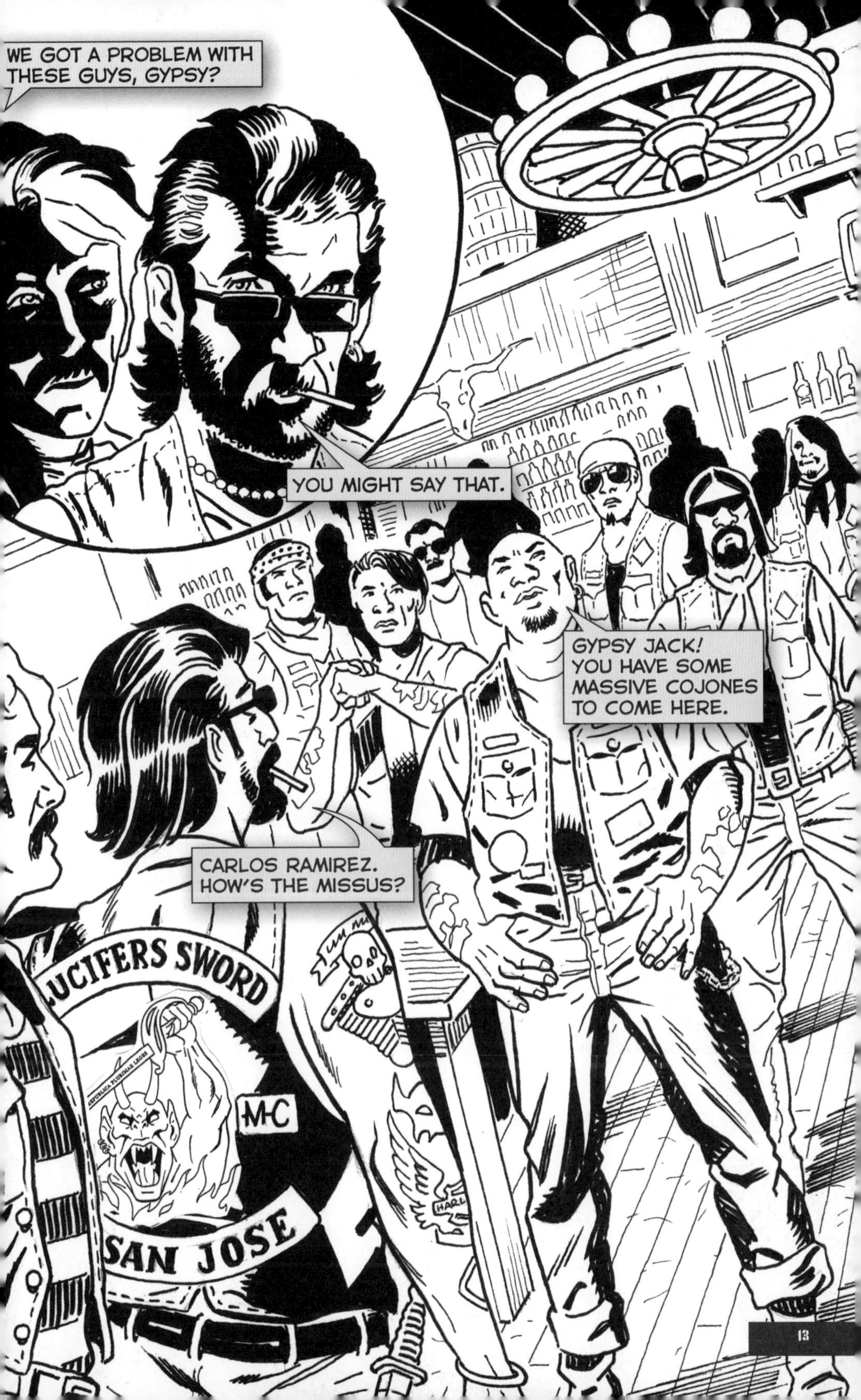
WE GOT A PROBLEM WITH THESE GUYS, GYPSY?
YOU MIGHT SAY THAT.
GYPSY JACK! YOU HAVE SOME MASSIVE COJONES TO COME HERE.
CARLOS RAMIREZ. HOW'S THE MISSUS?
LUCIFERS SWORD
MC
SAN JOSE

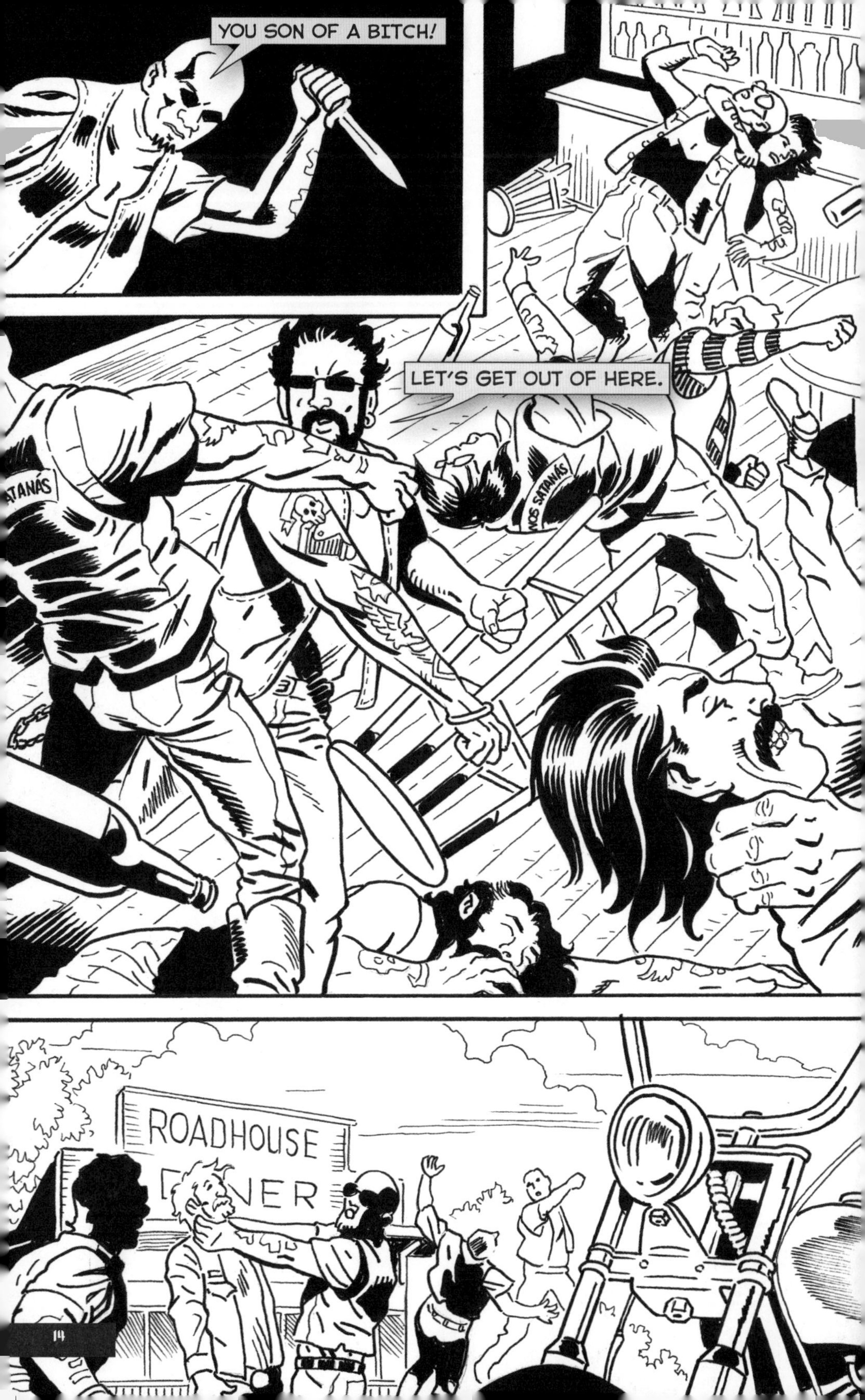
YOU SON OF A BITCH!
LET'S GET OUT OF HERE.
SATANÁS
NOS SATANÁS
ROADHOUSE

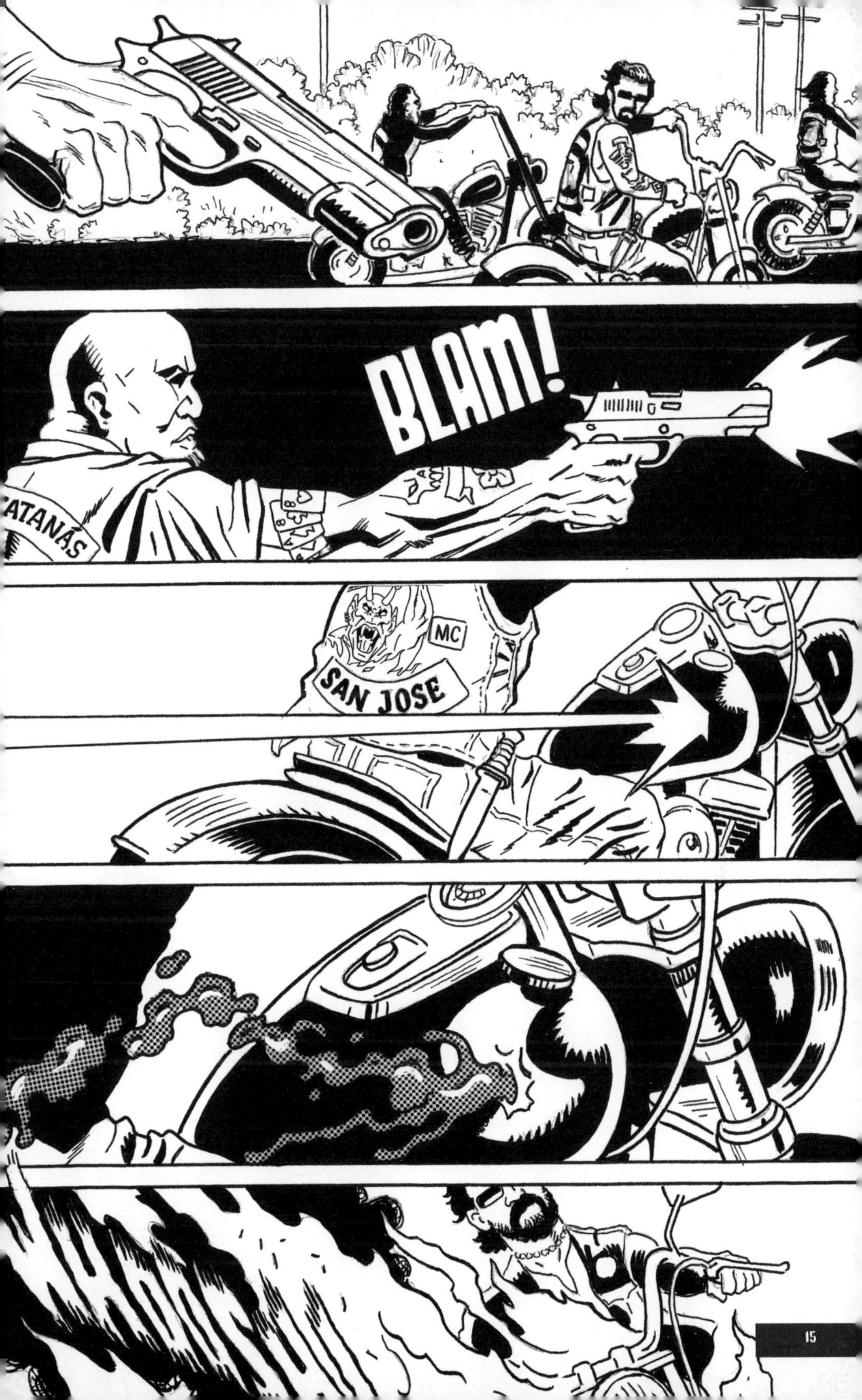
BLAM!
SATANÁS
MC
SAN JOSE

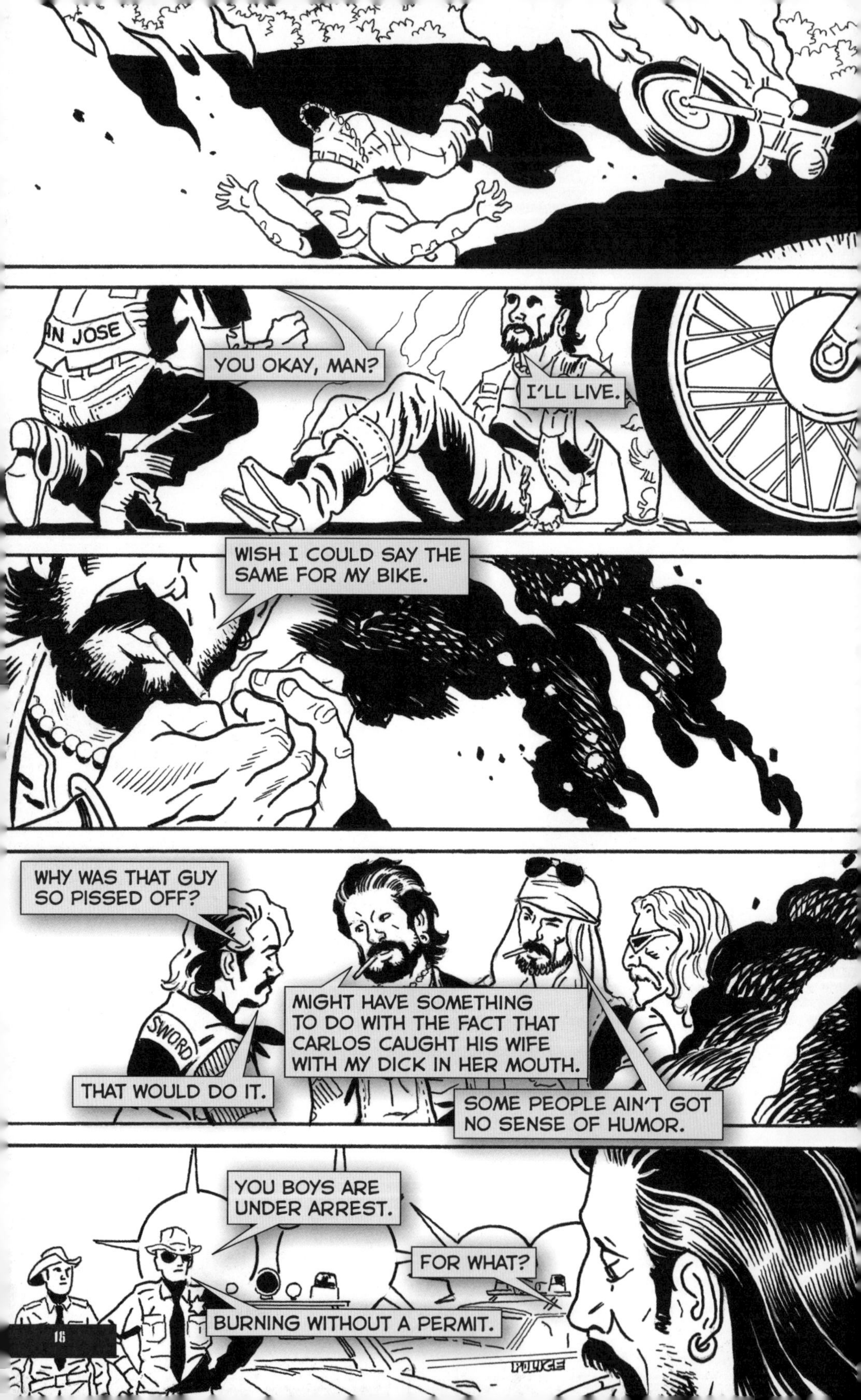

N JOSE
YOU OKAY, MAN?
I'LL LIVE.
WISH I COULD SAY THE SAME FOR MY BIKE.
WHY WAS THAT GUY SO PISSED OFF?
MIGHT HAVE SOMETHING TO DO WITH THE FACT THAT CARLOS CAUGHT HIS WIFE WITH MY DICK IN HER MOUTH.
SWORD
THAT WOULD DO IT.
SOME PEOPLE AIN'T GOT NO SENSE OF HUMOR.
YOU BOYS ARE UNDER ARREST.
FOR WHAT?
BURNING WITHOUT A PERMIT.
POLICE

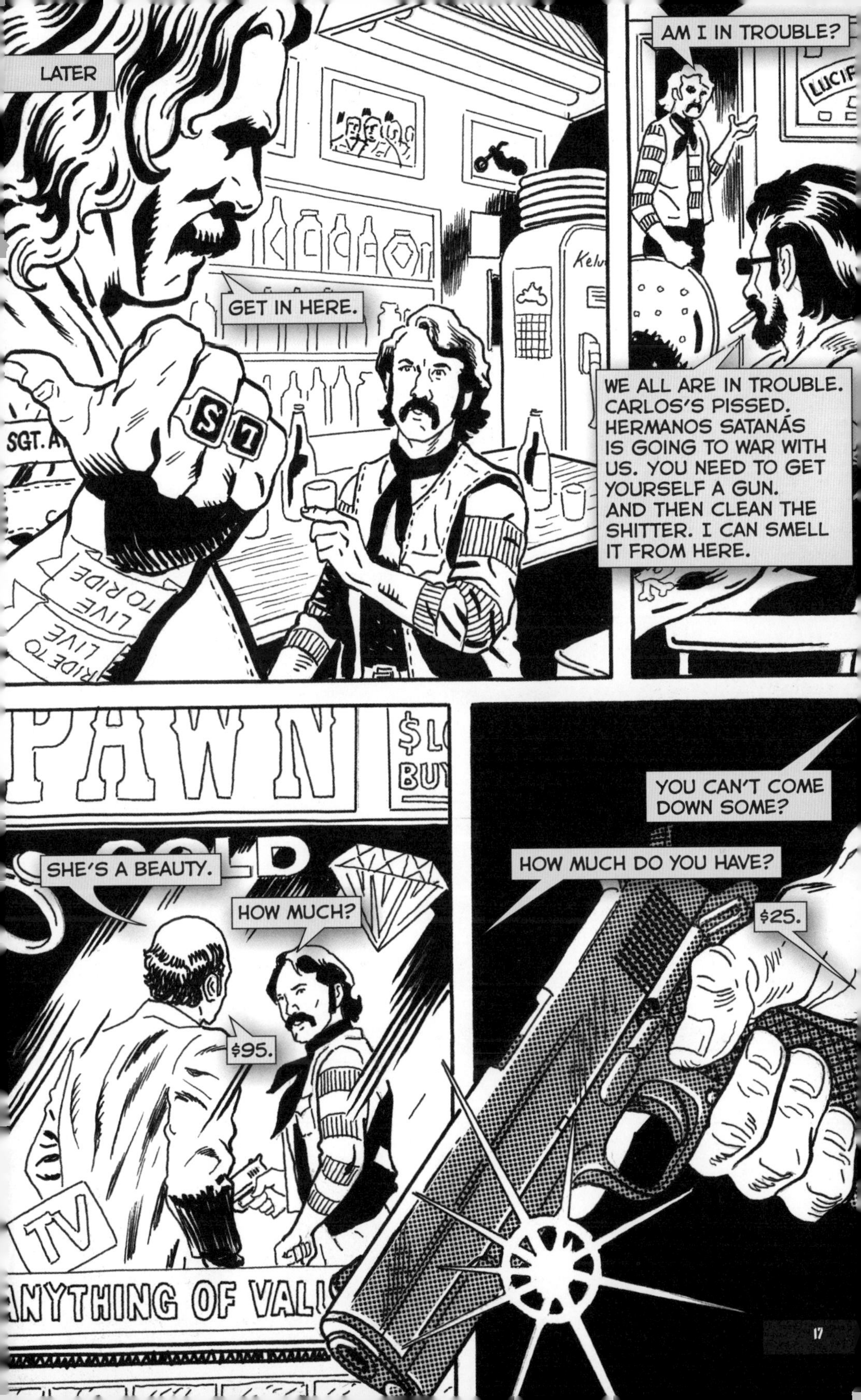
LATER
GET IN HERE.
SGT. A
LIVE TO RIDE
RIDE TO LIVE
AM I IN TROUBLE?
WE ALL ARE IN TROUBLE. CARLOS'S PISSED. HERMANOS SATANÁS IS GOING TO WAR WITH US. YOU NEED TO GET YOURSELF A GUN. AND THEN CLEAN THE SHITTER. I CAN SMELL IT FROM HERE.
PAWN
SHE'S A BEAUTY.
HOW MUCH?
$95.
TV
YOU CAN'T COME DOWN SOME?
HOW MUCH DO YOU HAVE?
$25.

#3 WAR

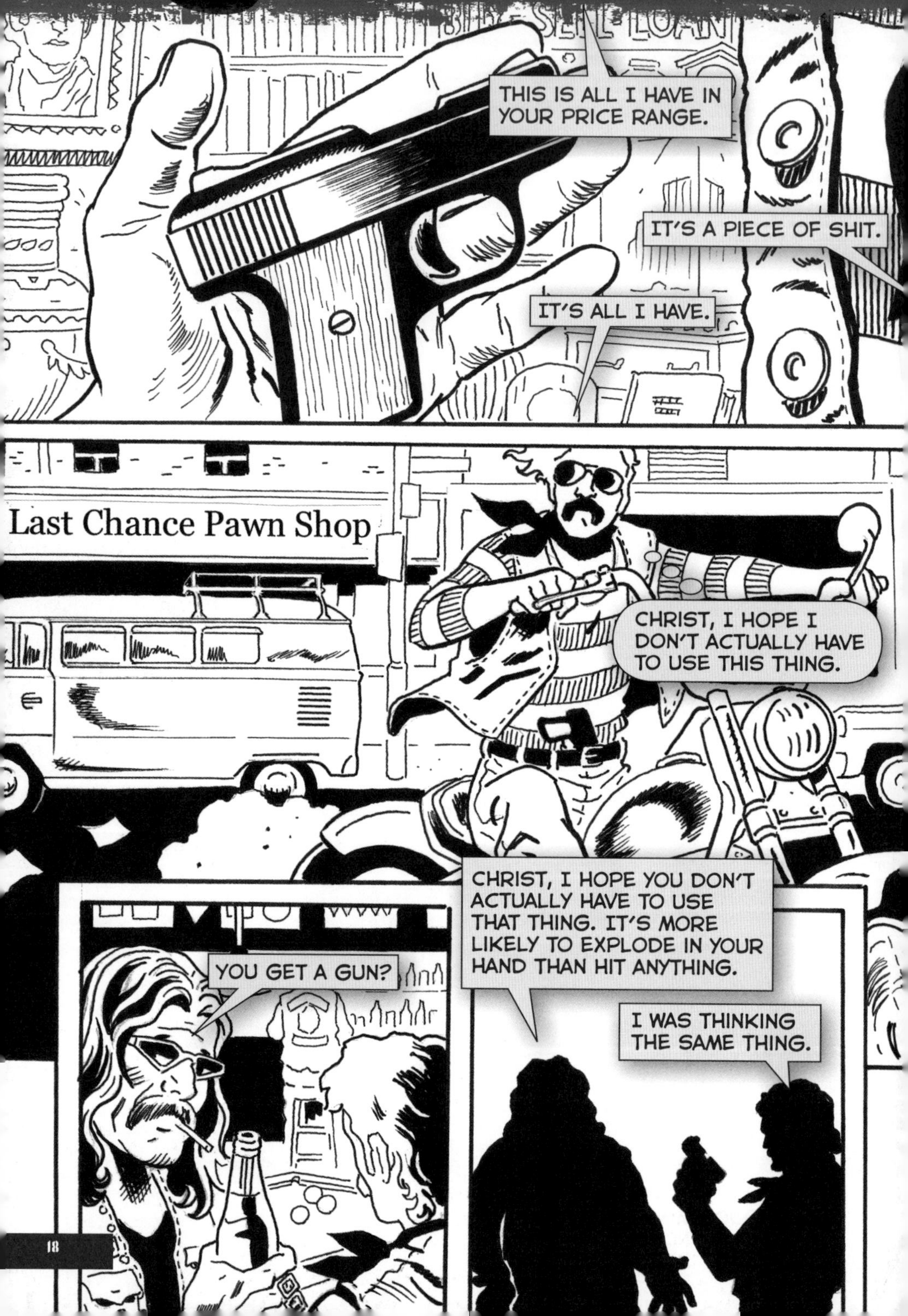
THIS IS ALL I HAVE IN YOUR PRICE RANGE.
IT'S A PIECE OF SHIT.
IT'S ALL I HAVE.
Last Chance Pawn Shop
CHRIST, I HOPE I DON'T ACTUALLY HAVE TO USE THIS THING.
YOU GET A GUN?
CHRIST, I HOPE YOU DON'T ACTUALLY HAVE TO USE THAT THING. IT'S MORE LIKELY TO EXPLODE IN YOUR HAND THAN HIT ANYTHING.
I WAS THINKING THE SAME THING.

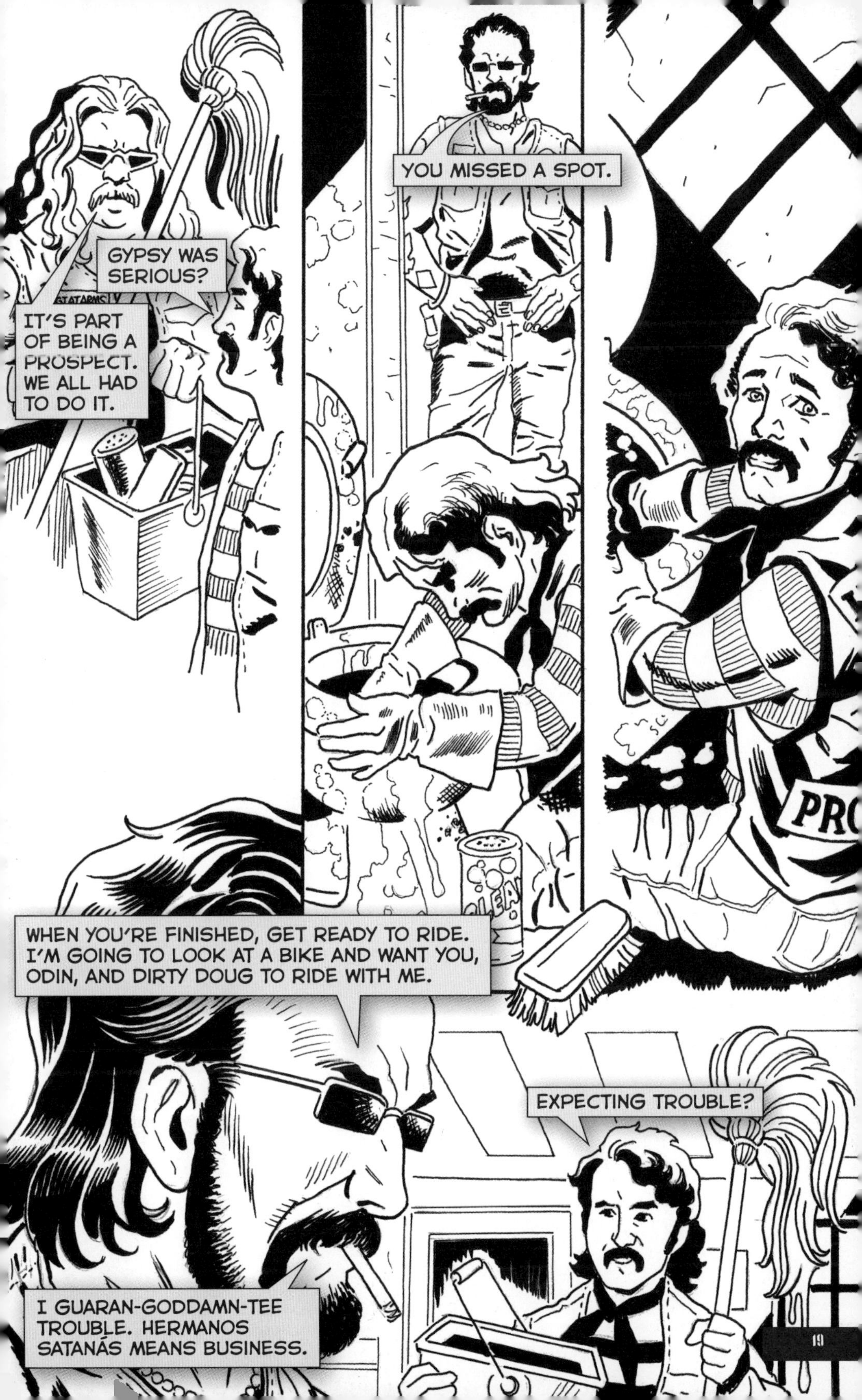
GYPSY WAS SERIOUS?
IT'S PART OF BEING A PROSPECT. WE ALL HAD TO DO IT.
YOU MISSED A SPOT.
PRO
WHEN YOU'RE FINISHED, GET READY TO RIDE. I'M GOING TO LOOK AT A BIKE AND WANT YOU, ODIN, AND DIRTY DOUG TO RIDE WITH ME.
EXPECTING TROUBLE?
I GUARAN-GODDAMN-TEE TROUBLE. HERMANOS SATANÁS MEANS BUSINESS.

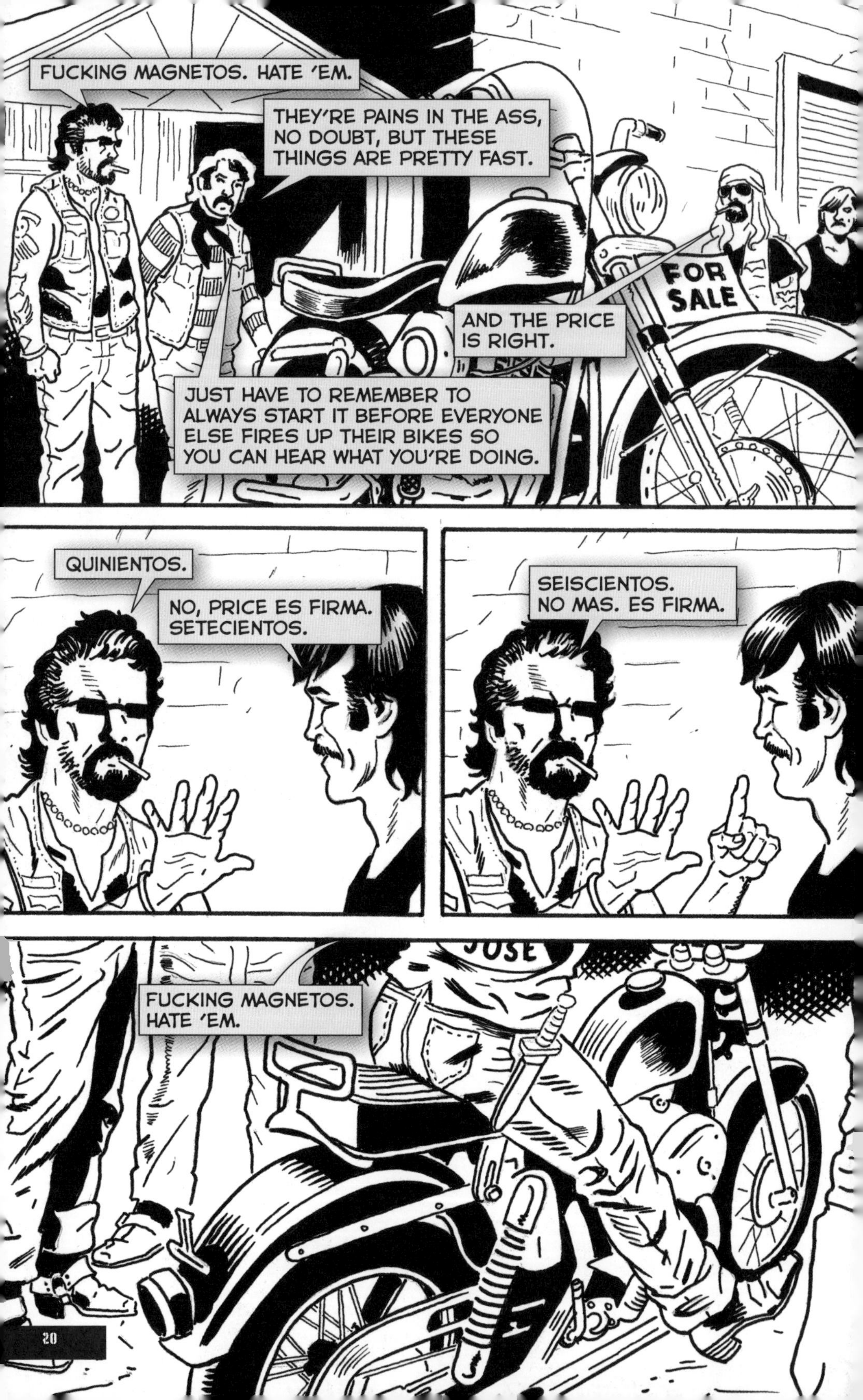
FUCKING MAGNETOS. HATE 'EM.
THEY'RE PAINS IN THE ASS, NO DOUBT, BUT THESE THINGS ARE PRETTY FAST.
FOR SALE
AND THE PRICE IS RIGHT.
JUST HAVE TO REMEMBER TO ALWAYS START IT BEFORE EVERYONE ELSE FIRES UP THEIR BIKES SO YOU CAN HEAR WHAT YOU'RE DOING.
QUINIENTOS.
NO, PRICE ES FIRMA. SETECIENTOS.
SEISCIENTOS. NO MAS. ES FIRMA.
JOSE
FUCKING MAGNETOS. HATE 'EM.

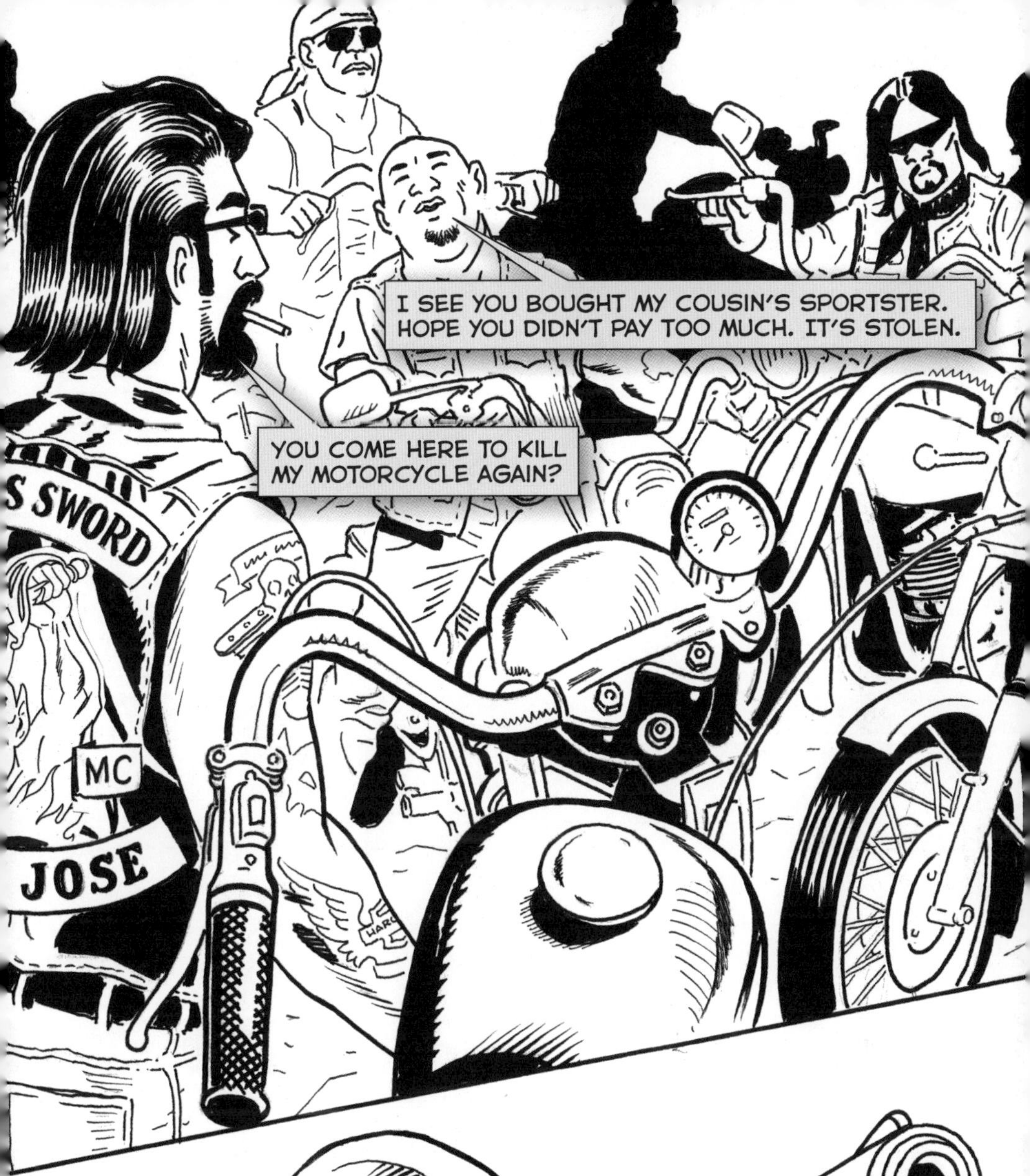
I SEE YOU BOUGHT MY COUSIN'S SPORTSTER. HOPE YOU DIDN'T PAY TOO MUCH. IT'S STOLEN.
YOU COME HERE TO KILL MY MOTORCYCLE AGAIN?
S SWORD
MC
JOSE

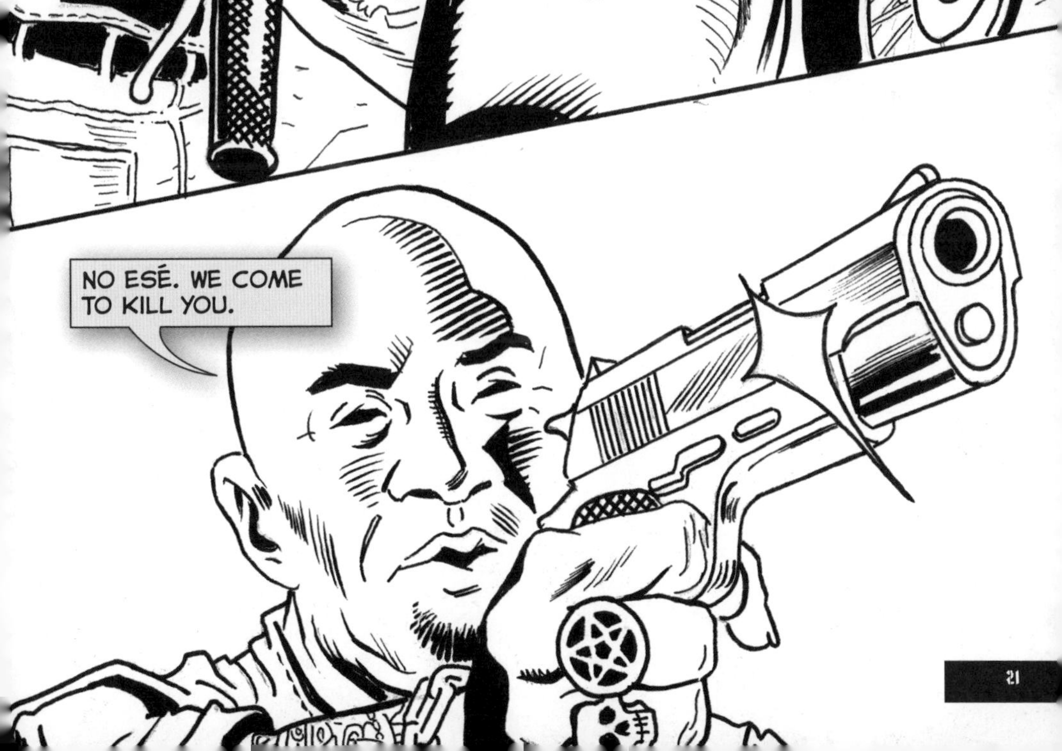
NO ESÉ. WE COME TO KILL YOU.

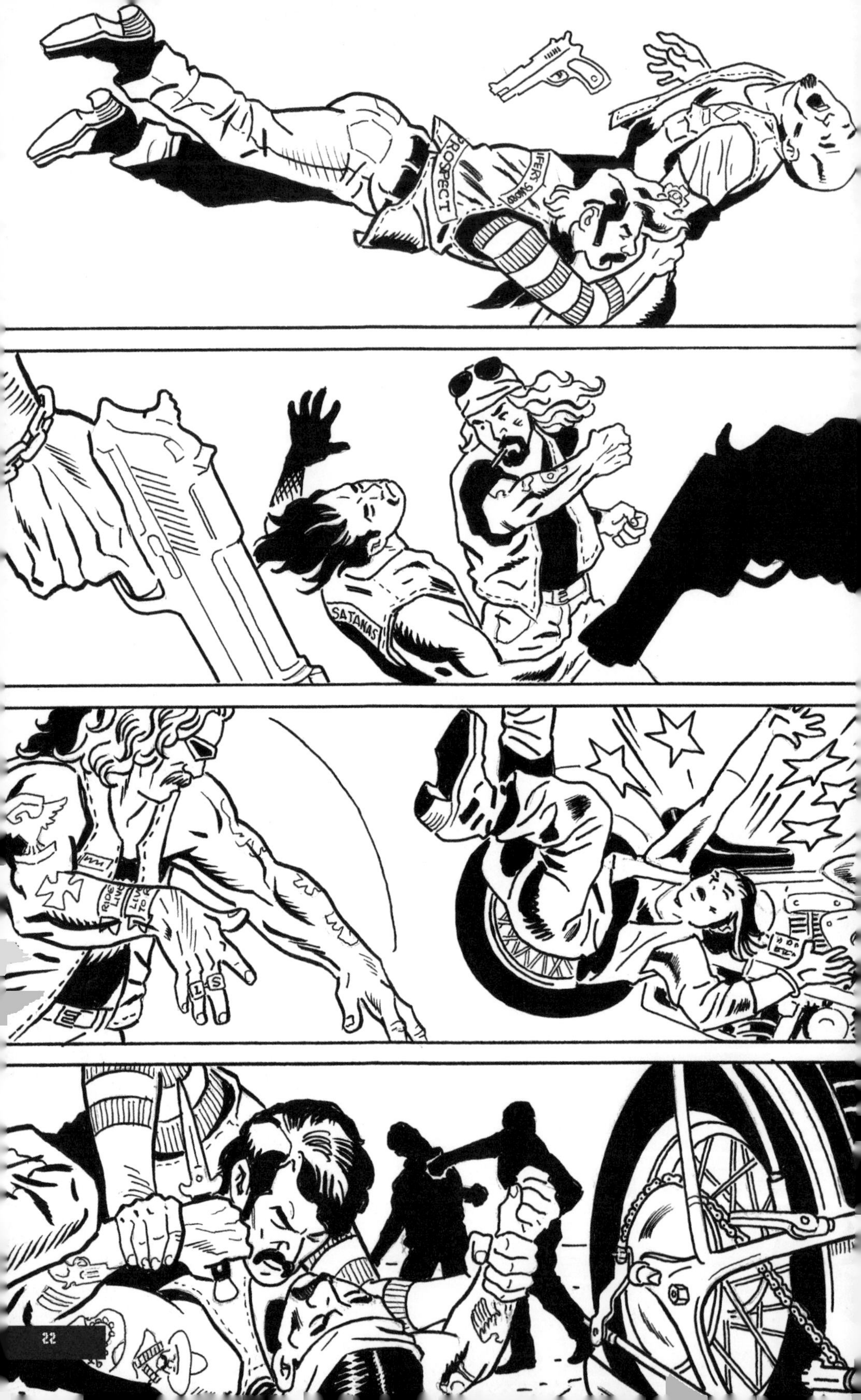
SATANAS

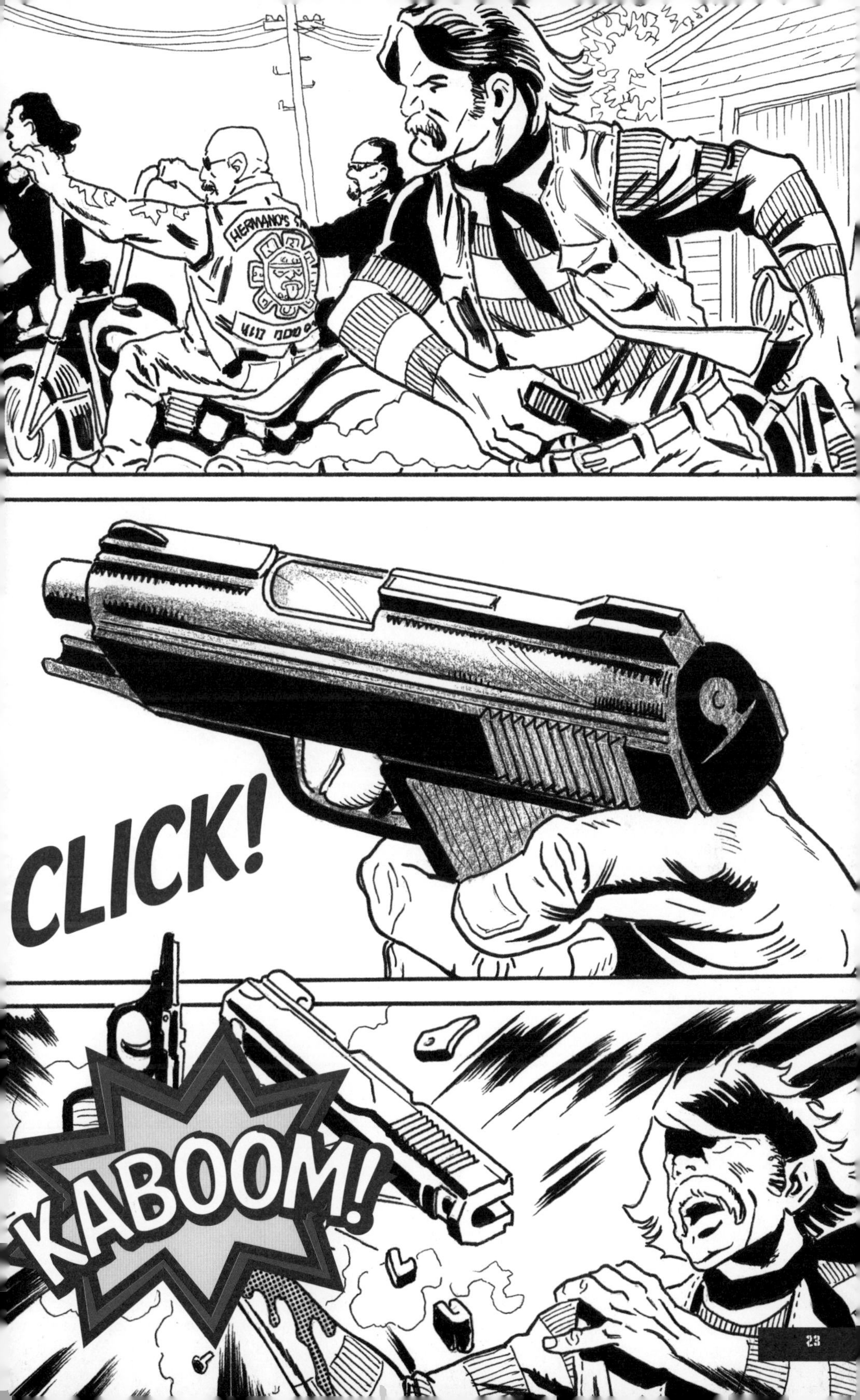
CLICK!
KABOOM!

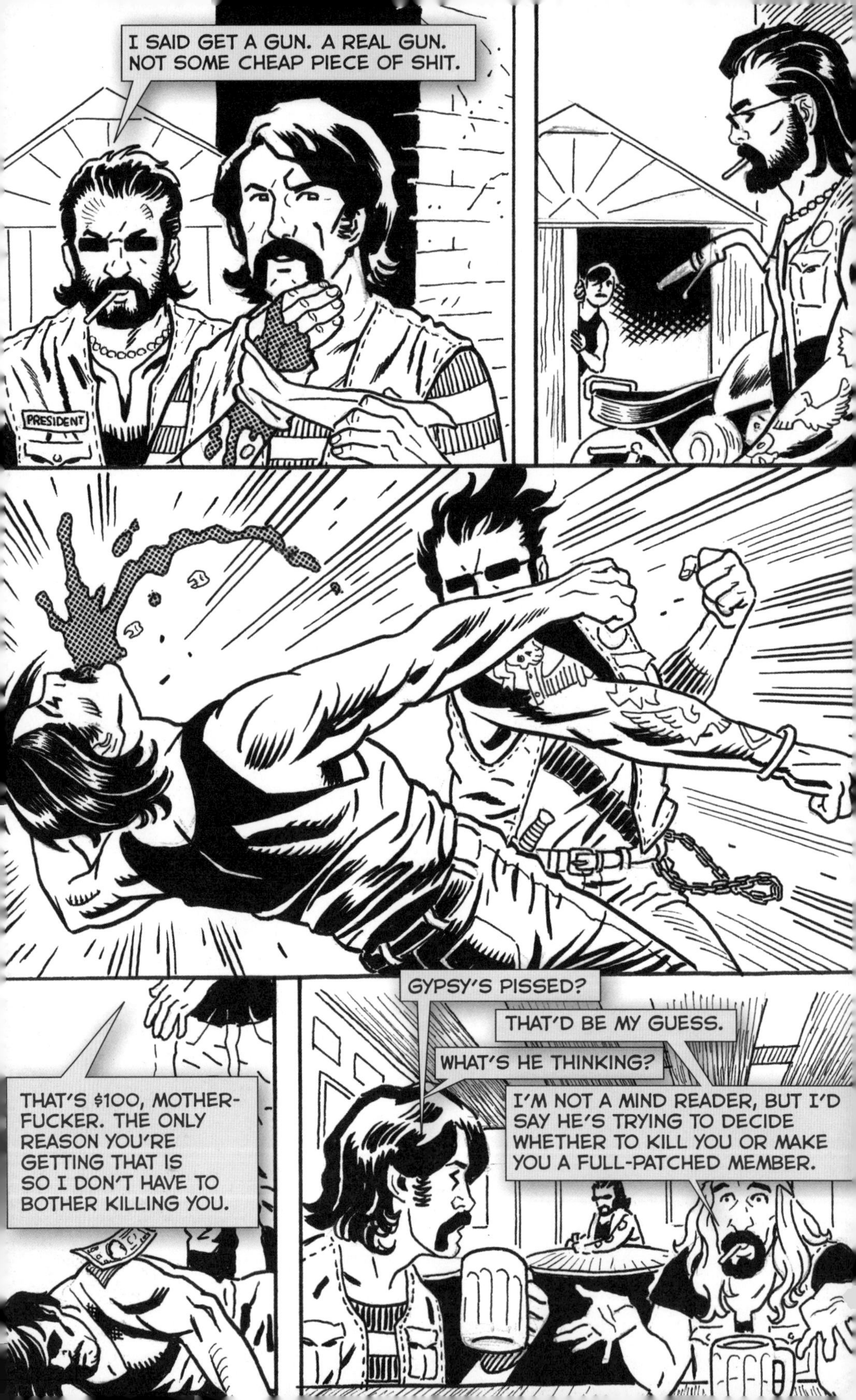

I SAID GET A GUN. A REAL GUN. NOT SOME CHEAP PIECE OF SHIT.
PRESIDENT
THAT'S $100, MOTHER-FUCKER. THE ONLY REASON YOU'RE GETTING THAT IS SO I DON'T HAVE TO BOTHER KILLING YOU.
GYPSY'S PISSED?
THAT'D BE MY GUESS.
WHAT'S HE THINKING?
I'M NOT A MIND READER, BUT I'D SAY HE'S TRYING TO DECIDE WHETHER TO KILL YOU OR MAKE YOU A FULL-PATCHED MEMBER.

GOING TO THE MATTRESSES #4

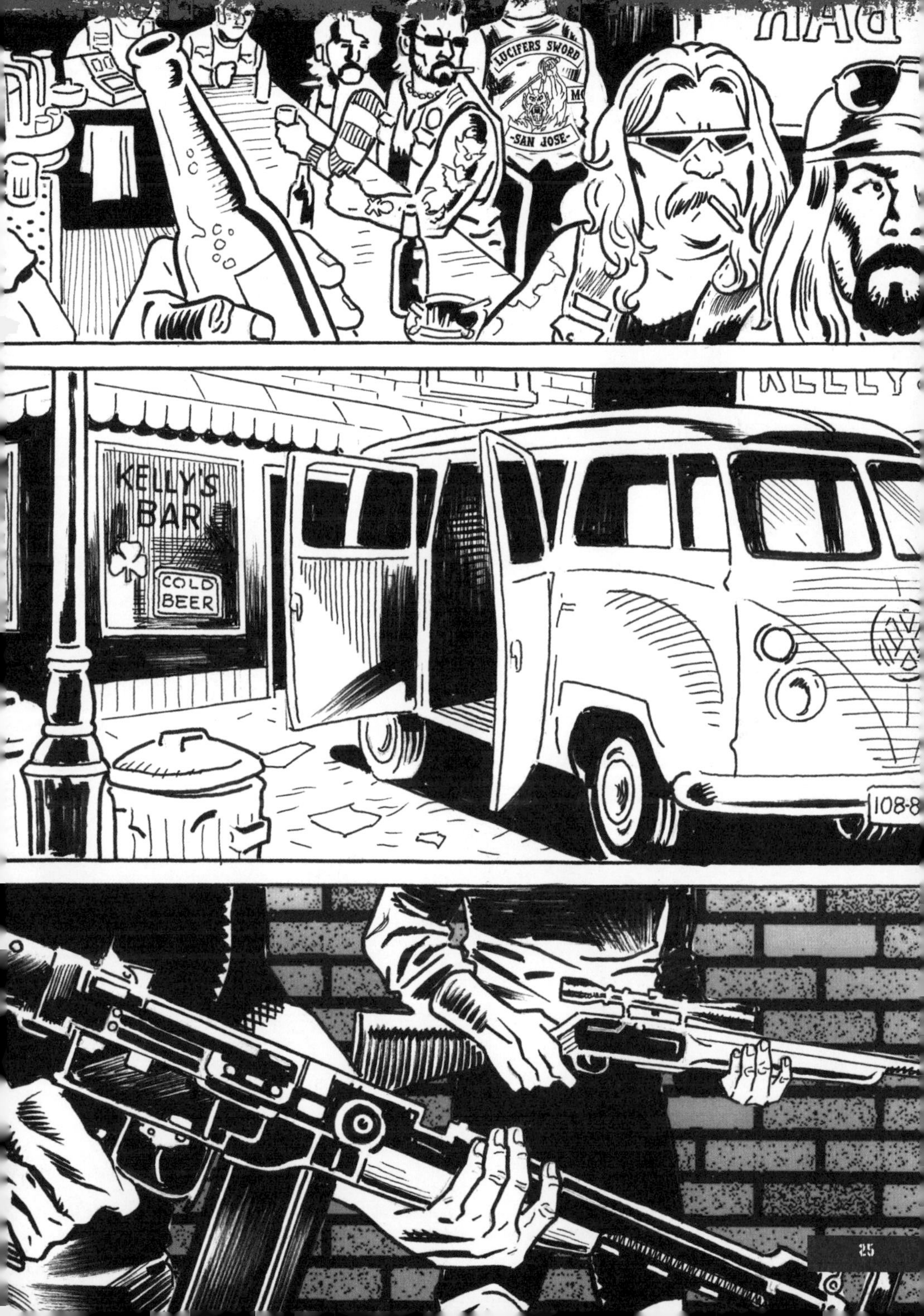
LUCIFERS SWORD
MC
SAN JOSE
KELLY'S BAR
COLD BEER
108-8

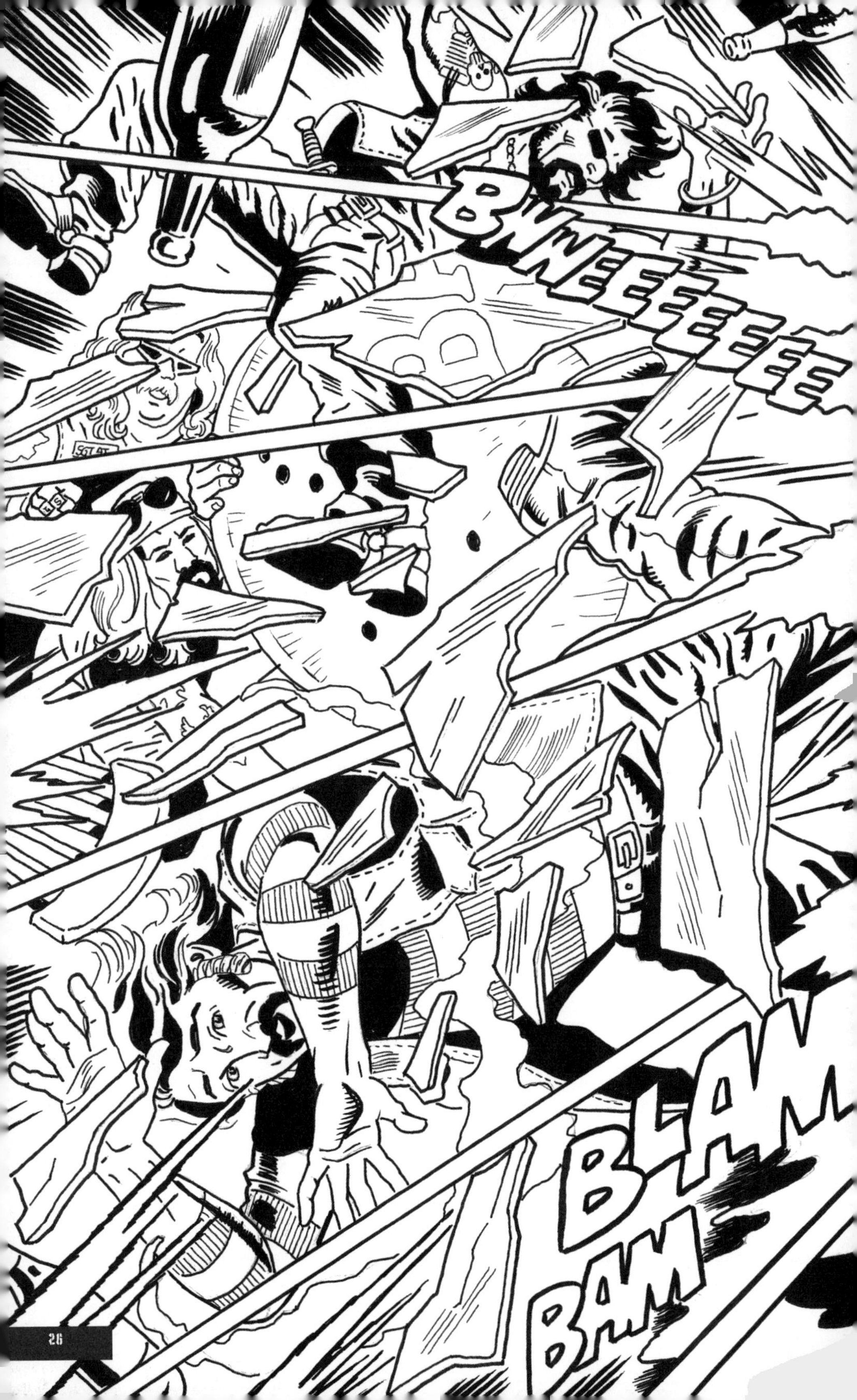
BNEEEEEEE
BLAM
BAM

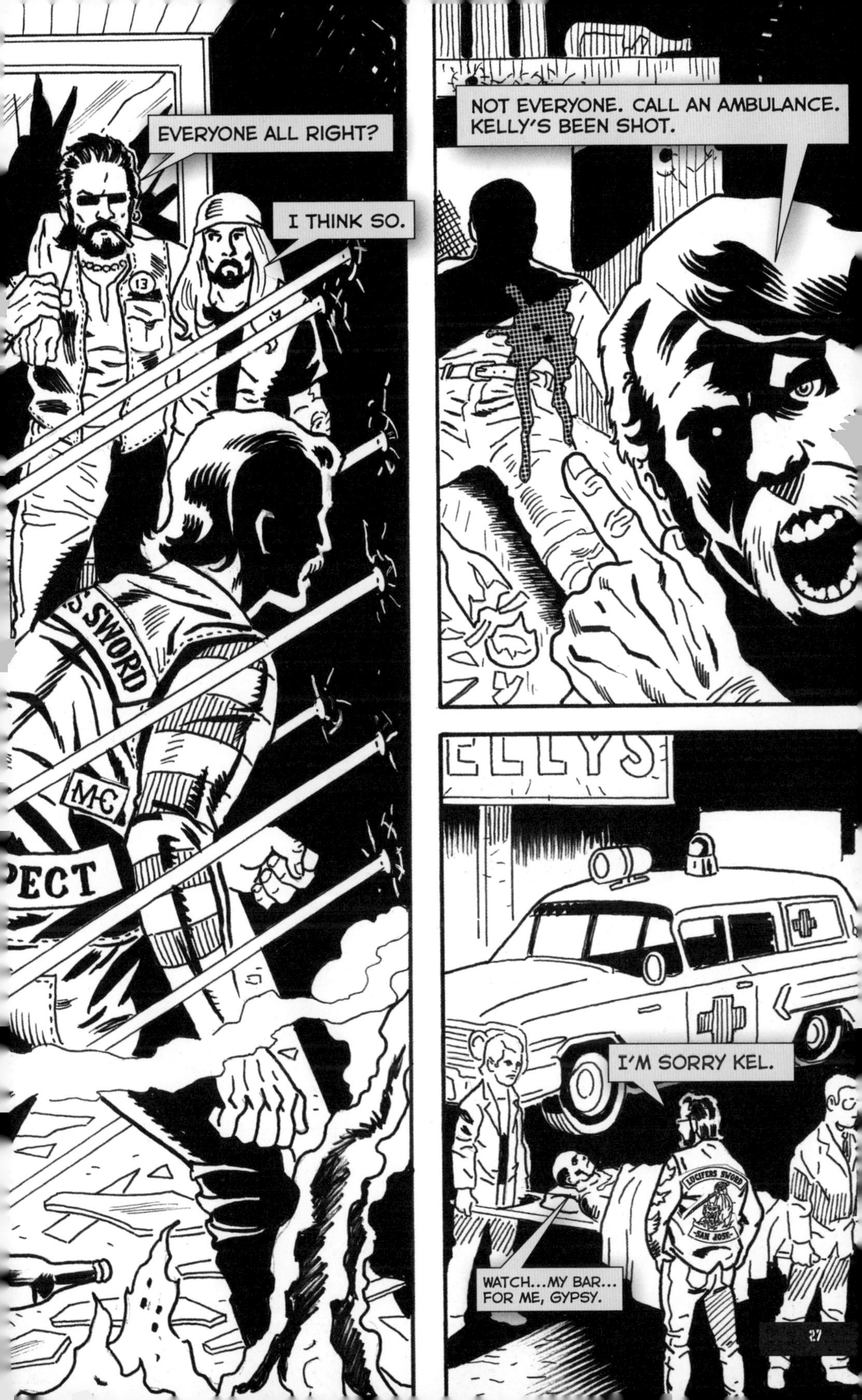
EVERYONE ALL RIGHT?
I THINK SO.
13
S SWORD
MC
PECT
NOT EVERYONE. CALL AN AMBULANCE. KELLY'S BEEN SHOT.
ELLYS
I'M SORRY KEL.
LUCIFERS SWORD
SAN JOSE
WATCH...MY BAR... FOR ME, GYPSY.

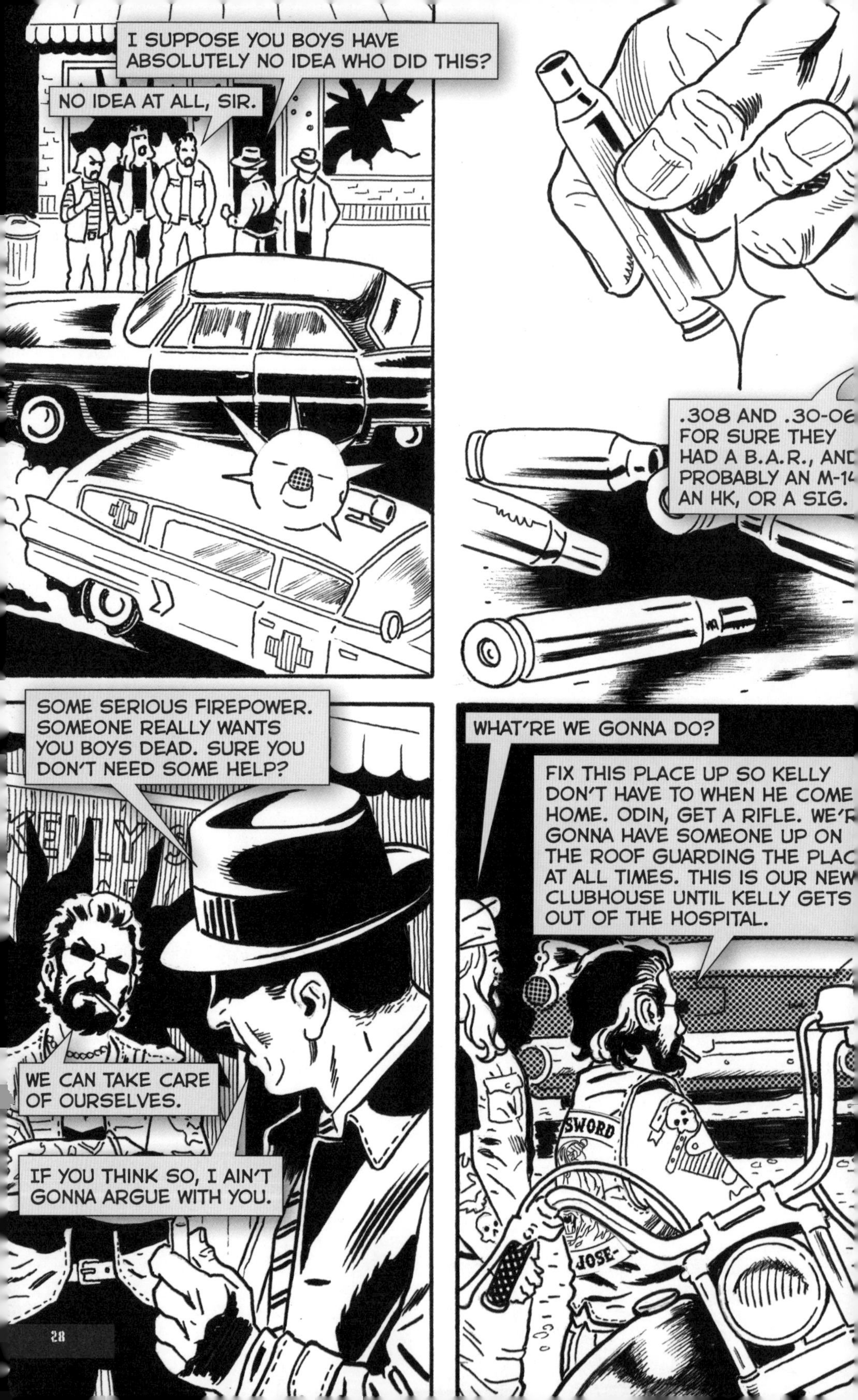
I SUPPOSE YOU BOYS HAVE ABSOLUTELY NO IDEA WHO DID THIS?
NO IDEA AT ALL, SIR.
.308 AND .30-06 FOR SURE THEY HAD A B.A.R., AND PROBABLY AN M-14 AN HK, OR A SIG.
SOME SERIOUS FIREPOWER. SOMEONE REALLY WANTS YOU BOYS DEAD. SURE YOU DON'T NEED SOME HELP?
WE CAN TAKE CARE OF OURSELVES.
IF YOU THINK SO, I AIN'T GONNA ARGUE WITH YOU.
WHAT'RE WE GONNA DO?
FIX THIS PLACE UP SO KELLY DON'T HAVE TO WHEN HE COME HOME. ODIN, GET A RIFLE. WE'R GONNA HAVE SOMEONE UP ON THE ROOF GUARDING THE PLAC AT ALL TIMES. THIS IS OUR NEW CLUBHOUSE UNTIL KELLY GETS OUT OF THE HOSPITAL.
SWORD
JOSE-

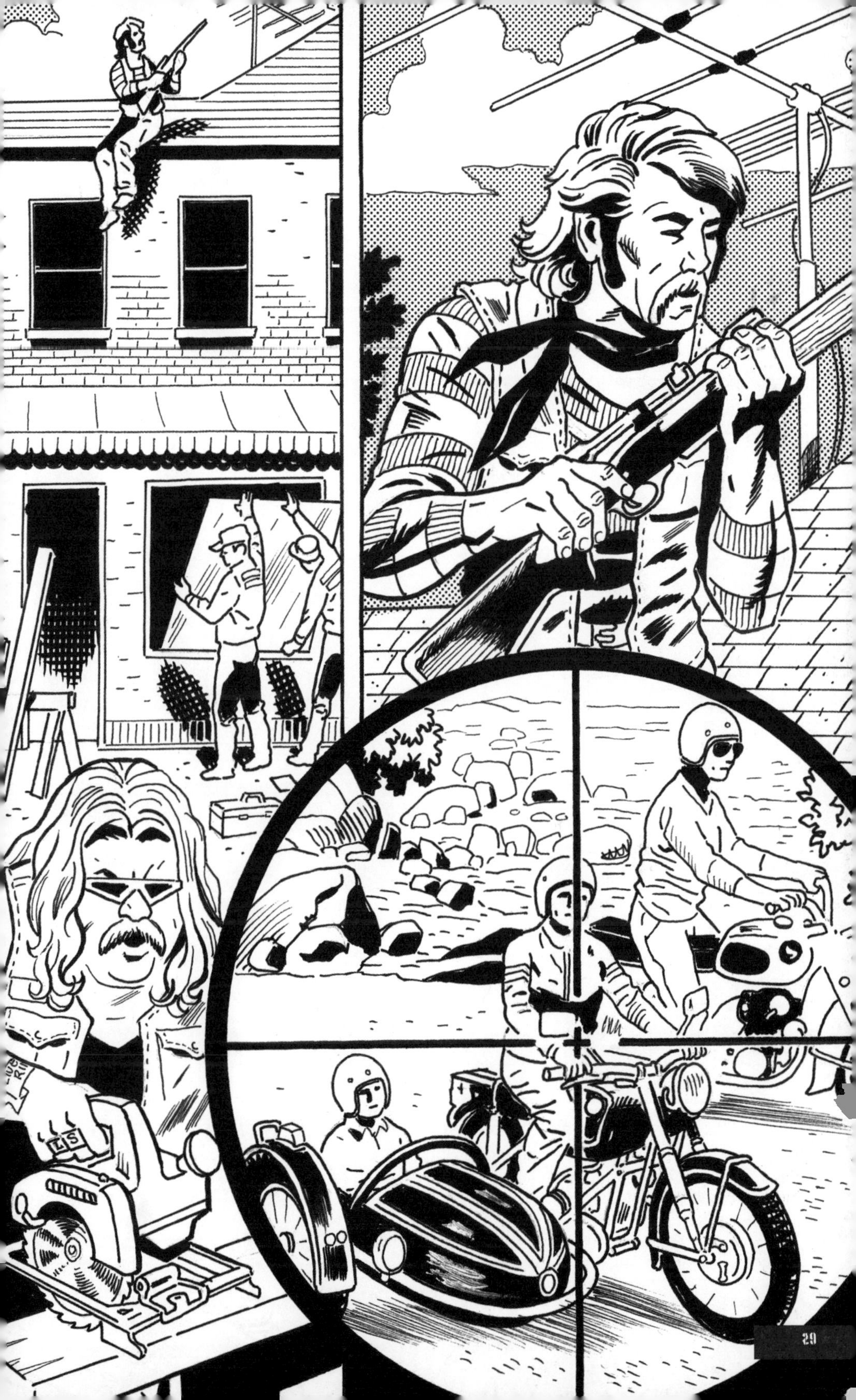

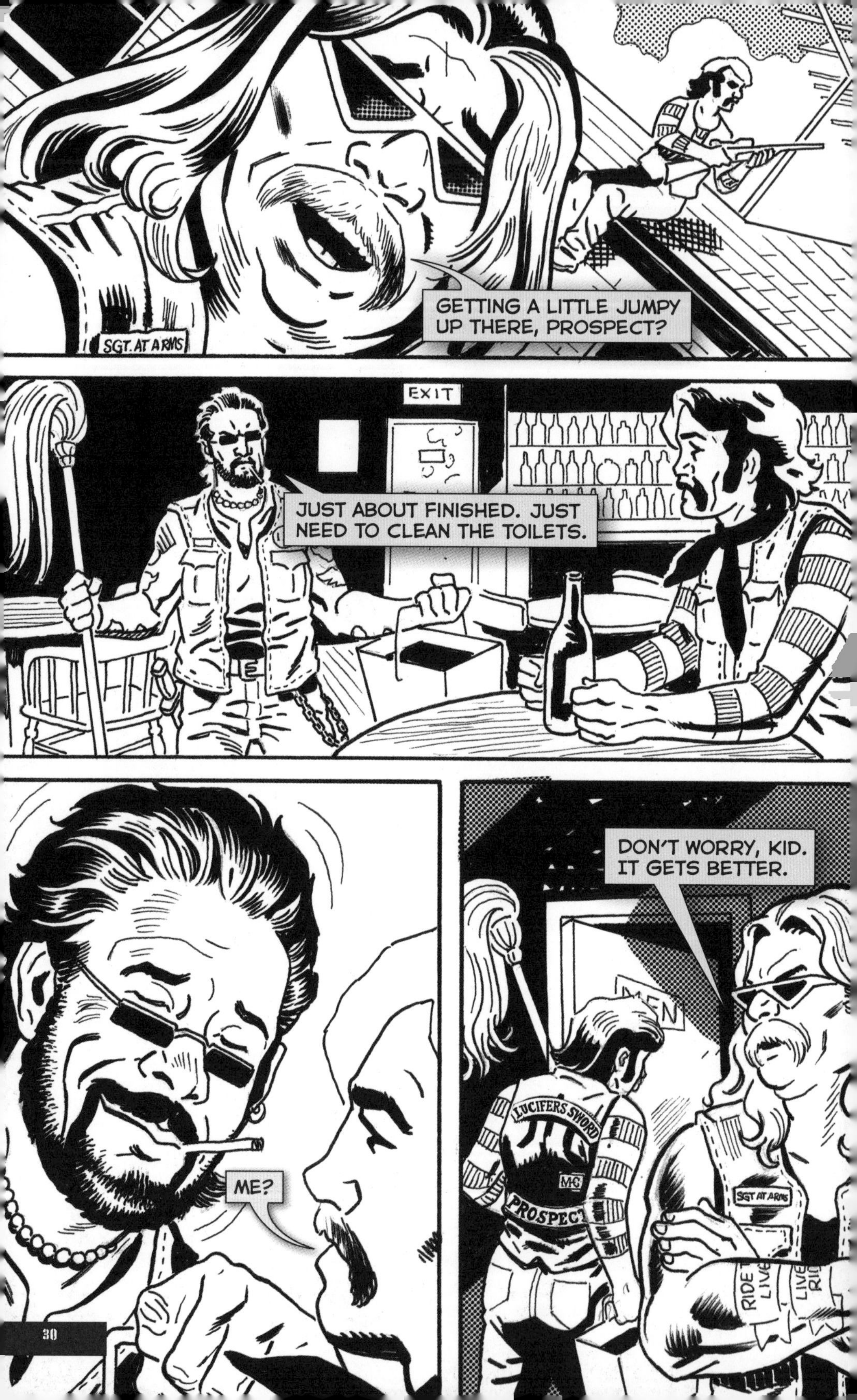
SGT. AT ARMS
GETTING A LITTLE JUMPY UP THERE, PROSPECT?
EXIT
JUST ABOUT FINISHED. JUST NEED TO CLEAN THE TOILETS.
ME?
DON'T WORRY, KID. IT GETS BETTER.
LUCIFERS SWORD
MC
PROSPECT
SGT AT ARMS

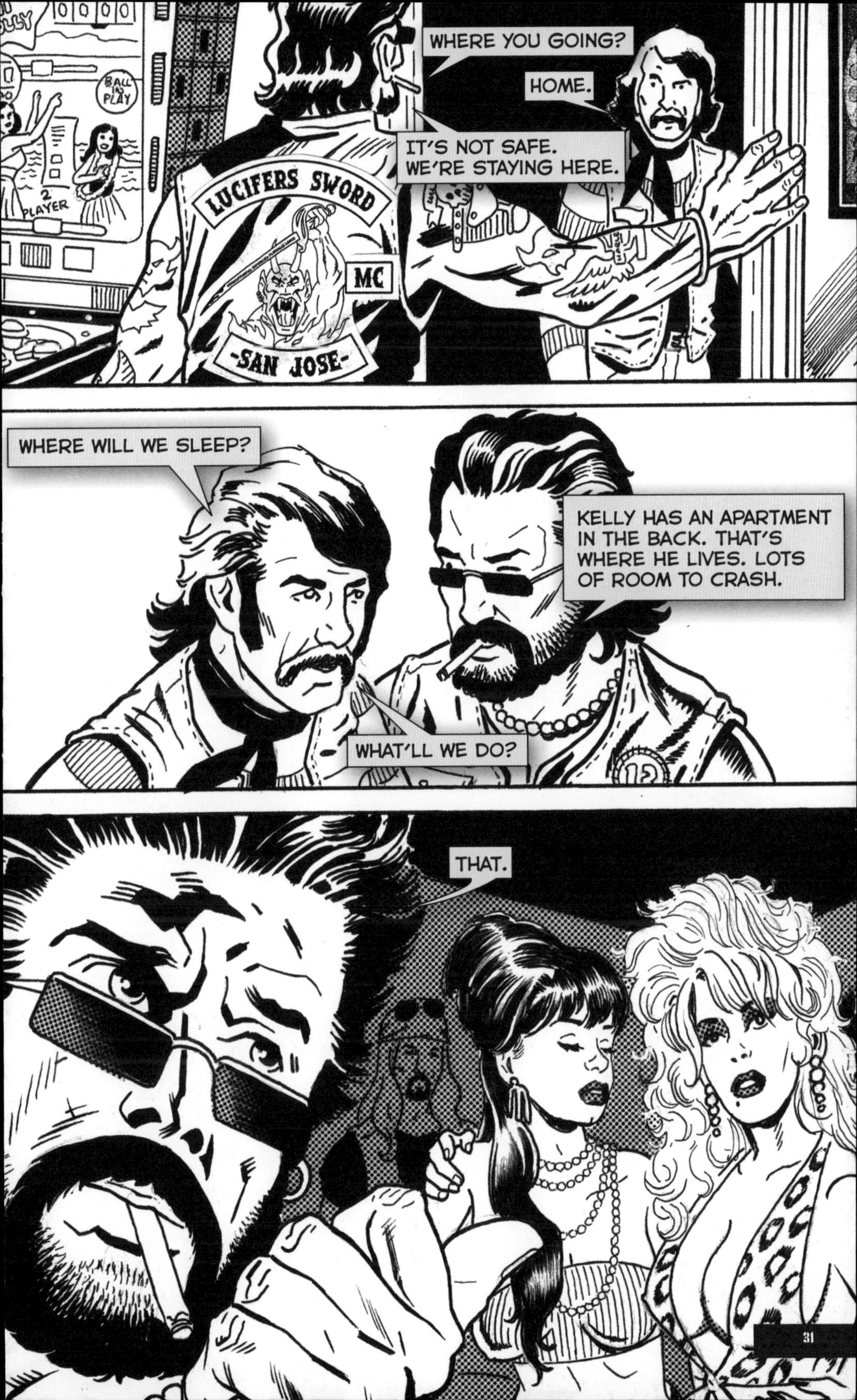
WHERE YOU GOING?
HOME.
IT'S NOT SAFE. WE'RE STAYING HERE.
LUCIFERS SWORD
MC
-SAN JOSE-
BALL IN PLAY
2 PLAYER
WHERE WILL WE SLEEP?
KELLY HAS AN APARTMENT IN THE BACK. THAT'S WHERE HE LIVES. LOTS OF ROOM TO CRASH.
WHAT'LL WE DO?
THAT.

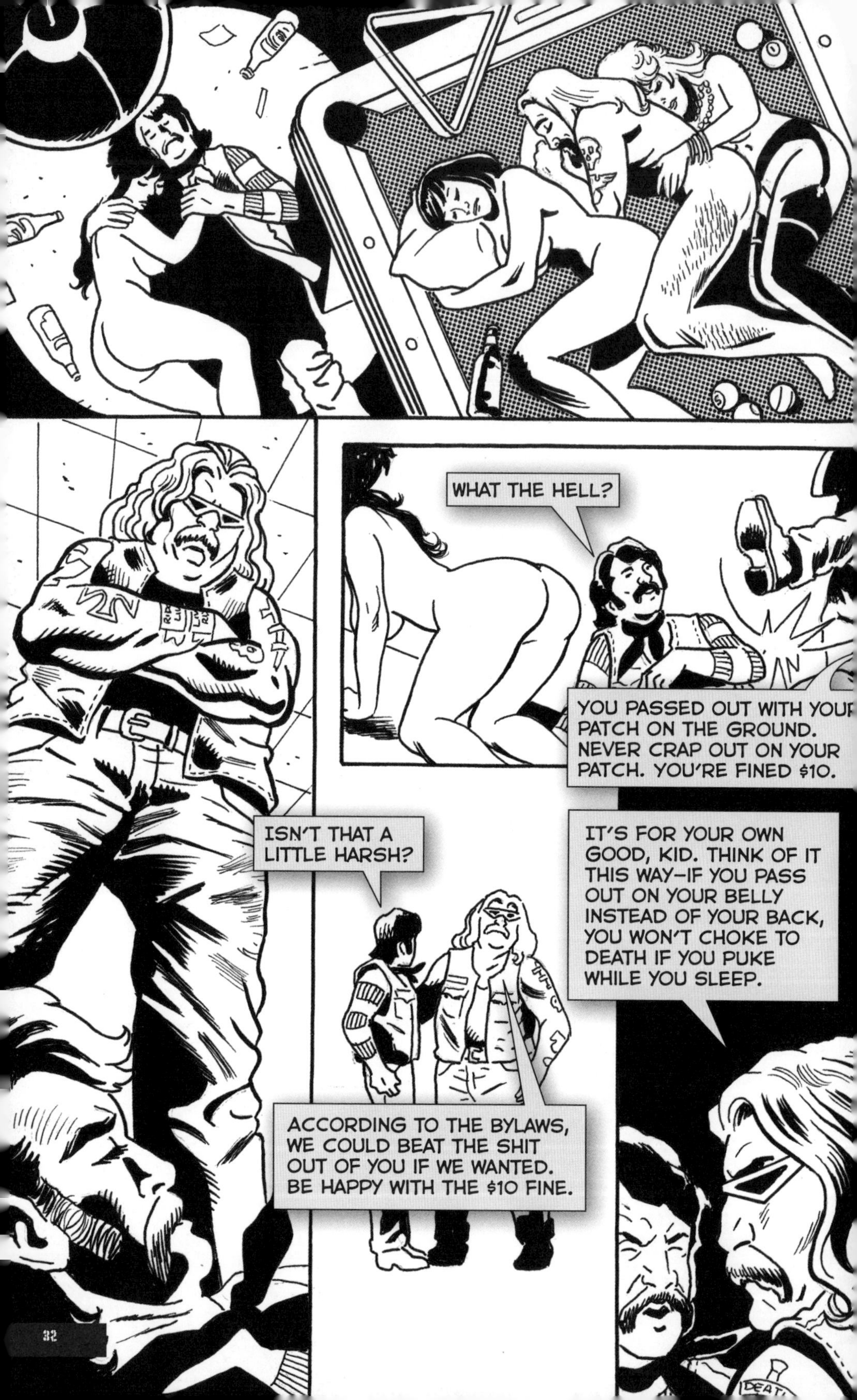
WHAT THE HELL?
YOU PASSED OUT WITH YOUR PATCH ON THE GROUND. NEVER CRAP OUT ON YOUR PATCH. YOU'RE FINED $10.
ISN'T THAT A LITTLE HARSH?
ACCORDING TO THE BYLAWS, WE COULD BEAT THE SHIT OUT OF YOU IF WE WANTED. BE HAPPY WITH THE $10 FINE.
IT'S FOR YOUR OWN GOOD, KID. THINK OF IT THIS WAY—IF YOU PASS OUT ON YOUR BELLY INSTEAD OF YOUR BACK, YOU WON'T CHOKE TO DEATH IF YOU PUKE WHILE YOU SLEEP.

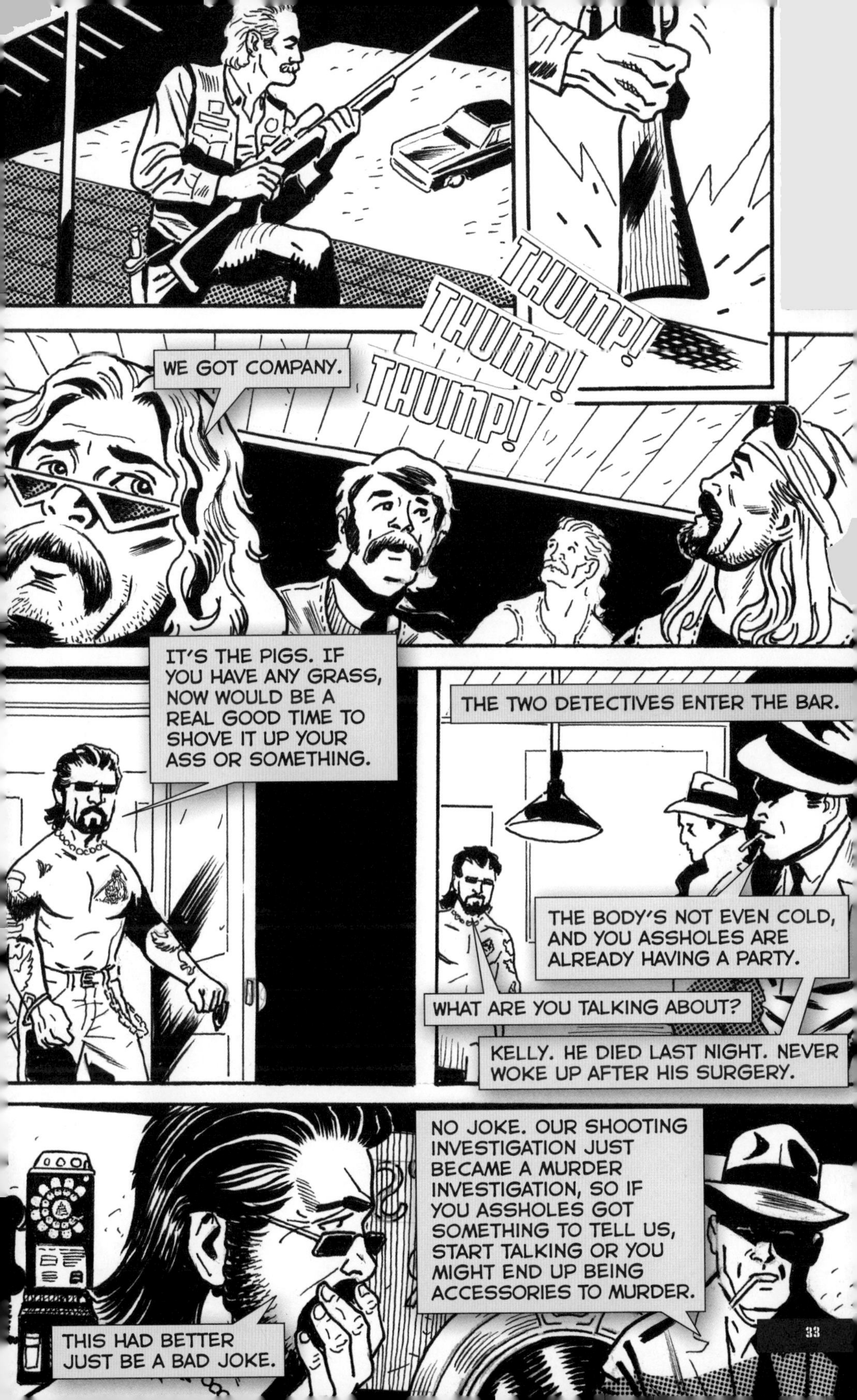
THUMP! THUMP! THUMP!
WE GOT COMPANY.
IT'S THE PIGS. IF YOU HAVE ANY GRASS, NOW WOULD BE A REAL GOOD TIME TO SHOVE IT UP YOUR ASS OR SOMETHING.
THE TWO DETECTIVES ENTER THE BAR.
THE BODY'S NOT EVEN COLD, AND YOU ASSHOLES ARE ALREADY HAVING A PARTY.
WHAT ARE YOU TALKING ABOUT?
KELLY. HE DIED LAST NIGHT. NEVER WOKE UP AFTER HIS SURGERY.
THIS HAD BETTER JUST BE A BAD JOKE.
NO JOKE. OUR SHOOTING INVESTIGATION JUST BECAME A MURDER INVESTIGATION, SO IF YOU ASSHOLES GOT SOMETHING TO TELL US, START TALKING OR YOU MIGHT END UP BEING ACCESSORIES TO MURDER.

#5 RETALIATION

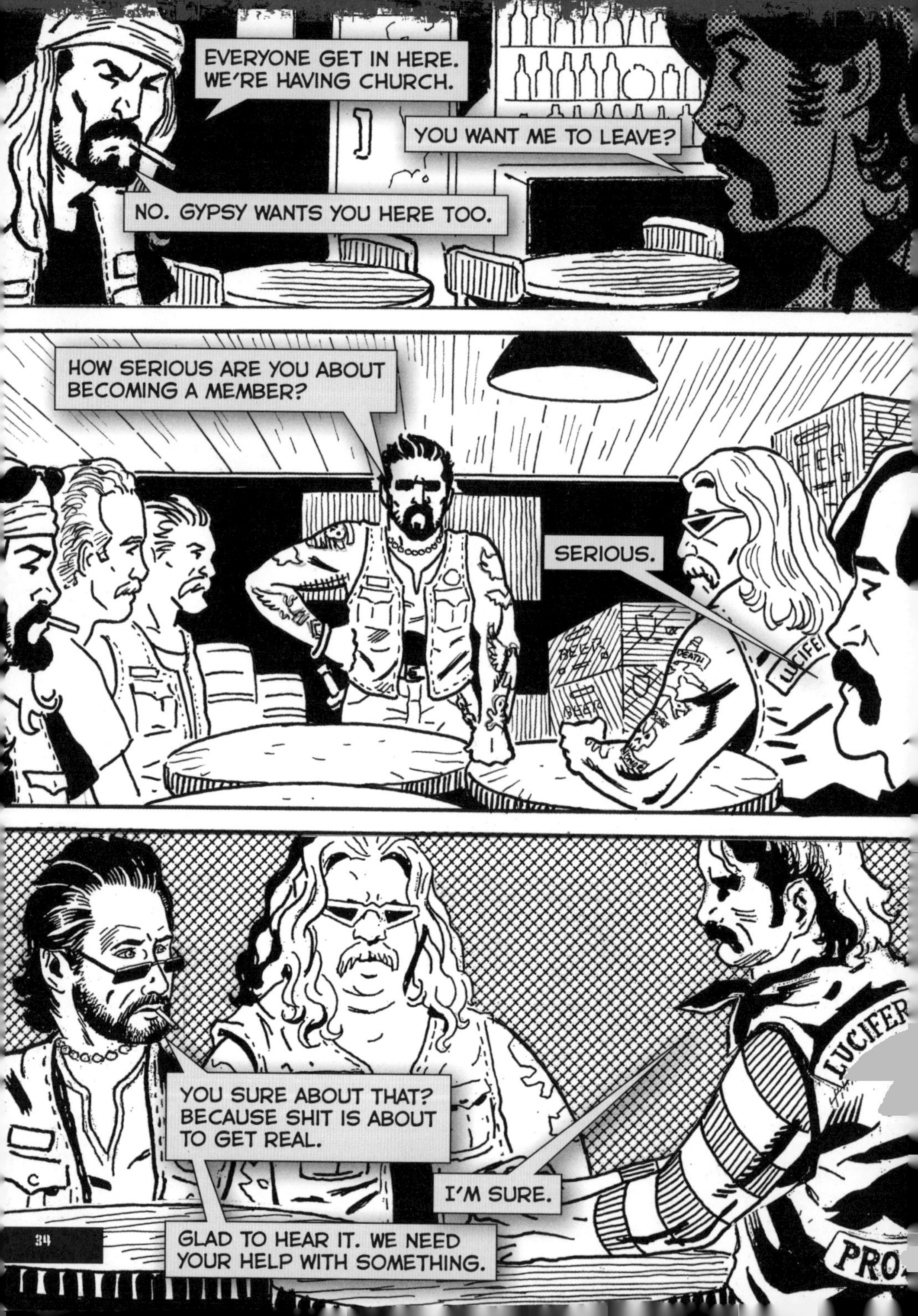
EVERYONE GET IN HERE. WE'RE HAVING CHURCH.
YOU WANT ME TO LEAVE?
NO. GYPSY WANTS YOU HERE TOO.
HOW SERIOUS ARE YOU ABOUT BECOMING A MEMBER?
SERIOUS.
YOU SURE ABOUT THAT? BECAUSE SHIT IS ABOUT TO GET REAL.
I'M SURE.
GLAD TO HEAR IT. WE NEED YOUR HELP WITH SOMETHING.
LUCIFER
PRO

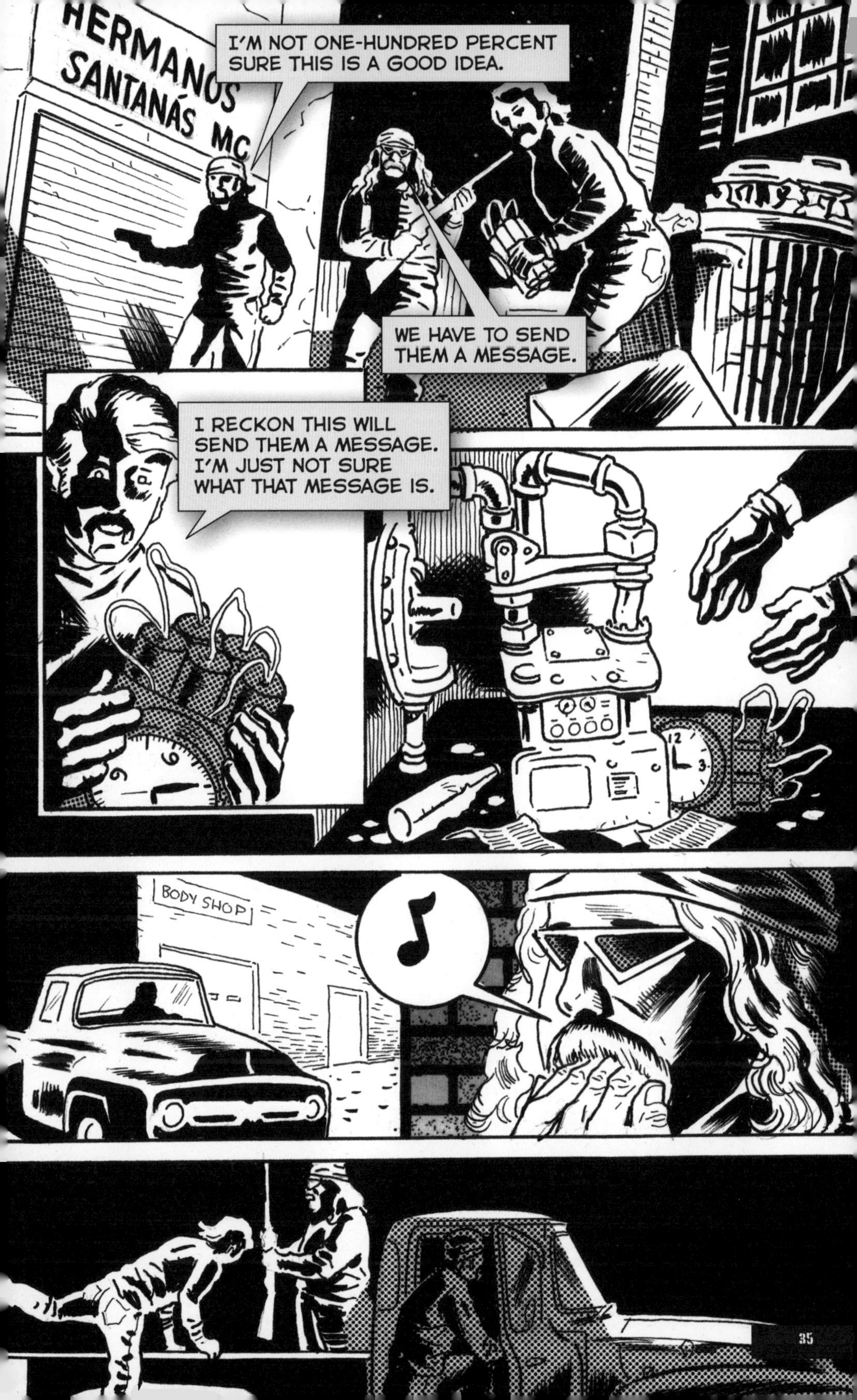
HERMANOS SANTANÁS MC
I'M NOT ONE-HUNDRED PERCENT SURE THIS IS A GOOD IDEA.
WE HAVE TO SEND THEM A MESSAGE.
I RECKON THIS WILL SEND THEM A MESSAGE. I'M JUST NOT SURE WHAT THAT MESSAGE IS.
BODY SHOP
♪

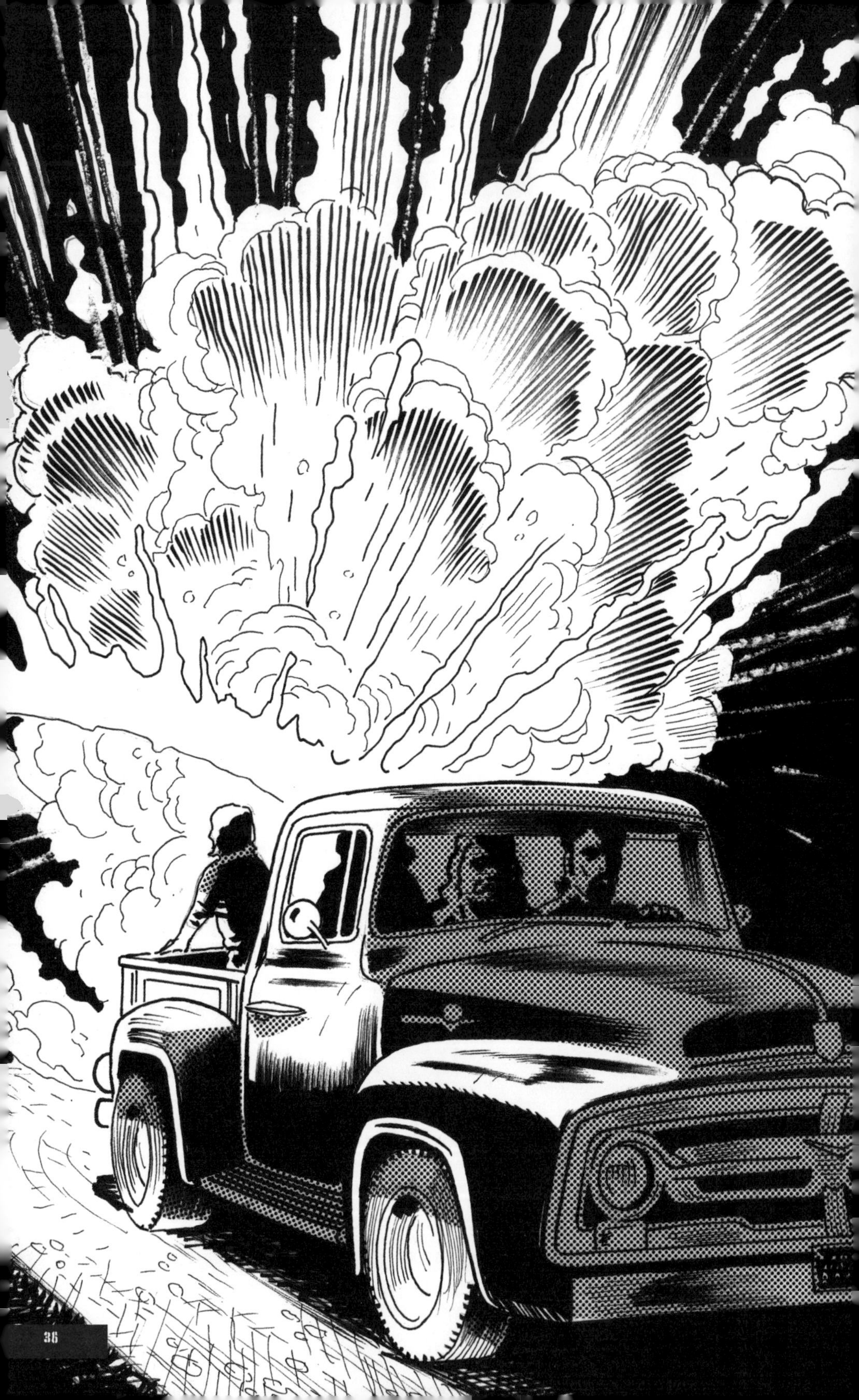

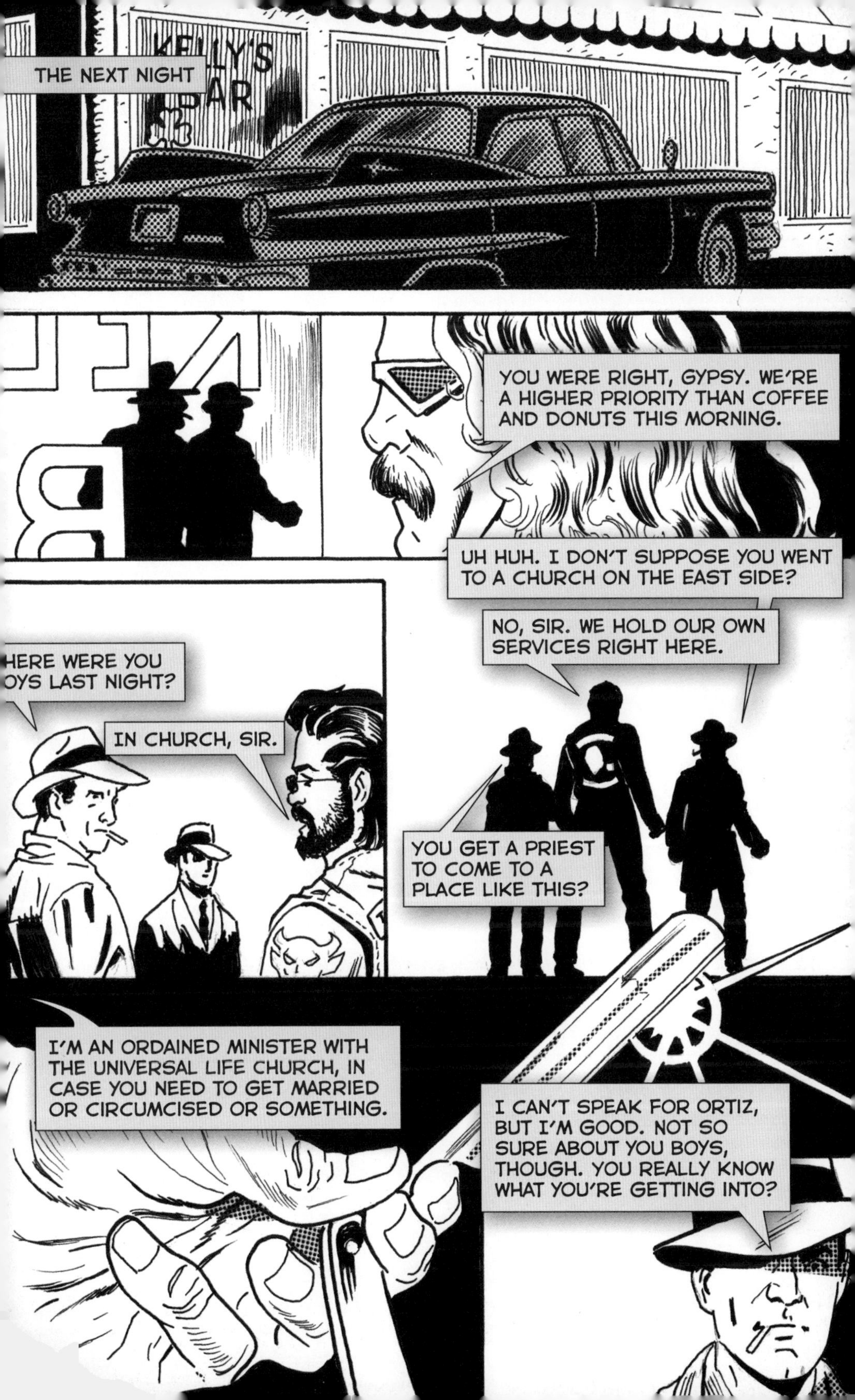

THE NEXT NIGHT
KELLY'S BAR
YOU WERE RIGHT, GYPSY. WE'RE A HIGHER PRIORITY THAN COFFEE AND DONUTS THIS MORNING.
HERE WERE YOU OYS LAST NIGHT?
IN CHURCH, SIR.
UH HUH. I DON'T SUPPOSE YOU WENT TO A CHURCH ON THE EAST SIDE?
NO, SIR. WE HOLD OUR OWN SERVICES RIGHT HERE.
YOU GET A PRIEST TO COME TO A PLACE LIKE THIS?
I'M AN ORDAINED MINISTER WITH THE UNIVERSAL LIFE CHURCH, IN CASE YOU NEED TO GET MARRIED OR CIRCUMCISED OR SOMETHING.
I CAN'T SPEAK FOR ORTIZ, BUT I'M GOOD. NOT SO SURE ABOUT YOU BOYS, THOUGH. YOU REALLY KNOW WHAT YOU'RE GETTING INTO?

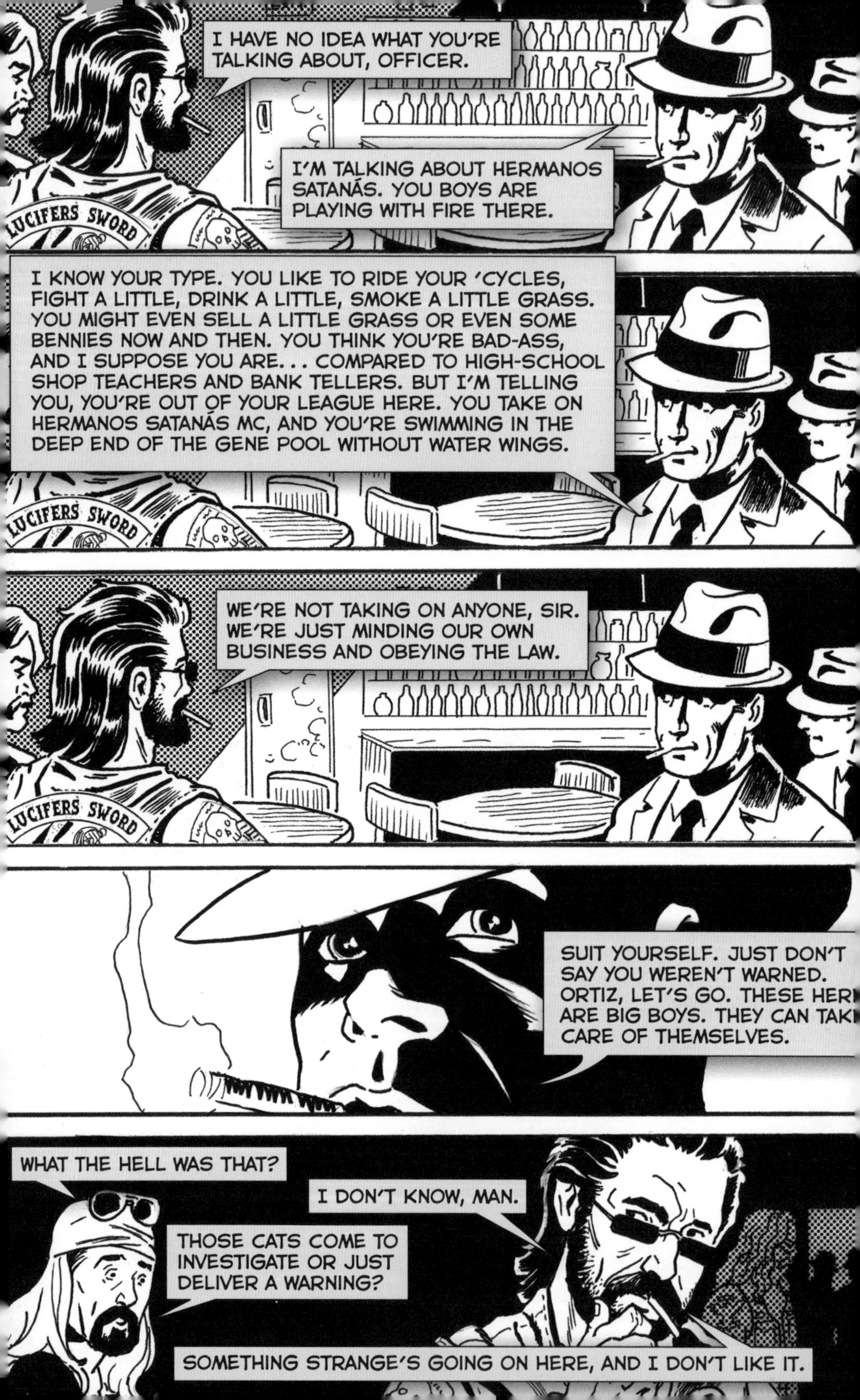

I HAVE NO IDEA WHAT YOU'RE TALKING ABOUT, OFFICER.
I'M TALKING ABOUT HERMANOS SATANÁS. YOU BOYS ARE PLAYING WITH FIRE THERE.
LUCIFERS SWORD
I KNOW YOUR TYPE. YOU LIKE TO RIDE YOUR 'CYCLES, FIGHT A LITTLE, DRINK A LITTLE, SMOKE A LITTLE GRASS. YOU MIGHT EVEN SELL A LITTLE GRASS OR EVEN SOME BENNIES NOW AND THEN. YOU THINK YOU'RE BAD-ASS, AND I SUPPOSE YOU ARE. . . COMPARED TO HIGH-SCHOOL SHOP TEACHERS AND BANK TELLERS. BUT I'M TELLING YOU, YOU'RE OUT OF YOUR LEAGUE HERE. YOU TAKE ON HERMANOS SATANÁS MC, AND YOU'RE SWIMMING IN THE DEEP END OF THE GENE POOL WITHOUT WATER WINGS.
LUCIFERS SWORD
WE'RE NOT TAKING ON ANYONE, SIR. WE'RE JUST MINDING OUR OWN BUSINESS AND OBEYING THE LAW.
LUCIFERS SWORD
SUIT YOURSELF. JUST DON'T SAY YOU WEREN'T WARNED. ORTIZ, LET'S GO. THESE HER ARE BIG BOYS. THEY CAN TAK CARE OF THEMSELVES.
WHAT THE HELL WAS THAT?
I DON'T KNOW, MAN.
THOSE CATS COME TO INVESTIGATE OR JUST DELIVER A WARNING?
SOMETHING STRANGE'S GOING ON HERE, AND I DON'T LIKE IT.

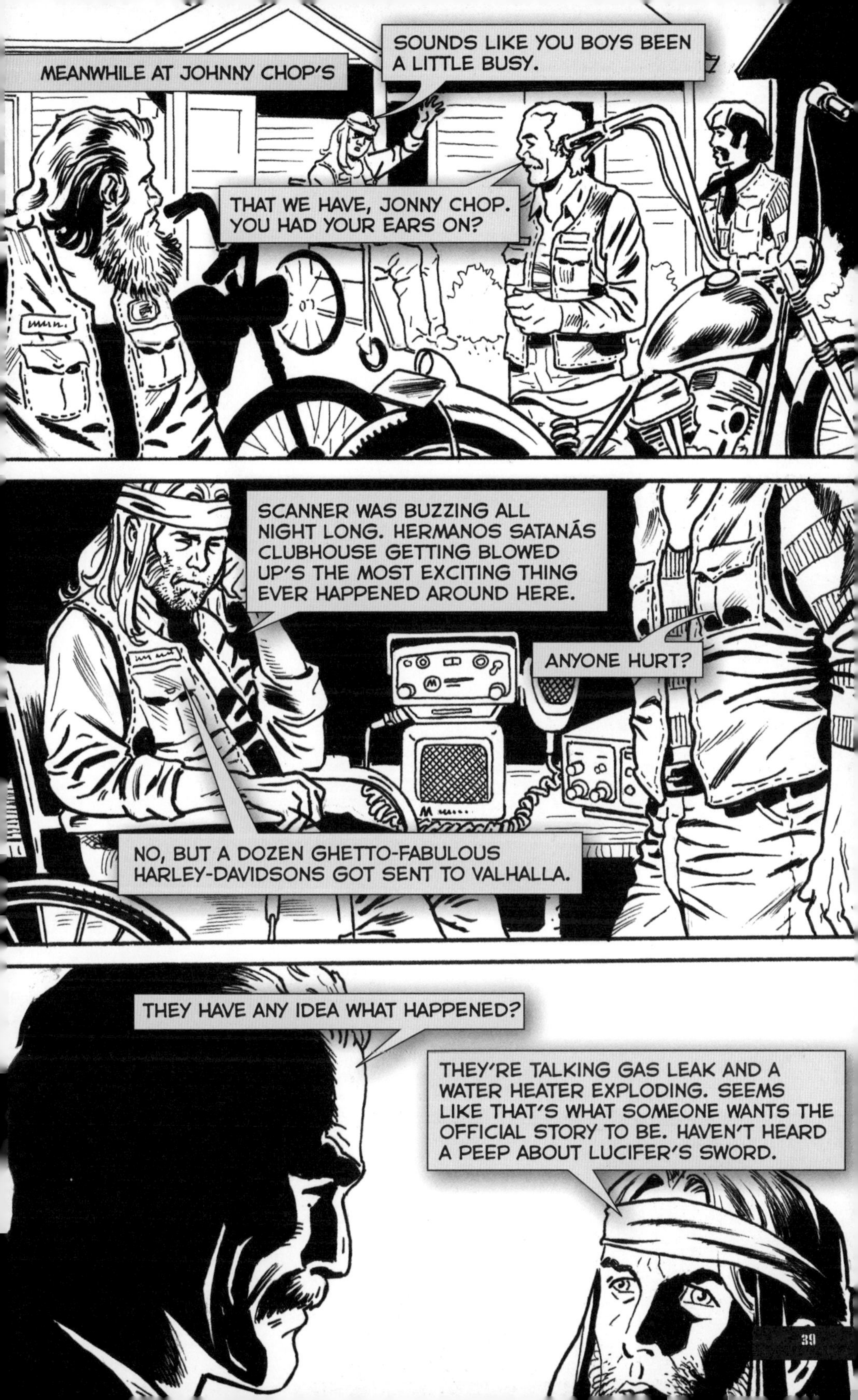
MEANWHILE AT JOHNNY CHOP'S
SOUNDS LIKE YOU BOYS BEEN A LITTLE BUSY.
THAT WE HAVE, JONNY CHOP. YOU HAD YOUR EARS ON?
SCANNER WAS BUZZING ALL NIGHT LONG. HERMANOS SATANÁS CLUBHOUSE GETTING BLOWED UP'S THE MOST EXCITING THING EVER HAPPENED AROUND HERE.
ANYONE HURT?
NO, BUT A DOZEN GHETTO-FABULOUS HARLEY-DAVIDSONS GOT SENT TO VALHALLA.
THEY HAVE ANY IDEA WHAT HAPPENED?
THEY'RE TALKING GAS LEAK AND A WATER HEATER EXPLODING. SEEMS LIKE THAT'S WHAT SOMEONE WANTS THE OFFICIAL STORY TO BE. HAVEN'T HEARD A PEEP ABOUT LUCIFER'S SWORD.

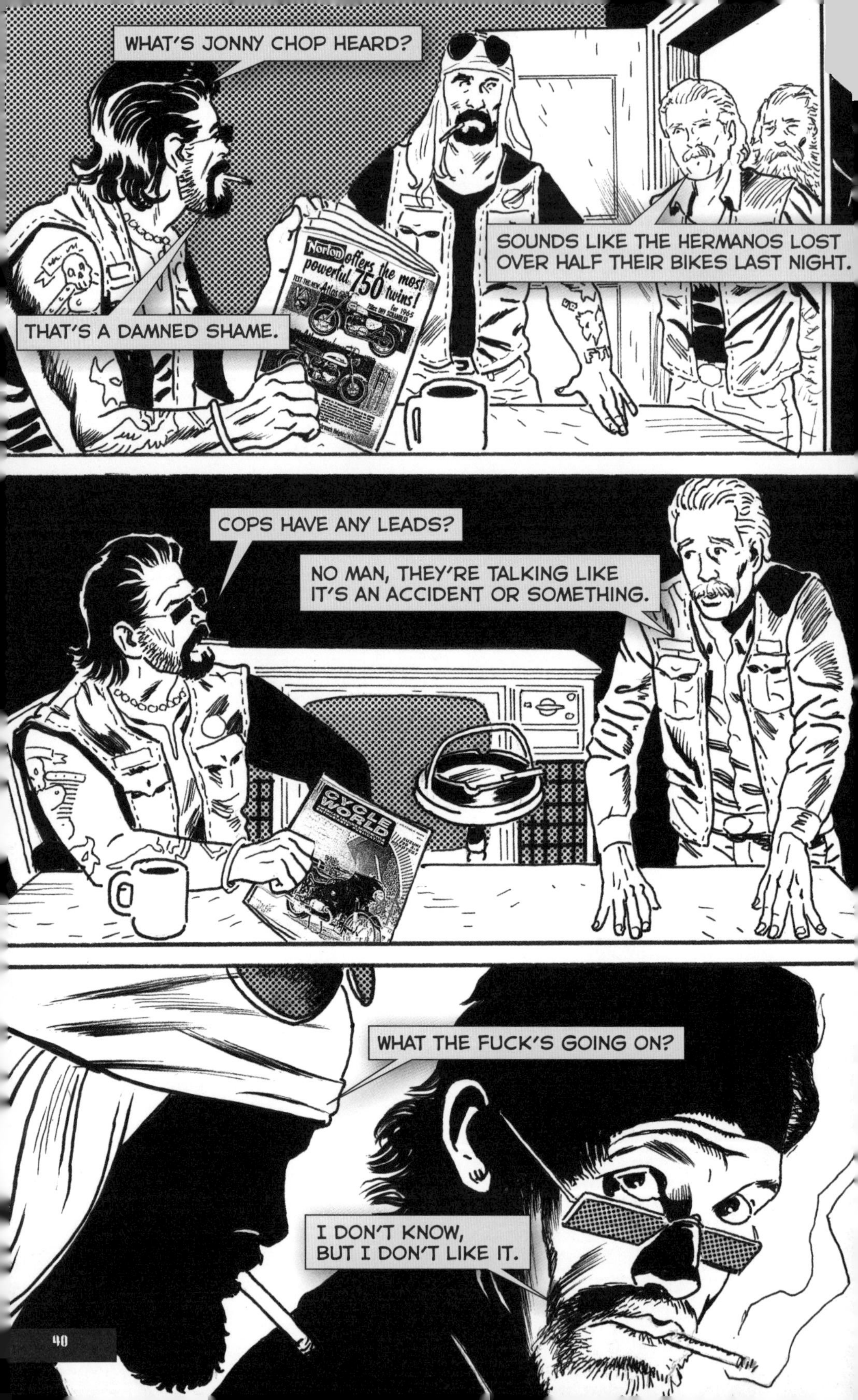
WHAT'S JONNY CHOP HEARD?
SOUNDS LIKE THE HERMANOS LOST OVER HALF THEIR BIKES LAST NIGHT.
THAT'S A DAMNED SHAME.
Norton offers the most powerful 750 twins!
COPS HAVE ANY LEADS?
NO MAN, THEY'RE TALKING LIKE IT'S AN ACCIDENT OR SOMETHING.
CYCLE WORLD
WHAT THE FUCK'S GOING ON?
I DON'T KNOW, BUT I DON'T LIKE IT.

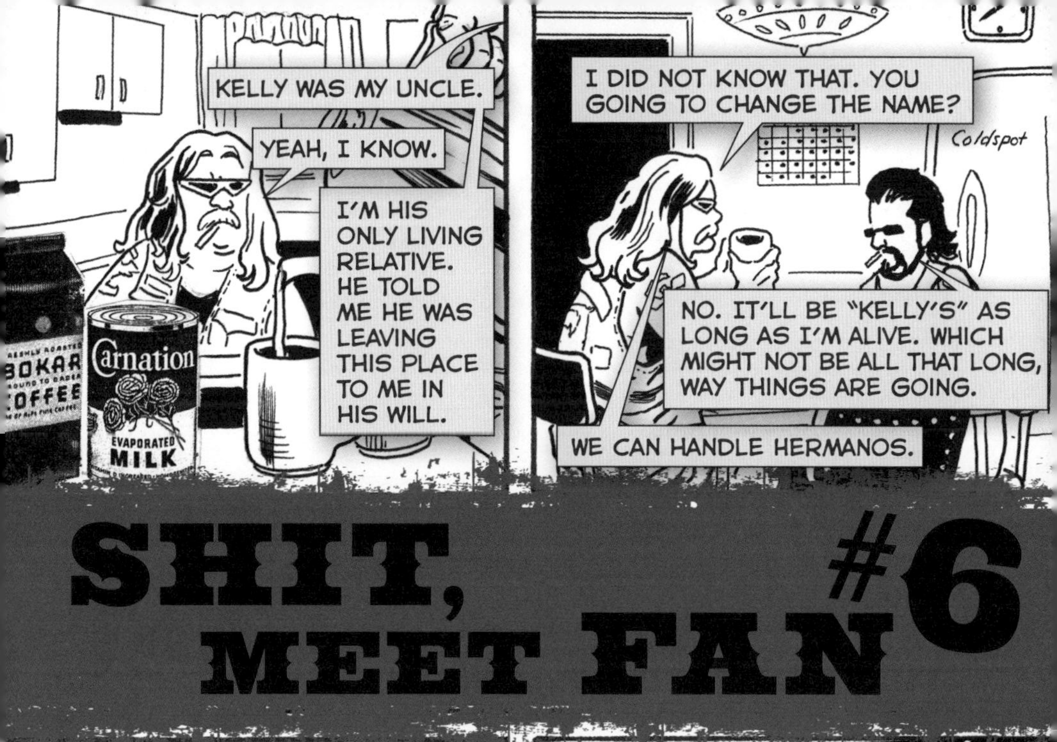

KELLY WAS MY UNCLE.
YEAH, I KNOW.
I'M HIS ONLY LIVING RELATIVE. HE TOLD ME HE WAS LEAVING THIS PLACE TO ME IN HIS WILL.
BOKAR COFFEE
Carnation EVAPORATED MILK
I DID NOT KNOW THAT. YOU GOING TO CHANGE THE NAME?
Coldspot
NO. IT'LL BE "KELLY'S" AS LONG AS I'M ALIVE. WHICH MIGHT NOT BE ALL THAT LONG, WAY THINGS ARE GOING.
WE CAN HANDLE HERMANOS.

SHIT, MEET FAN #6

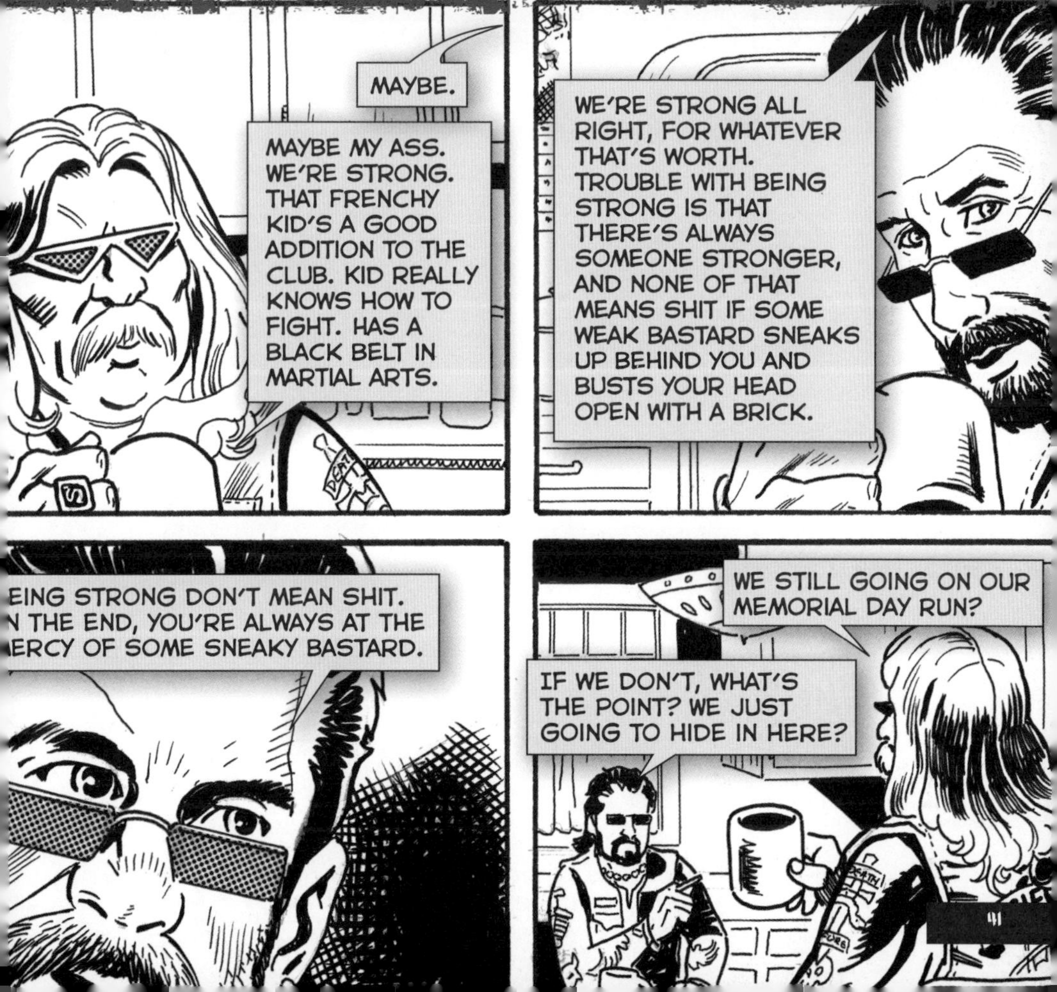

MAYBE.
MAYBE MY ASS. WE'RE STRONG. THAT FRENCHY KID'S A GOOD ADDITION TO THE CLUB. KID REALLY KNOWS HOW TO FIGHT. HAS A BLACK BELT IN MARTIAL ARTS.
WE'RE STRONG ALL RIGHT, FOR WHATEVER THAT'S WORTH. TROUBLE WITH BEING STRONG IS THAT THERE'S ALWAYS SOMEONE STRONGER, AND NONE OF THAT MEANS SHIT IF SOME WEAK BASTARD SNEAKS UP BEHIND YOU AND BUSTS YOUR HEAD OPEN WITH A BRICK.
EING STRONG DON'T MEAN SHIT. N THE END, YOU'RE ALWAYS AT THE ERCY OF SOME SNEAKY BASTARD.
WE STILL GOING ON OUR MEMORIAL DAY RUN?
IF WE DON'T, WHAT'S THE POINT? WE JUST GOING TO HIDE IN HERE?

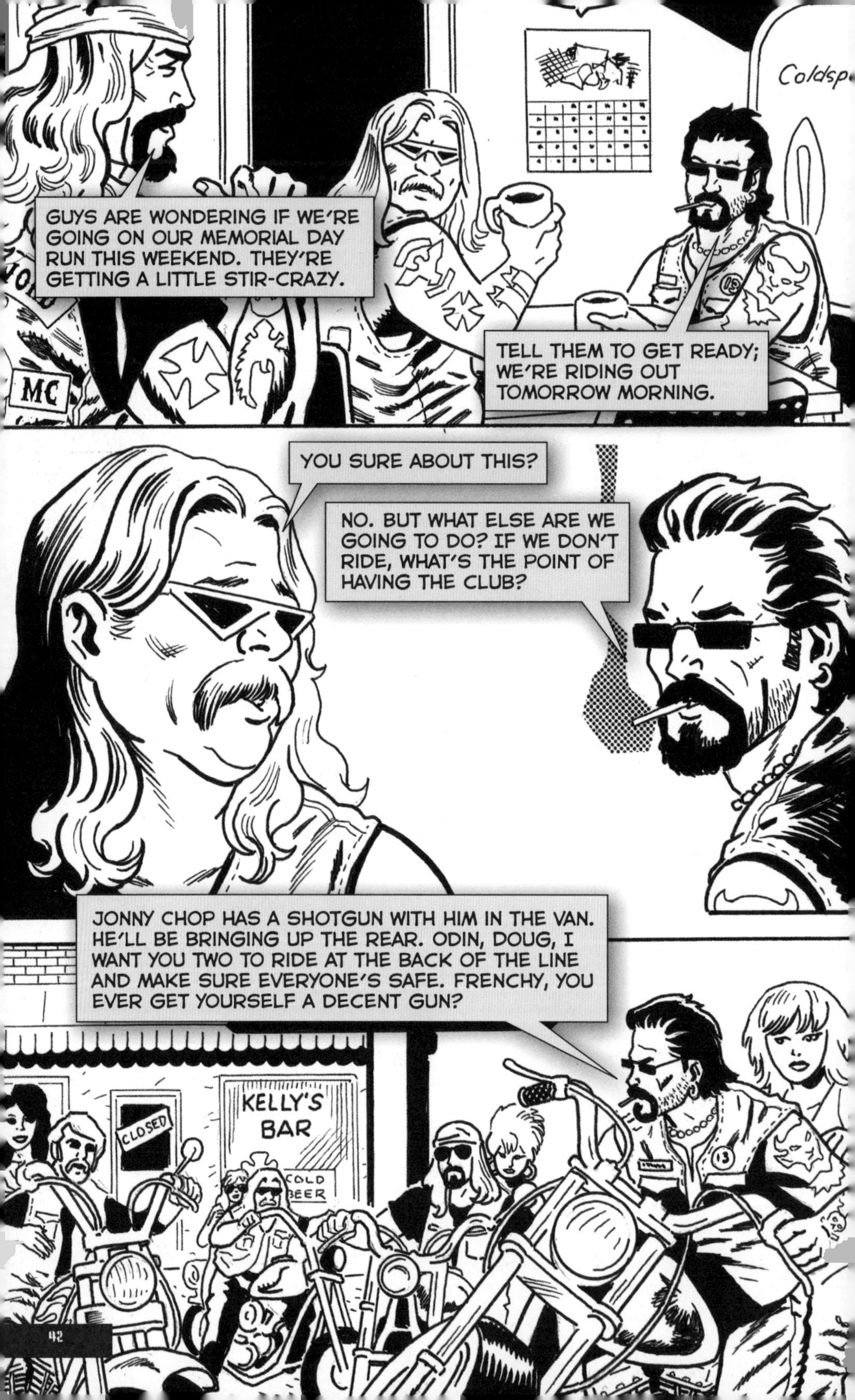
GUYS ARE WONDERING IF WE'RE GOING ON OUR MEMORIAL DAY RUN THIS WEEKEND. THEY'RE GETTING A LITTLE STIR-CRAZY.
MC
TELL THEM TO GET READY; WE'RE RIDING OUT TOMORROW MORNING.
YOU SURE ABOUT THIS?
NO. BUT WHAT ELSE ARE WE GOING TO DO? IF WE DON'T RIDE, WHAT'S THE POINT OF HAVING THE CLUB?
JONNY CHOP HAS A SHOTGUN WITH HIM IN THE VAN. HE'LL BE BRINGING UP THE REAR. ODIN, DOUG, I WANT YOU TWO TO RIDE AT THE BACK OF THE LINE AND MAKE SURE EVERYONE'S SAFE. FRENCHY, YOU EVER GET YOURSELF A DECENT GUN?
KELLY'S BAR
CLOSED
COLD BEER

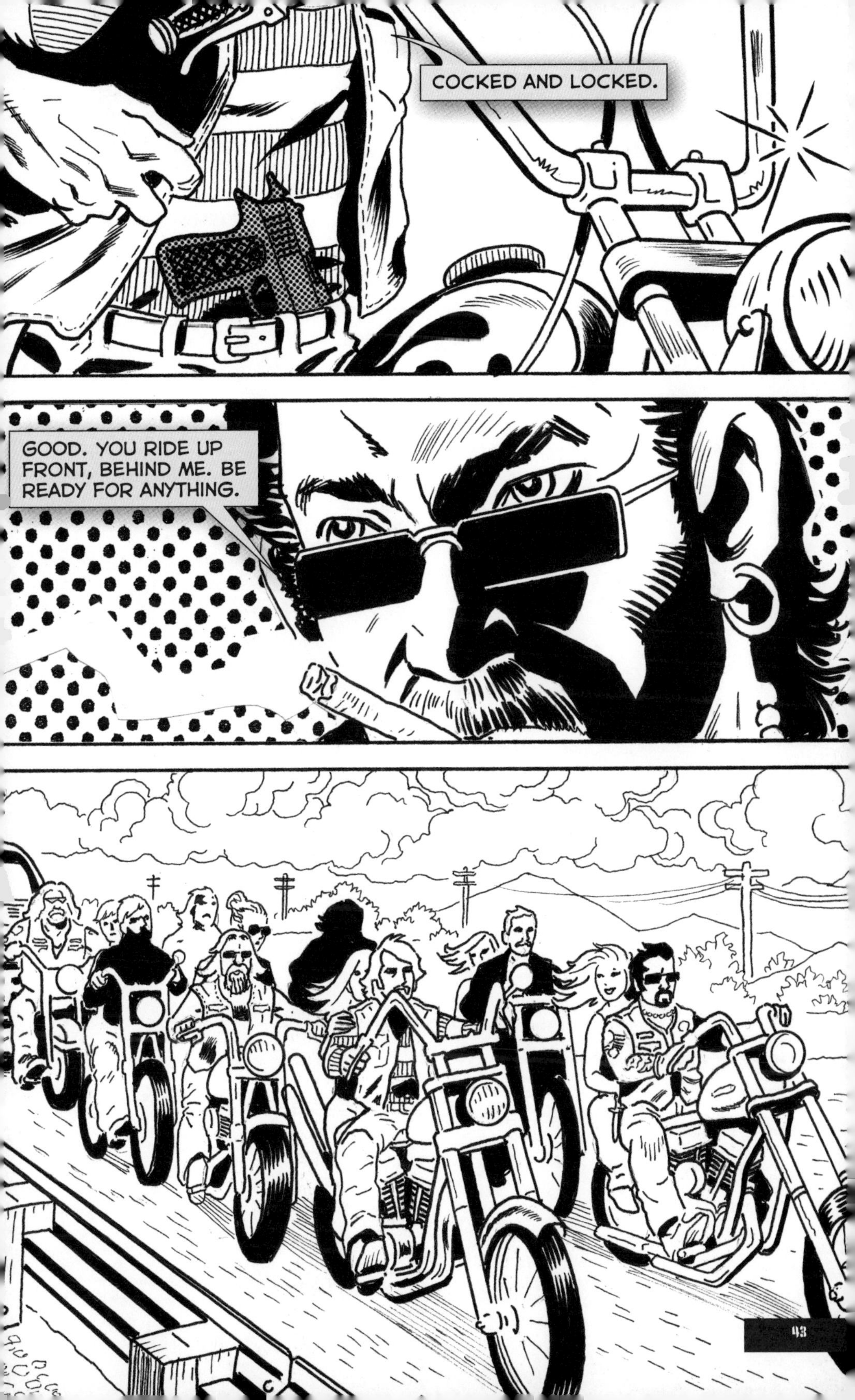
COCKED AND LOCKED.
GOOD. YOU RIDE UP FRONT, BEHIND ME. BE READY FOR ANYTHING.

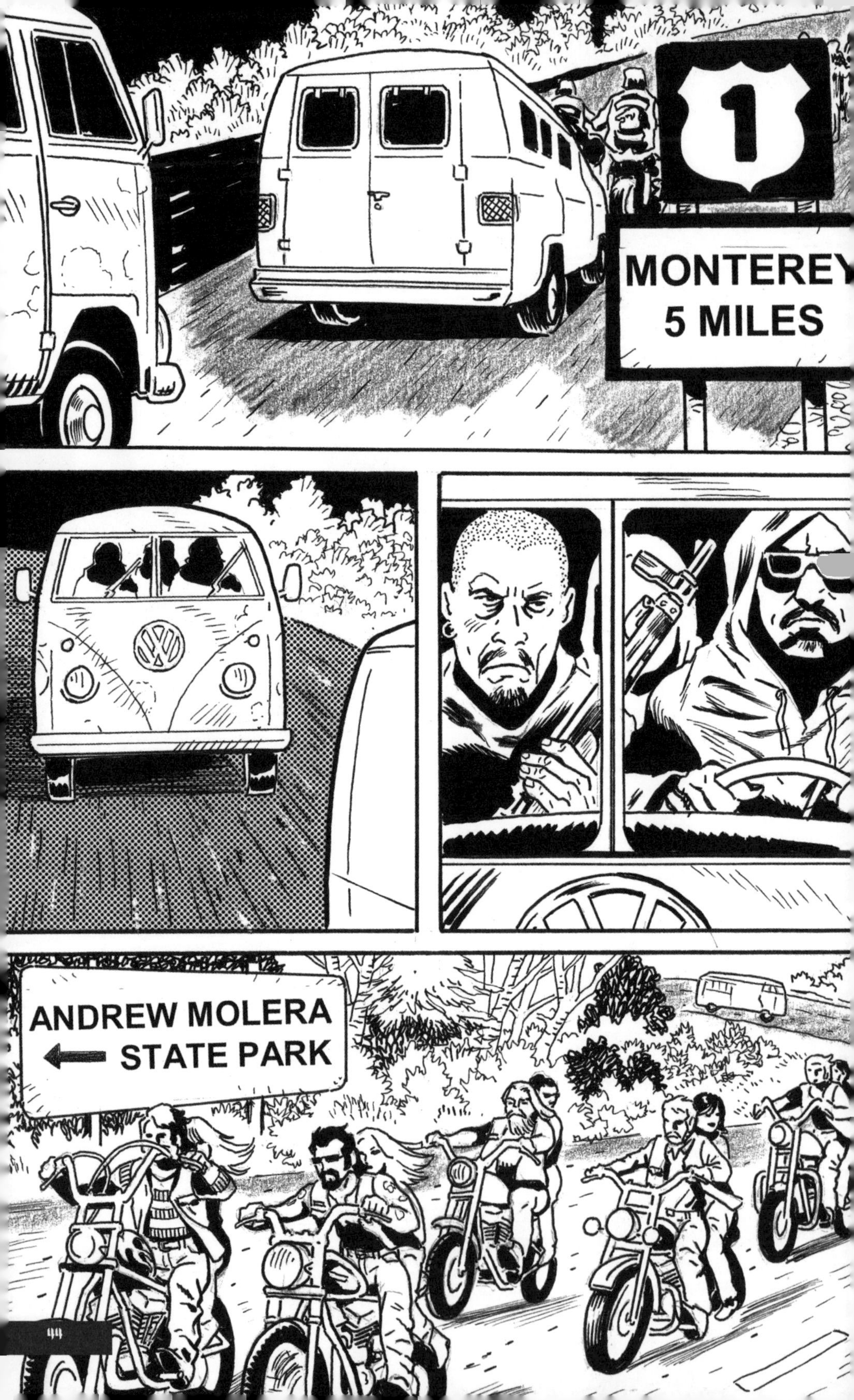
1
MONTEREY
5 MILES
ANDREW MOLERA
STATE PARK

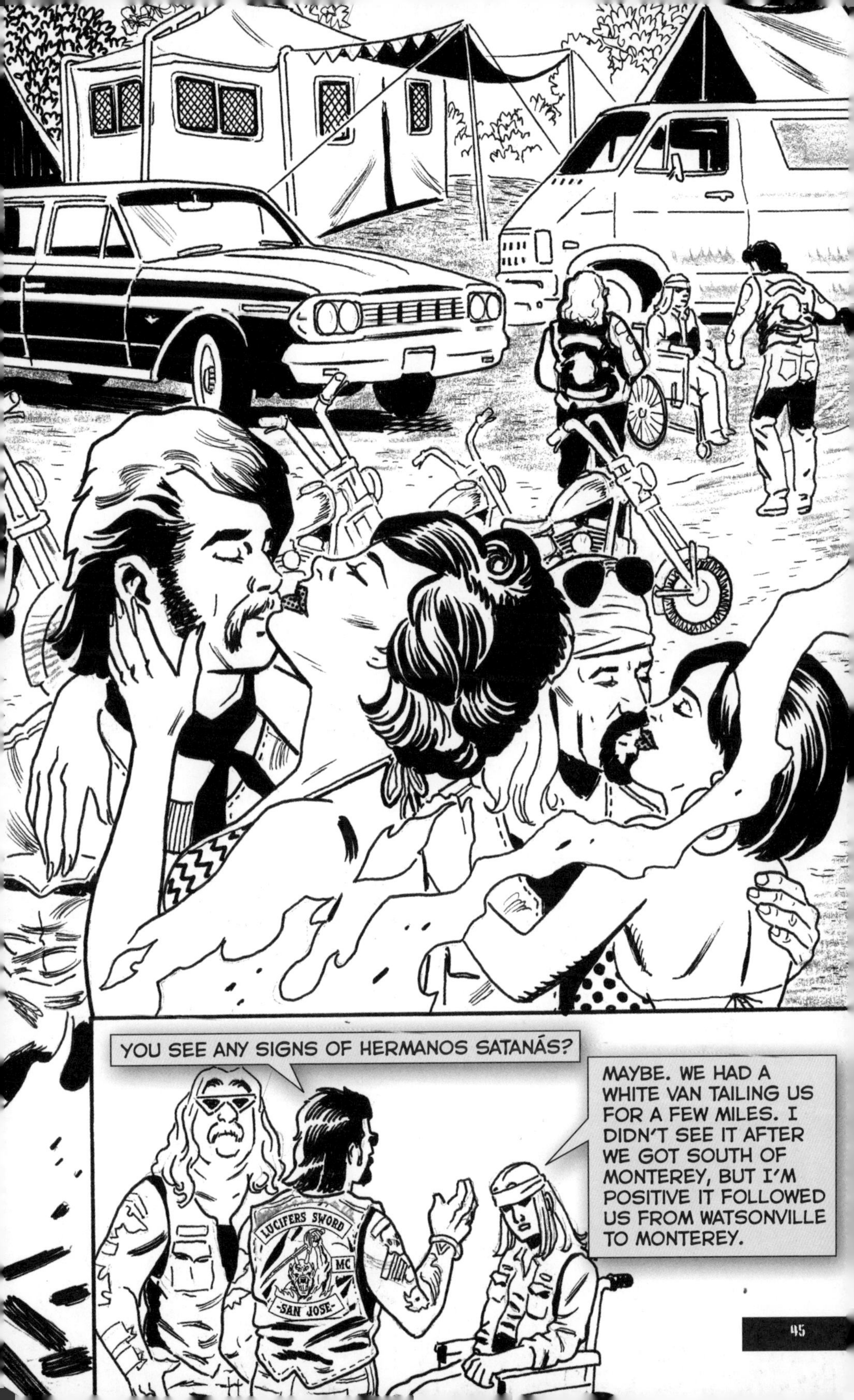
YOU SEE ANY SIGNS OF HERMANOS SATANÁS?
MAYBE. WE HAD A WHITE VAN TAILING US FOR A FEW MILES. I DIDN'T SEE IT AFTER WE GOT SOUTH OF MONTEREY, BUT I'M POSITIVE IT FOLLOWED US FROM WATSONVILLE TO MONTEREY.
LUCIFERS SWORD
MC
SAN JOSE

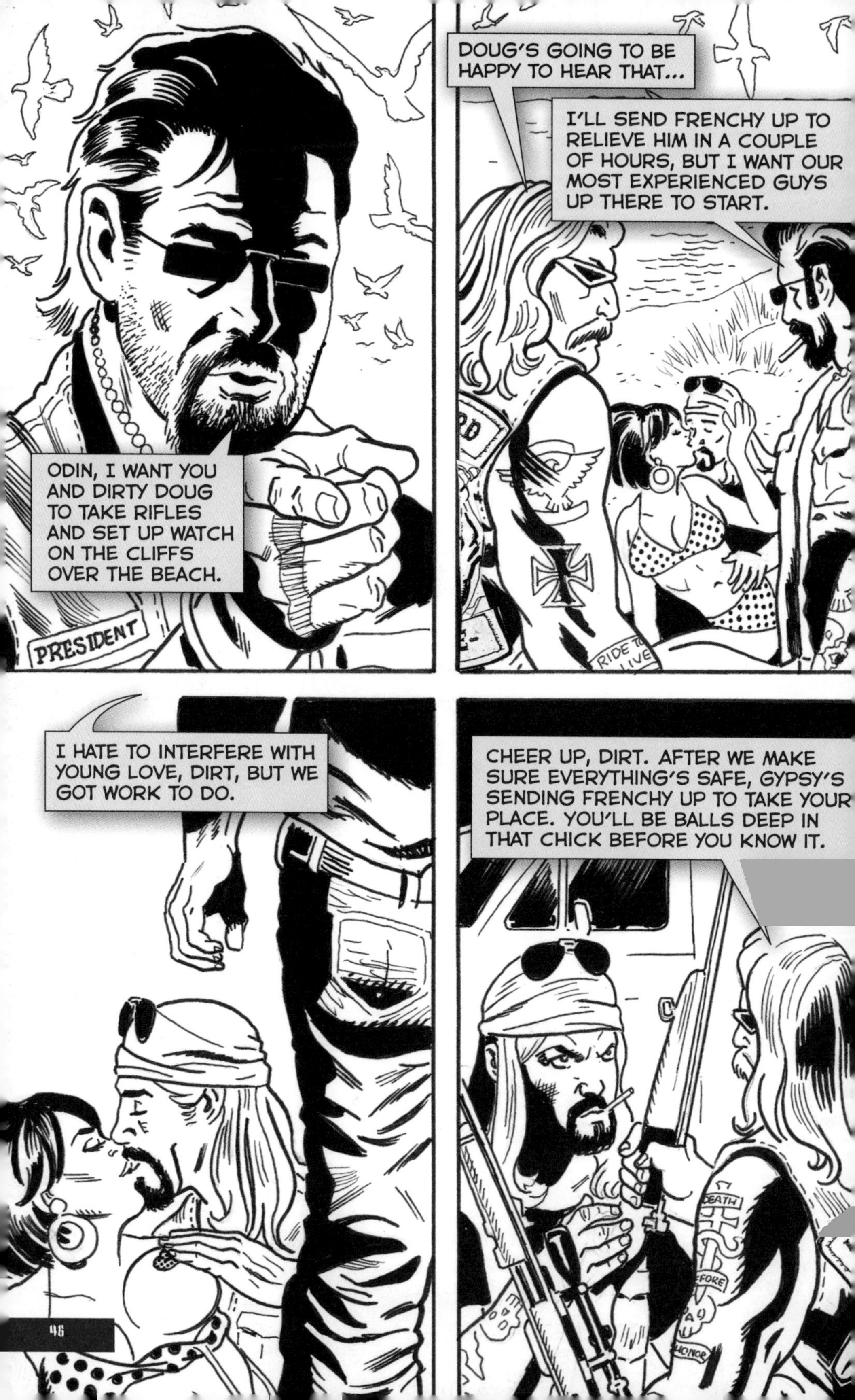
ODIN, I WANT YOU AND DIRTY DOUG TO TAKE RIFLES AND SET UP WATCH ON THE CLIFFS OVER THE BEACH.
PRESIDENT
DOUG'S GOING TO BE HAPPY TO HEAR THAT...
I'LL SEND FRENCHY UP TO RELIEVE HIM IN A COUPLE OF HOURS, BUT I WANT OUR MOST EXPERIENCED GUYS UP THERE TO START.
RIDE TO LIVE
I HATE TO INTERFERE WITH YOUNG LOVE, DIRT, BUT WE GOT WORK TO DO.
CHEER UP, DIRT. AFTER WE MAKE SURE EVERYTHING'S SAFE, GYPSY'S SENDING FRENCHY UP TO TAKE YOUR PLACE. YOU'LL BE BALLS DEEP IN THAT CHICK BEFORE YOU KNOW IT.
DEATH
HONOR

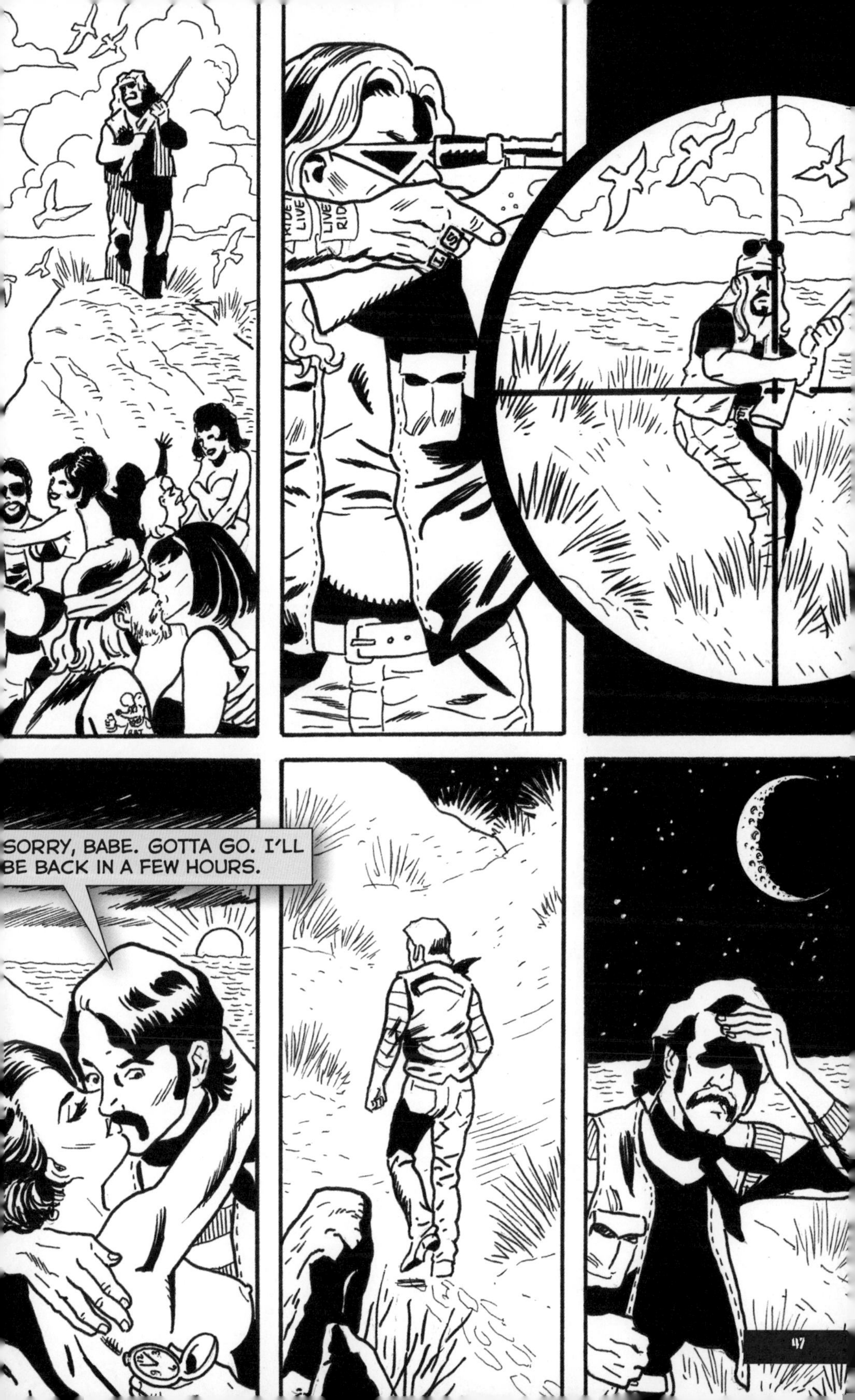
SORRY, BABE. GOTTA GO. I'LL BE BACK IN A FEW HOURS.

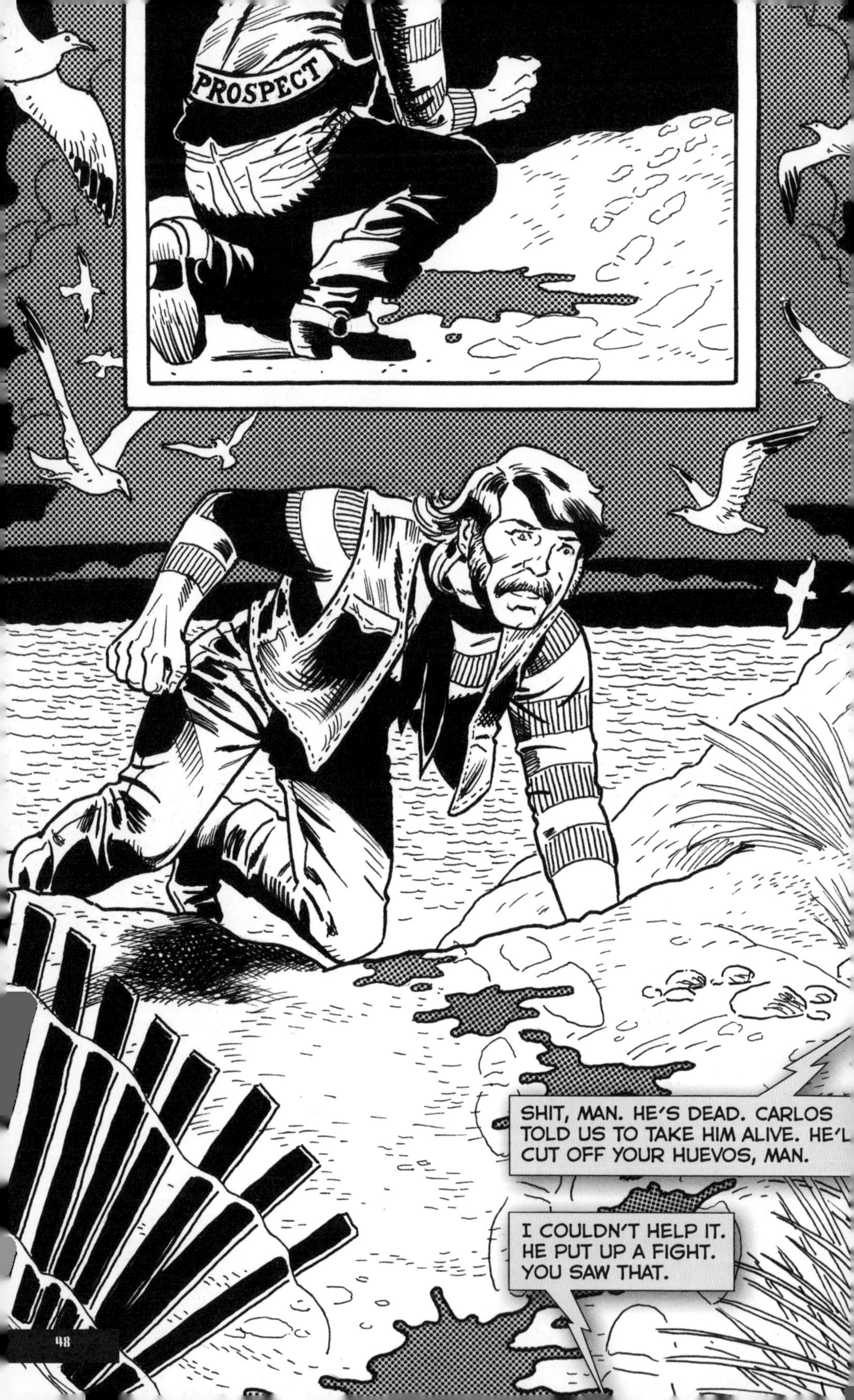
PROSPECT
SHIT, MAN. HE'S DEAD. CARLOS TOLD US TO TAKE HIM ALIVE. HE'L CUT OFF YOUR HUEVOS, MAN.
I COULDN'T HELP IT. HE PUT UP A FIGHT. YOU SAW THAT.

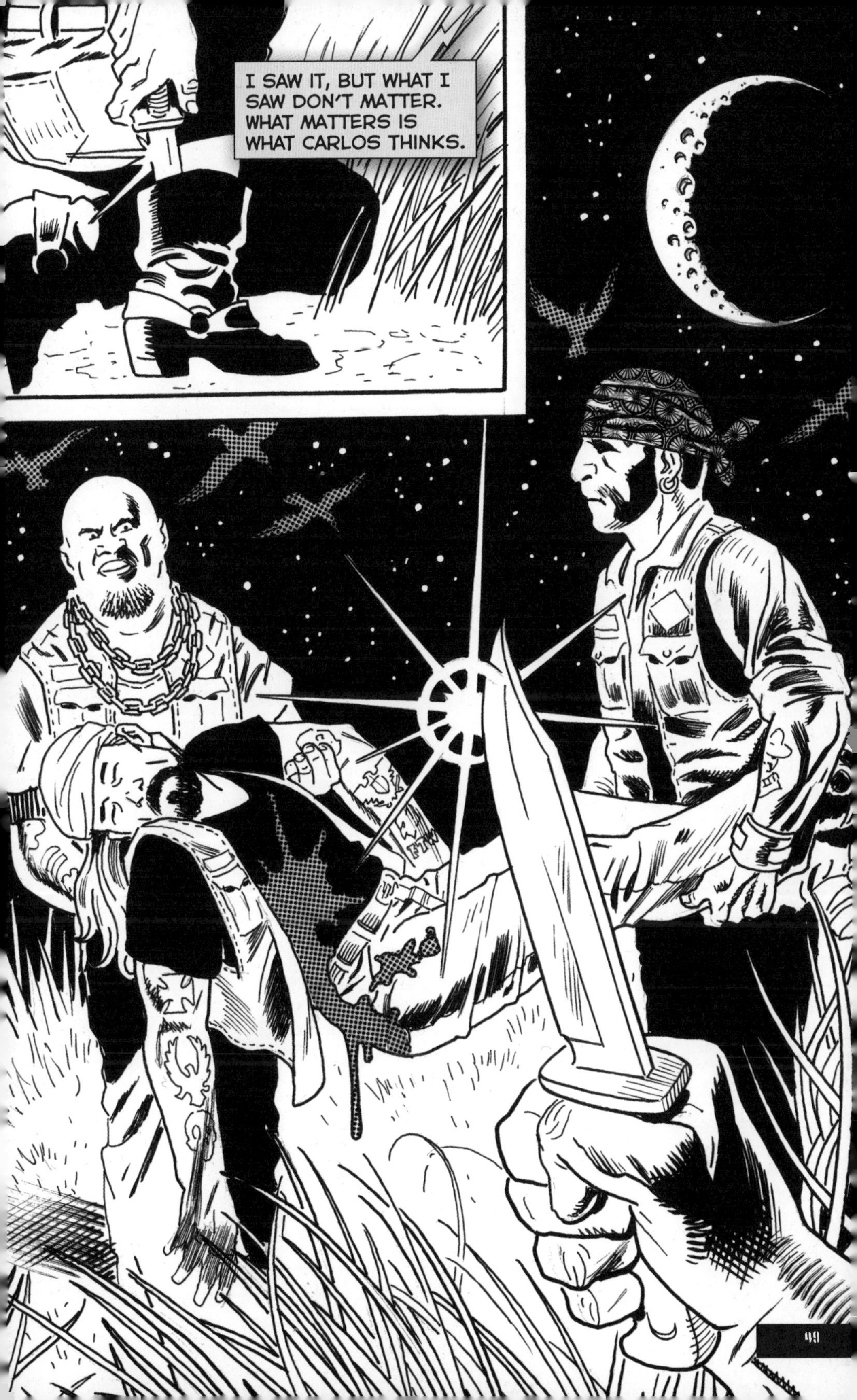
I SAW IT, BUT WHAT I SAW DON'T MATTER. WHAT MATTERS IS WHAT CARLOS THINKS.

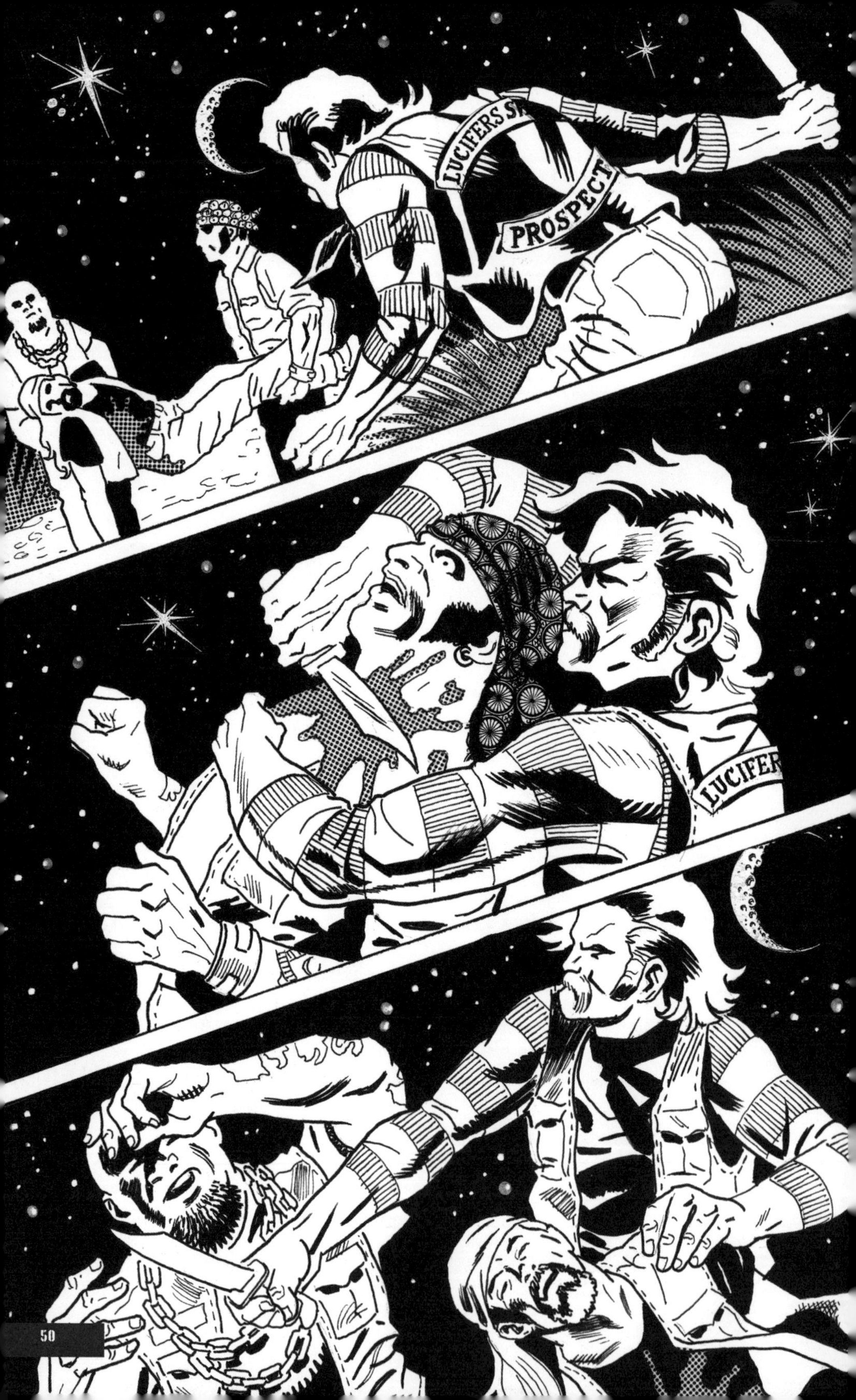
PROSPECT
LUCIFER

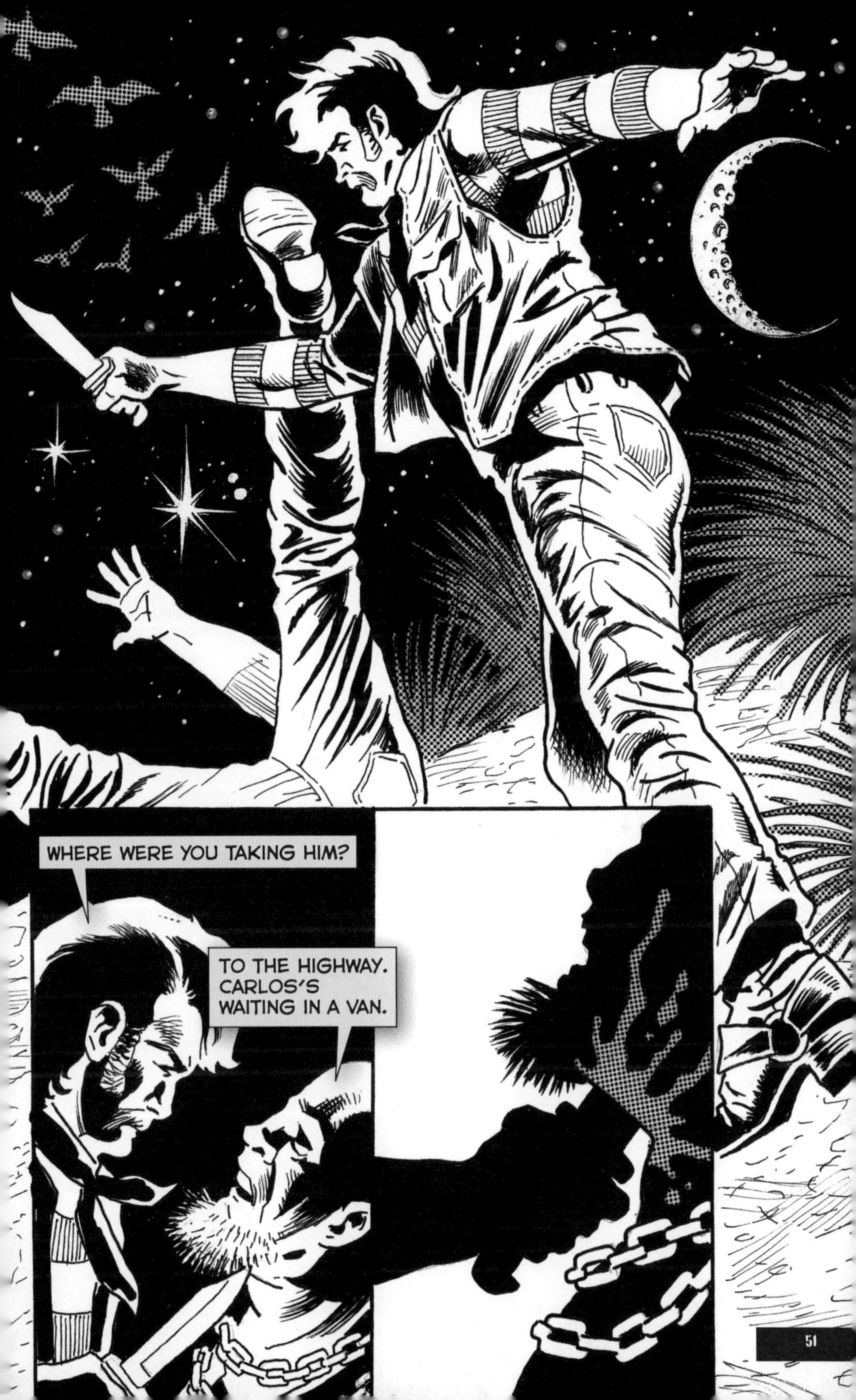
WHERE WERE YOU TAKING HIM?
TO THE HIGHWAY. CARLOS'S WAITING IN A VAN.

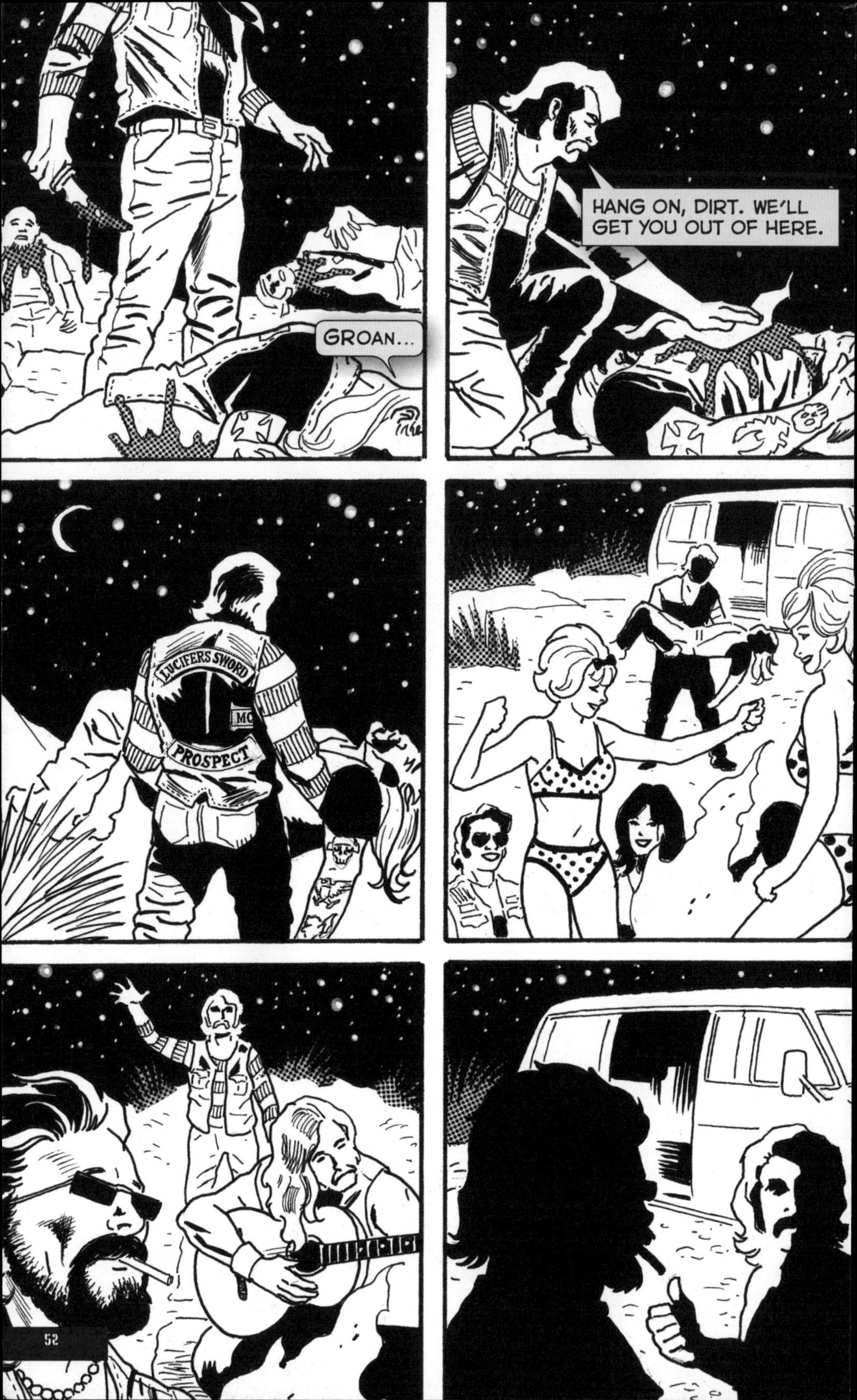
GROAN...
HANG ON, DIRT. WE'LL GET YOU OUT OF HERE.
LUCIFERS SWORD
MC
PROSPECT

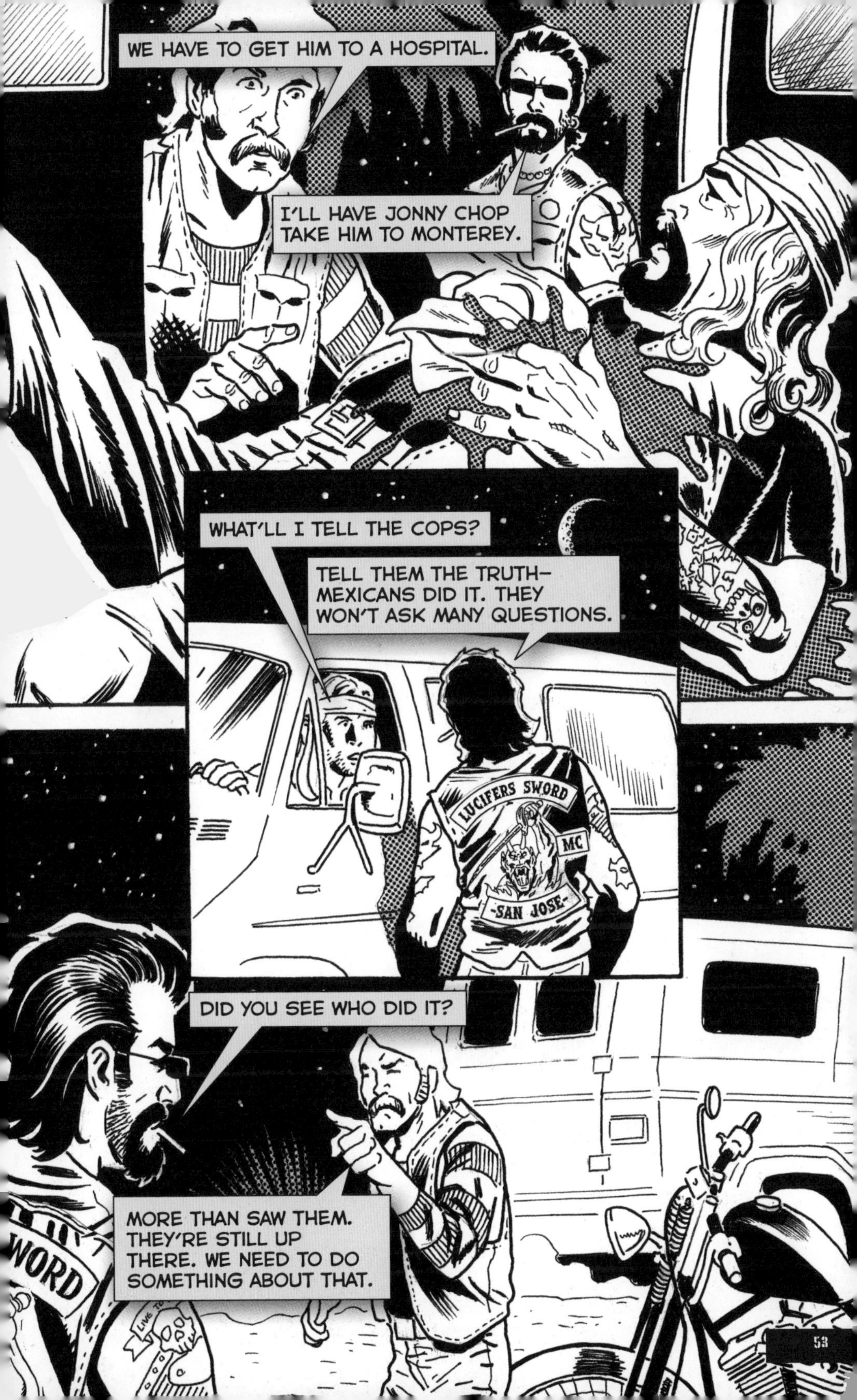
WE HAVE TO GET HIM TO A HOSPITAL.
I'LL HAVE JONNY CHOP TAKE HIM TO MONTEREY.
WHAT'LL I TELL THE COPS?
TELL THEM THE TRUTH—MEXICANS DID IT. THEY WON'T ASK MANY QUESTIONS.
LUCIFERS SWORD
MC
SAN JOSE
DID YOU SEE WHO DID IT?
MORE THAN SAW THEM. THEY'RE STILL UP THERE. WE NEED TO DO SOMETHING ABOUT THAT.

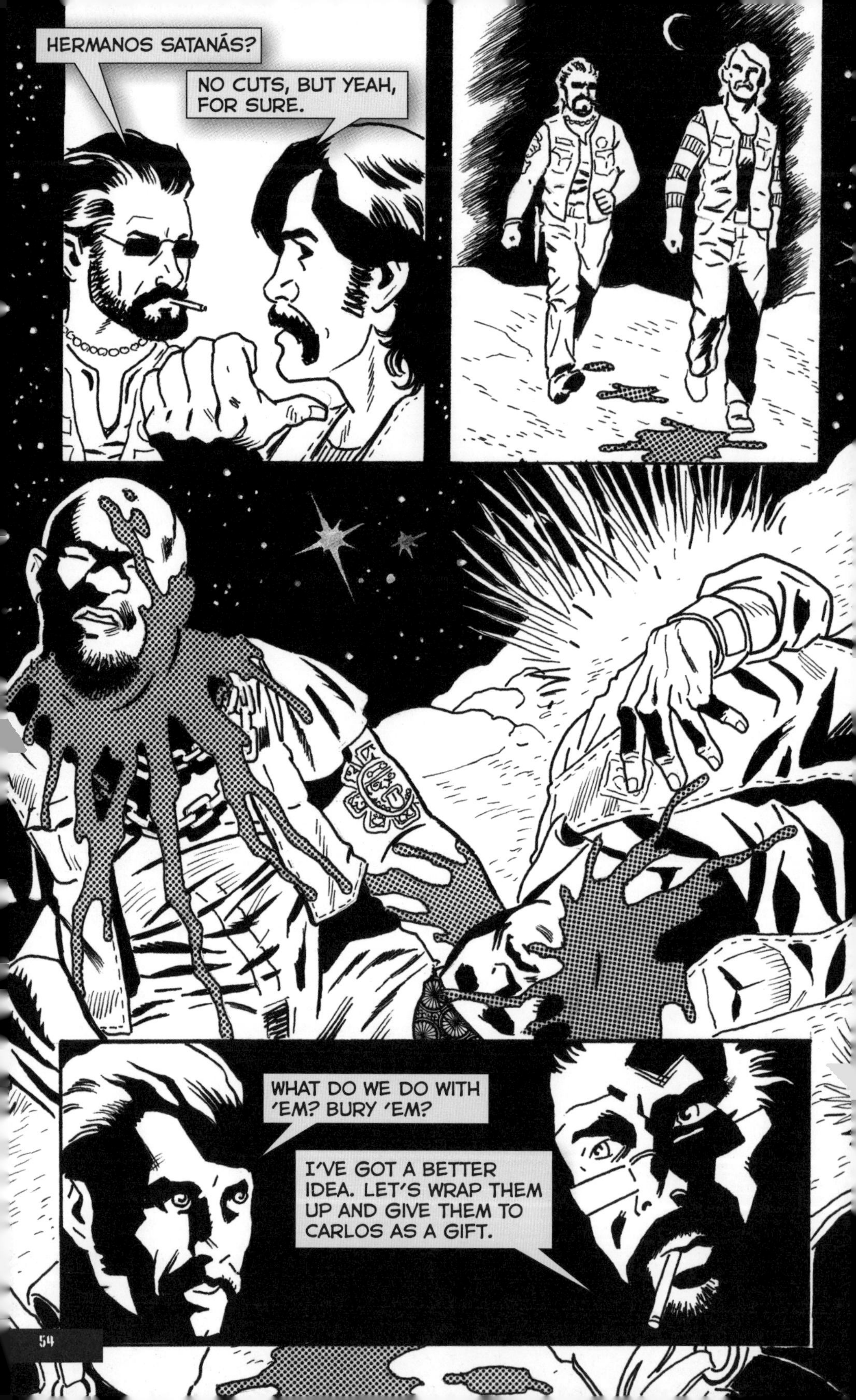
HERMANOS SATANÁS?
NO CUTS, BUT YEAH, FOR SURE.
WHAT DO WE DO WITH 'EM? BURY 'EM?
I'VE GOT A BETTER IDEA. LET'S WRAP THEM UP AND GIVE THEM TO CARLOS AS A GIFT.

FAN, MEET SHIT #7

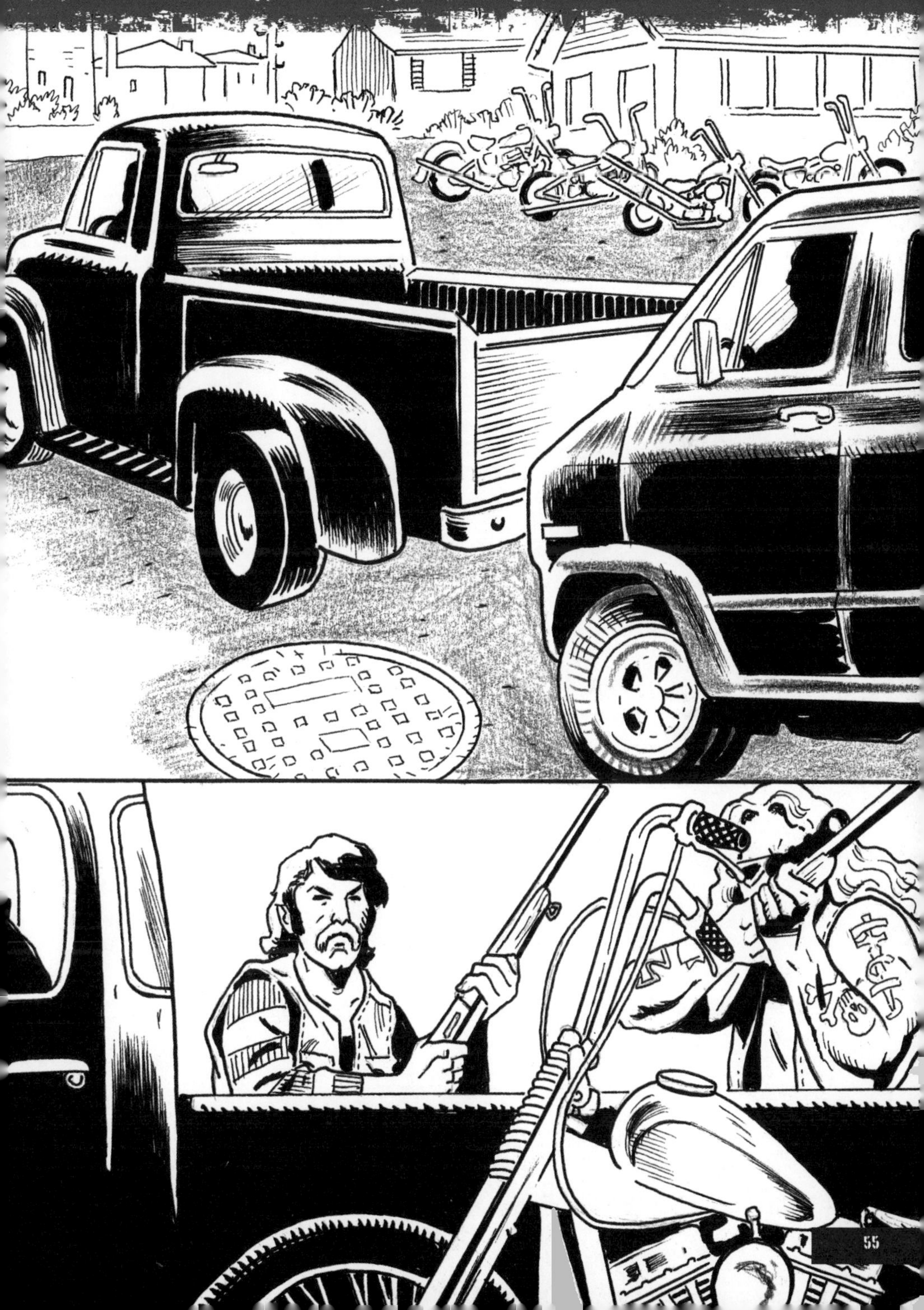

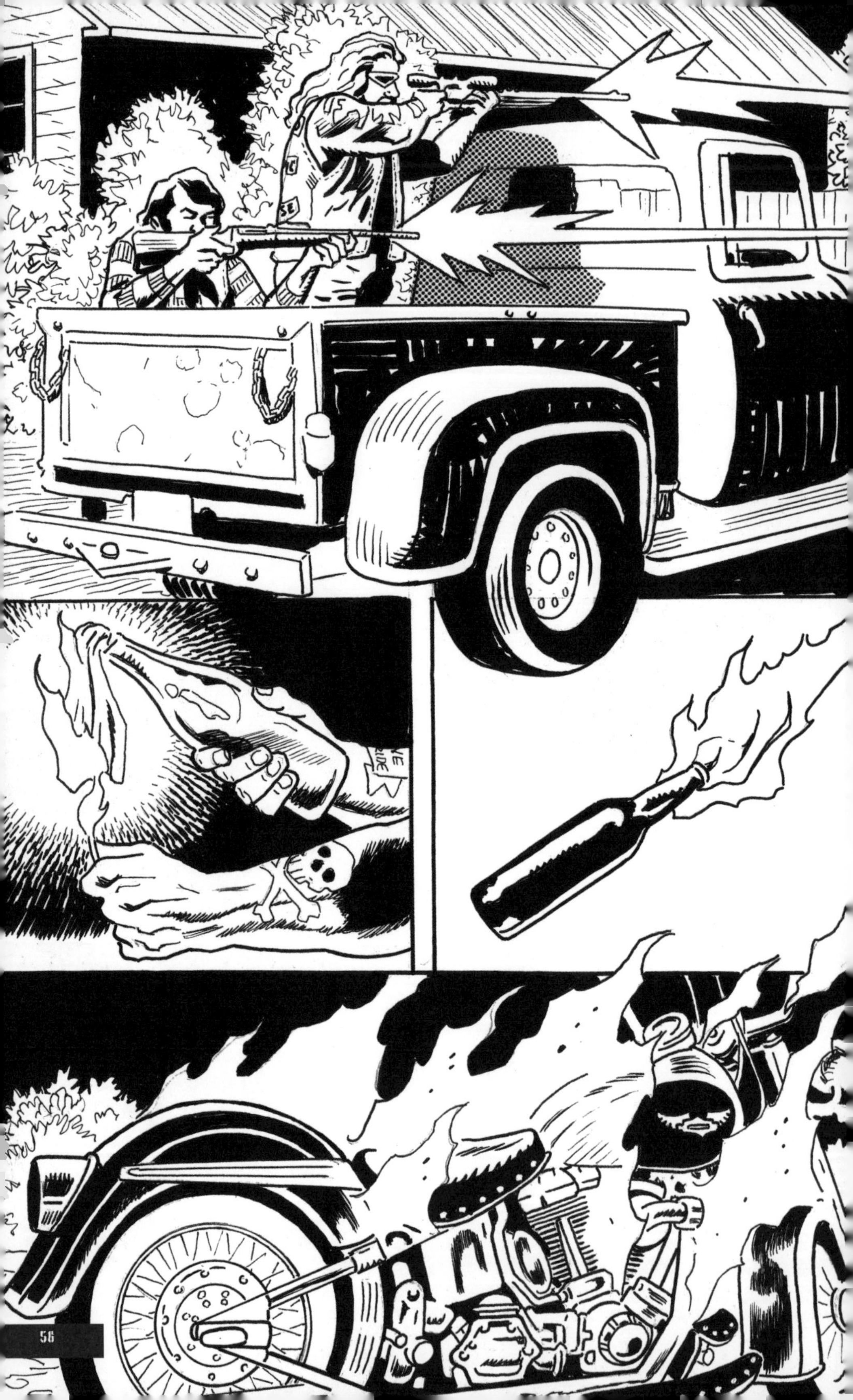

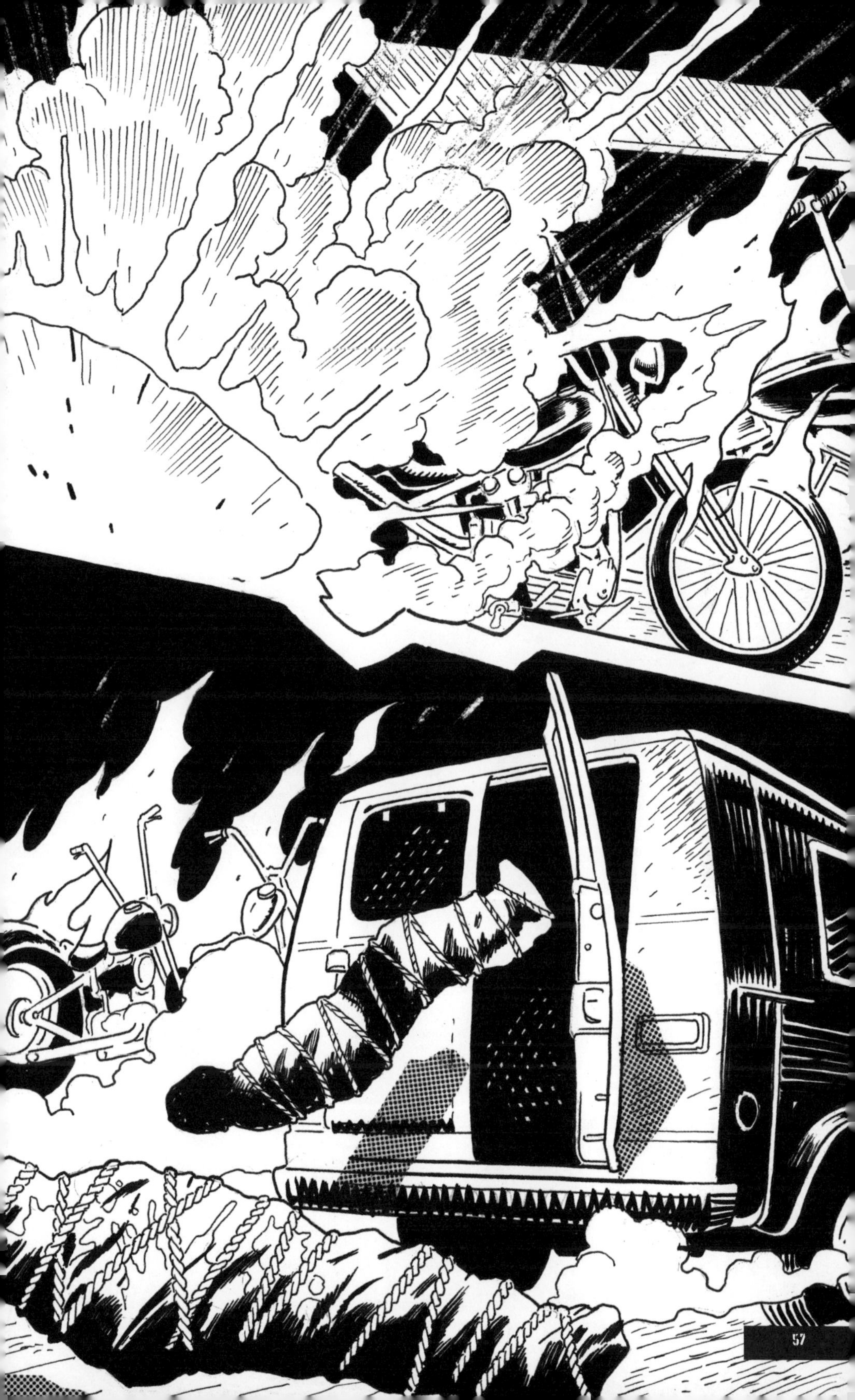

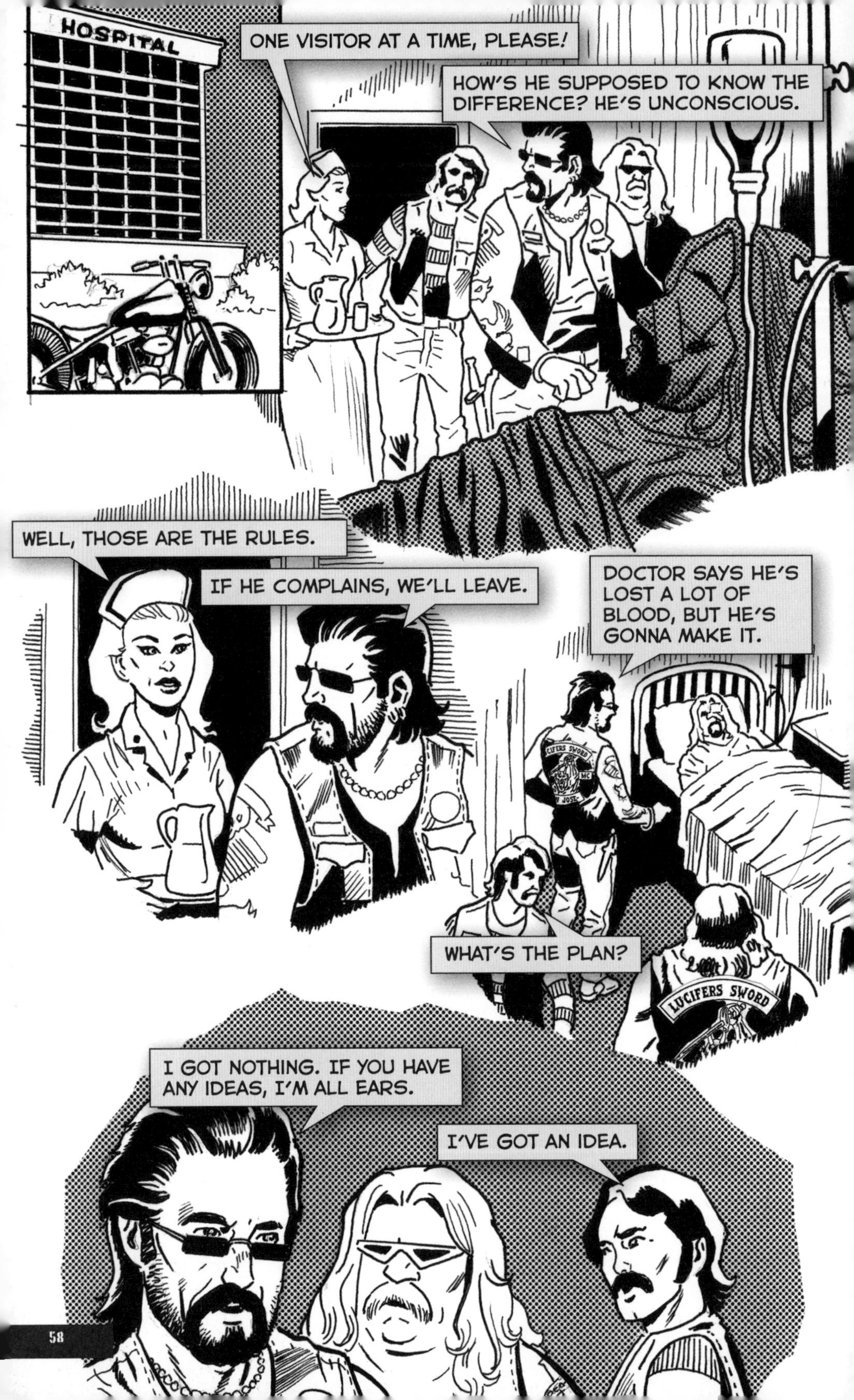
HOSPITAL
ONE VISITOR AT A TIME, PLEASE!
HOW'S HE SUPPOSED TO KNOW THE DIFFERENCE? HE'S UNCONSCIOUS.
WELL, THOSE ARE THE RULES.
IF HE COMPLAINS, WE'LL LEAVE.
DOCTOR SAYS HE'S LOST A LOT OF BLOOD, BUT HE'S GONNA MAKE IT.
WHAT'S THE PLAN?
LUCIFERS SWORD
I GOT NOTHING. IF YOU HAVE ANY IDEAS, I'M ALL EARS.
I'VE GOT AN IDEA.

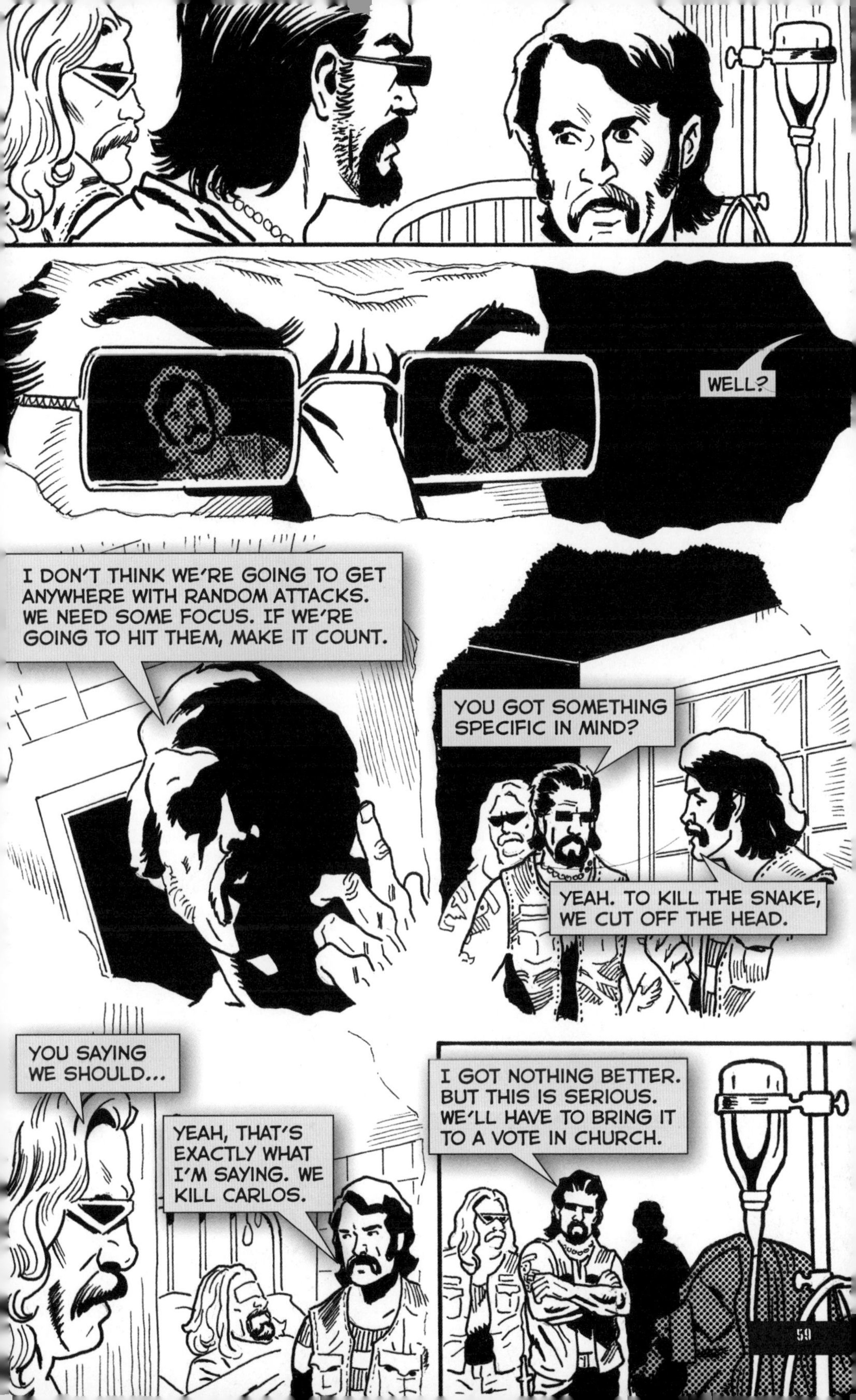
WELL?
I DON'T THINK WE'RE GOING TO GET ANYWHERE WITH RANDOM ATTACKS. WE NEED SOME FOCUS. IF WE'RE GOING TO HIT THEM, MAKE IT COUNT.
YOU GOT SOMETHING SPECIFIC IN MIND?
YEAH. TO KILL THE SNAKE, WE CUT OFF THE HEAD.
YOU SAYING WE SHOULD...
YEAH, THAT'S EXACTLY WHAT I'M SAYING. WE KILL CARLOS.
I GOT NOTHING BETTER. BUT THIS IS SERIOUS. WE'LL HAVE TO BRING IT TO A VOTE IN CHURCH.

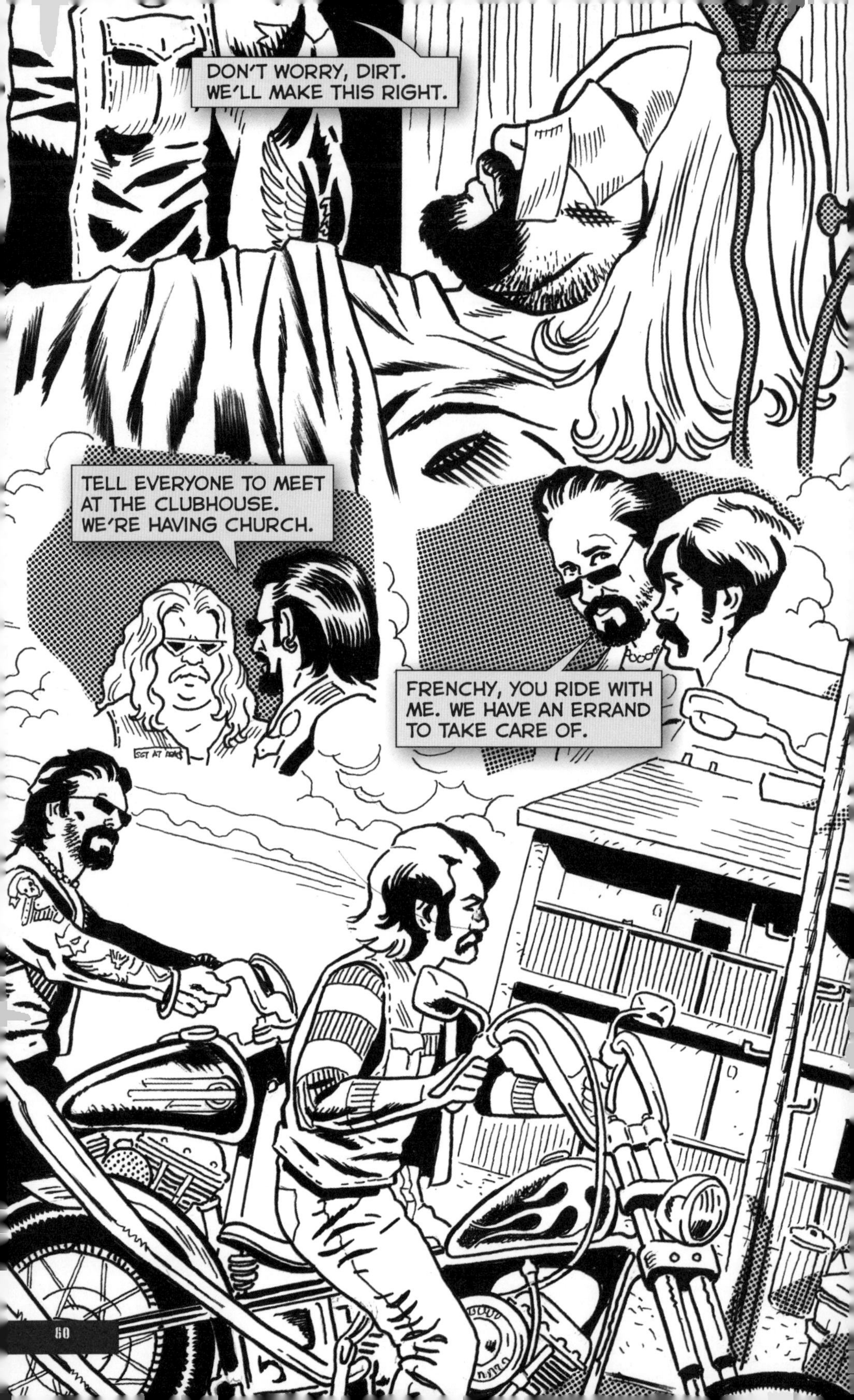
DON'T WORRY, DIRT. WE'LL MAKE THIS RIGHT.
TELL EVERYONE TO MEET AT THE CLUBHOUSE. WE'RE HAVING CHURCH.
FRENCHY, YOU RIDE WITH ME. WE HAVE AN ERRAND TO TAKE CARE OF.

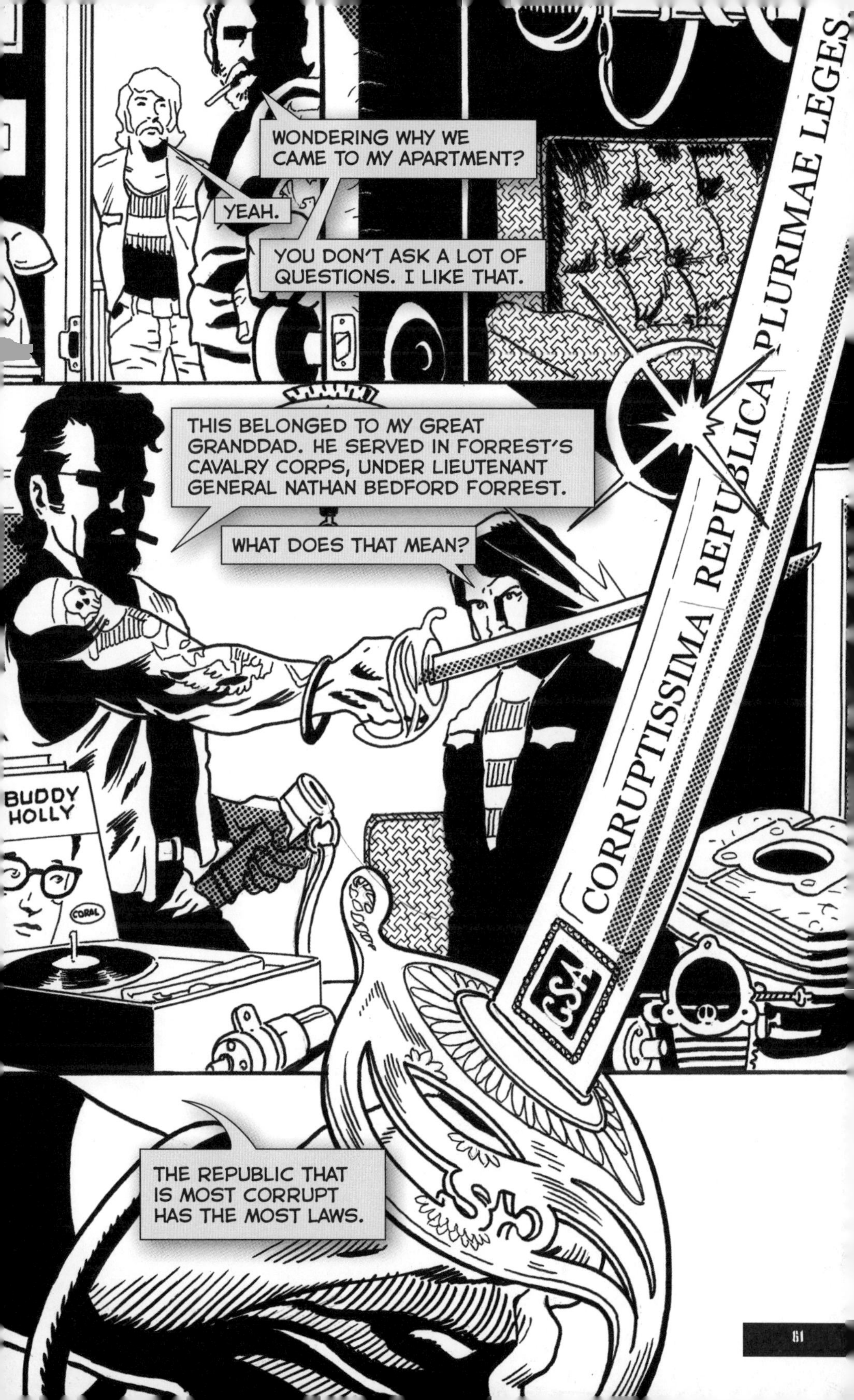
WONDERING WHY WE CAME TO MY APARTMENT?
YEAH.
YOU DON'T ASK A LOT OF QUESTIONS. I LIKE THAT.
THIS BELONGED TO MY GREAT GRANDDAD. HE SERVED IN FORREST'S CAVALRY CORPS, UNDER LIEUTENANT GENERAL NATHAN BEDFORD FORREST.
WHAT DOES THAT MEAN?
CORRUPTISSIMA REPUBLICA PLURIMAE LEGES.
CSA
BUDDY HOLLY
CORAL
THE REPUBLIC THAT IS MOST CORRUPT HAS THE MOST LAWS.

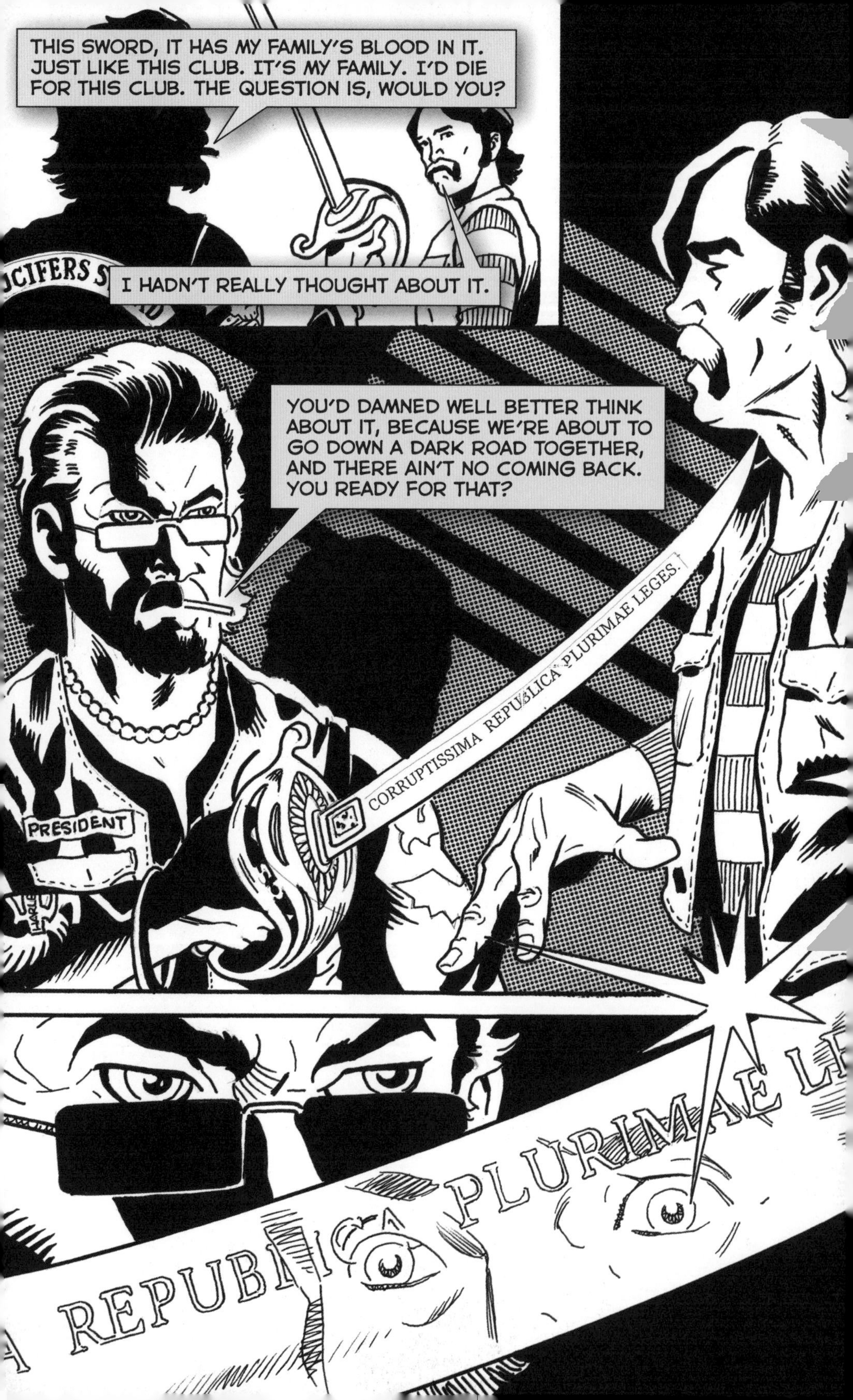
THIS SWORD, IT HAS MY FAMILY'S BLOOD IN IT. JUST LIKE THIS CLUB. IT'S MY FAMILY. I'D DIE FOR THIS CLUB. THE QUESTION IS, WOULD YOU?
I HADN'T REALLY THOUGHT ABOUT IT.
YOU'D DAMNED WELL BETTER THINK ABOUT IT, BECAUSE WE'RE ABOUT TO GO DOWN A DARK ROAD TOGETHER, AND THERE AIN'T NO COMING BACK. YOU READY FOR THAT?
PRESIDENT
CORRUPTISSIMA REPUBLICA PLURIMAE LEGES.
REPUBLICA PLURIMAE

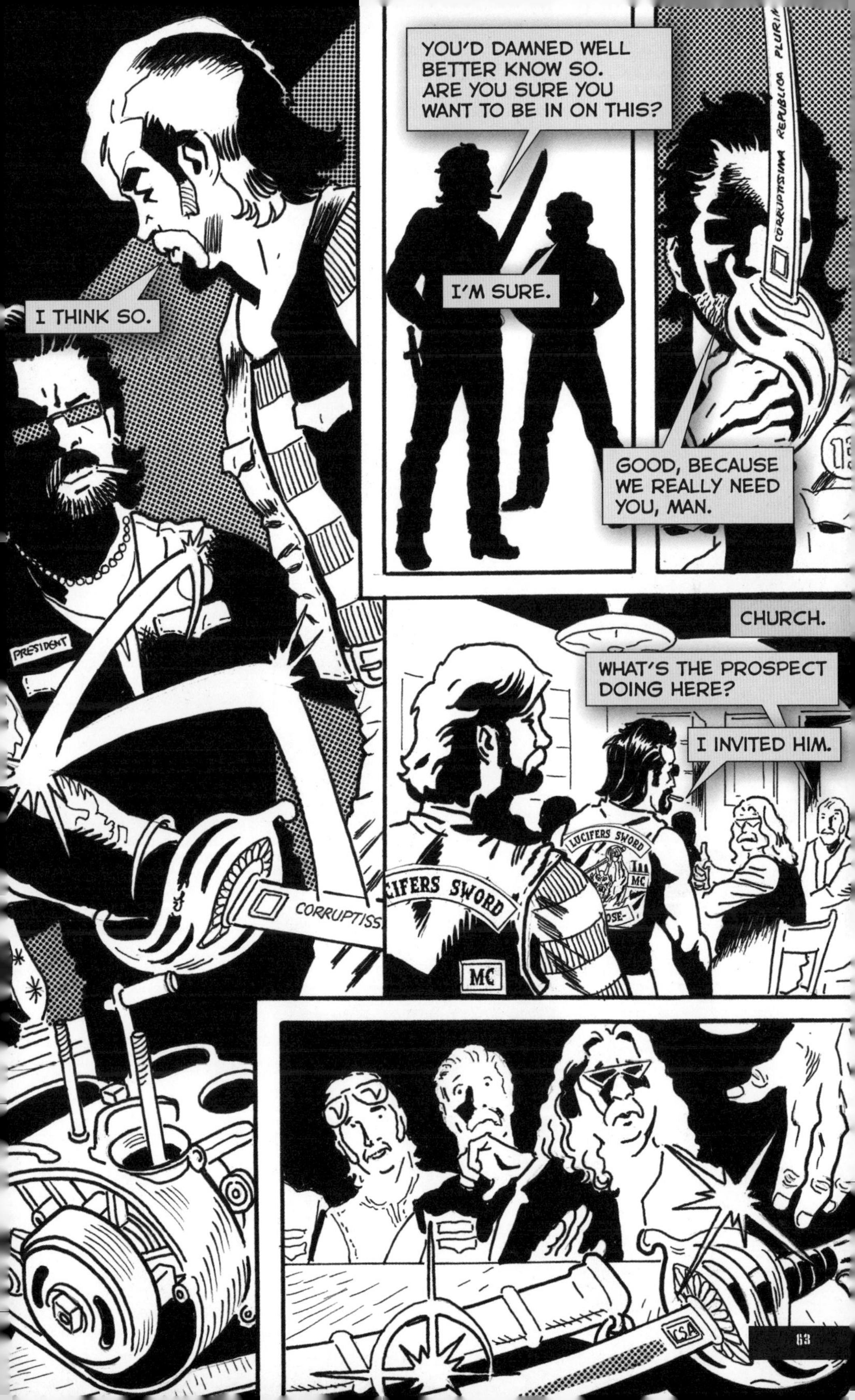
YOU'D DAMNED WELL BETTER KNOW SO. ARE YOU SURE YOU WANT TO BE IN ON THIS?
I THINK SO.
I'M SURE.
GOOD, BECAUSE WE REALLY NEED YOU, MAN.
CORRUPTISSIMA REPUBLICA PLURI
PRESIDENT
CORRUPTISS
CHURCH.
WHAT'S THE PROSPECT DOING HERE?
I INVITED HIM.
CIFERS SWORD
MC
LUCIFERS SWORD
MC
CSA

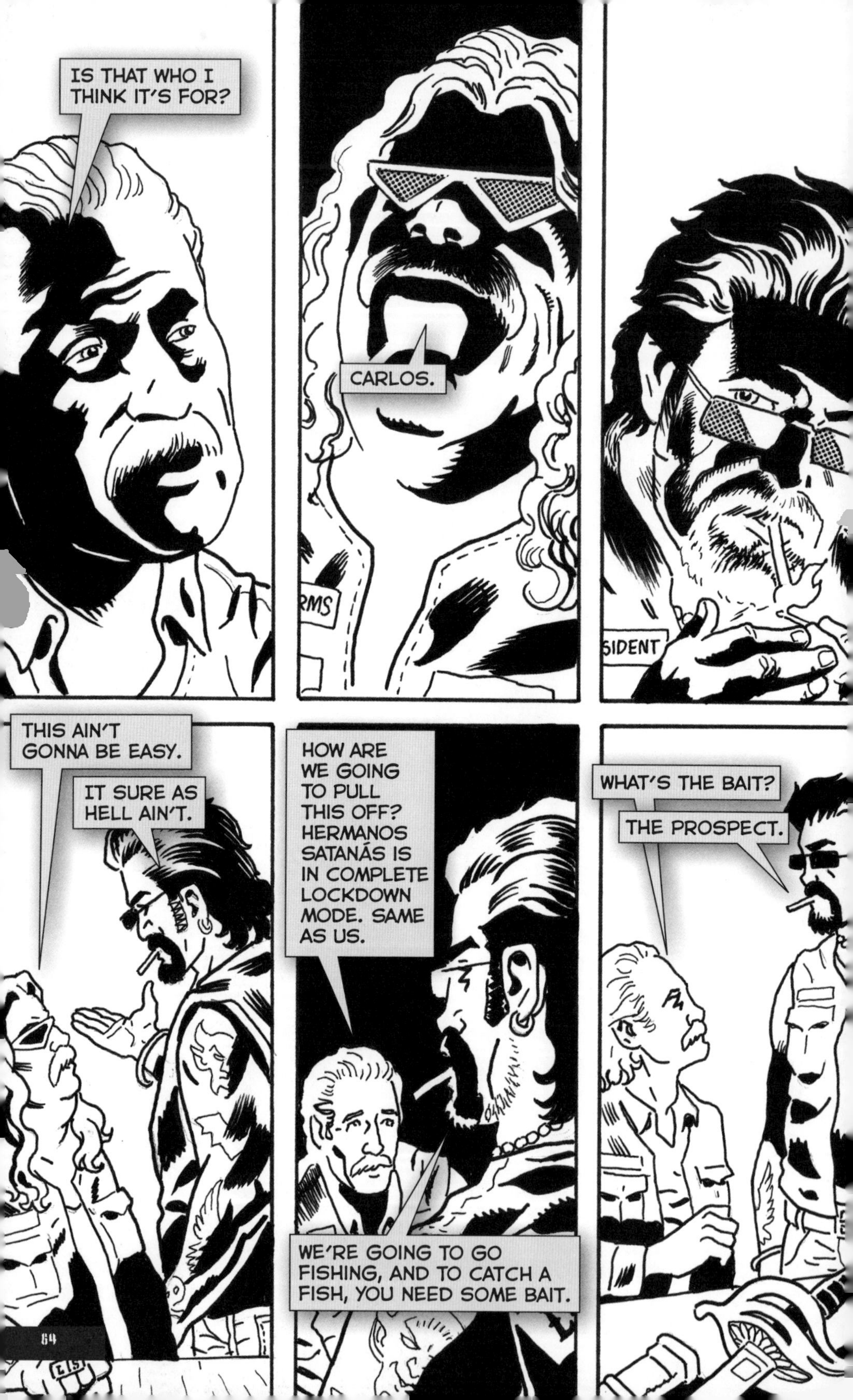
IS THAT WHO I THINK IT'S FOR?
CARLOS.
THIS AIN'T GONNA BE EASY.
IT SURE AS HELL AIN'T.
HOW ARE WE GOING TO PULL THIS OFF? HERMANOS SATANÁS IS IN COMPLETE LOCKDOWN MODE. SAME AS US.
WE'RE GOING TO GO FISHING, AND TO CATCH A FISH, YOU NEED SOME BAIT.
WHAT'S THE BAIT?
THE PROSPECT.

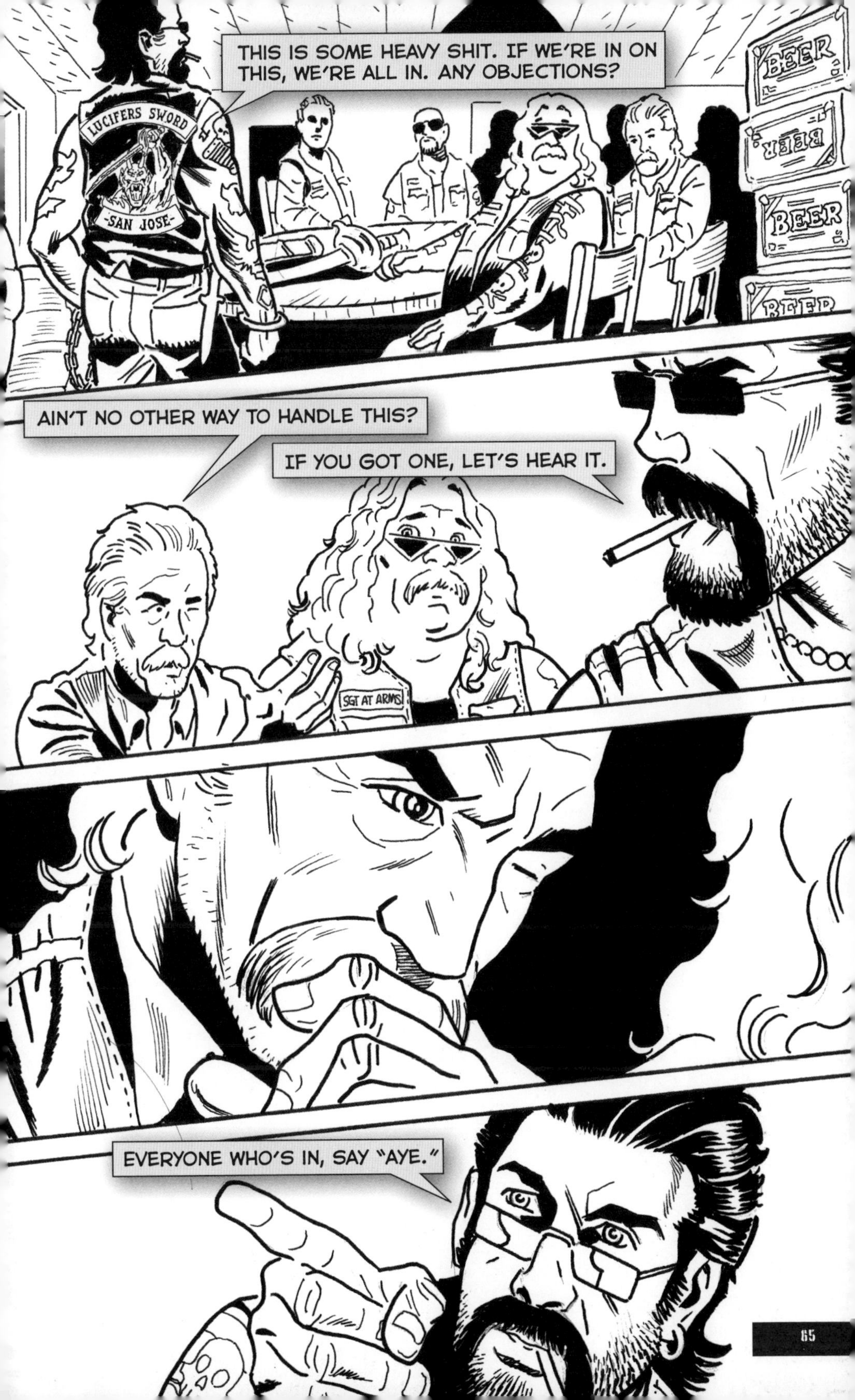
THIS IS SOME HEAVY SHIT. IF WE'RE IN ON THIS, WE'RE ALL IN. ANY OBJECTIONS?
LUCIFERS SWORD
SAN JOSE
BEER
BEER
BEER
AIN'T NO OTHER WAY TO HANDLE THIS?
IF YOU GOT ONE, LET'S HEAR IT.
SGT AT ARMS
EVERYONE WHO'S IN, SAY "AYE."

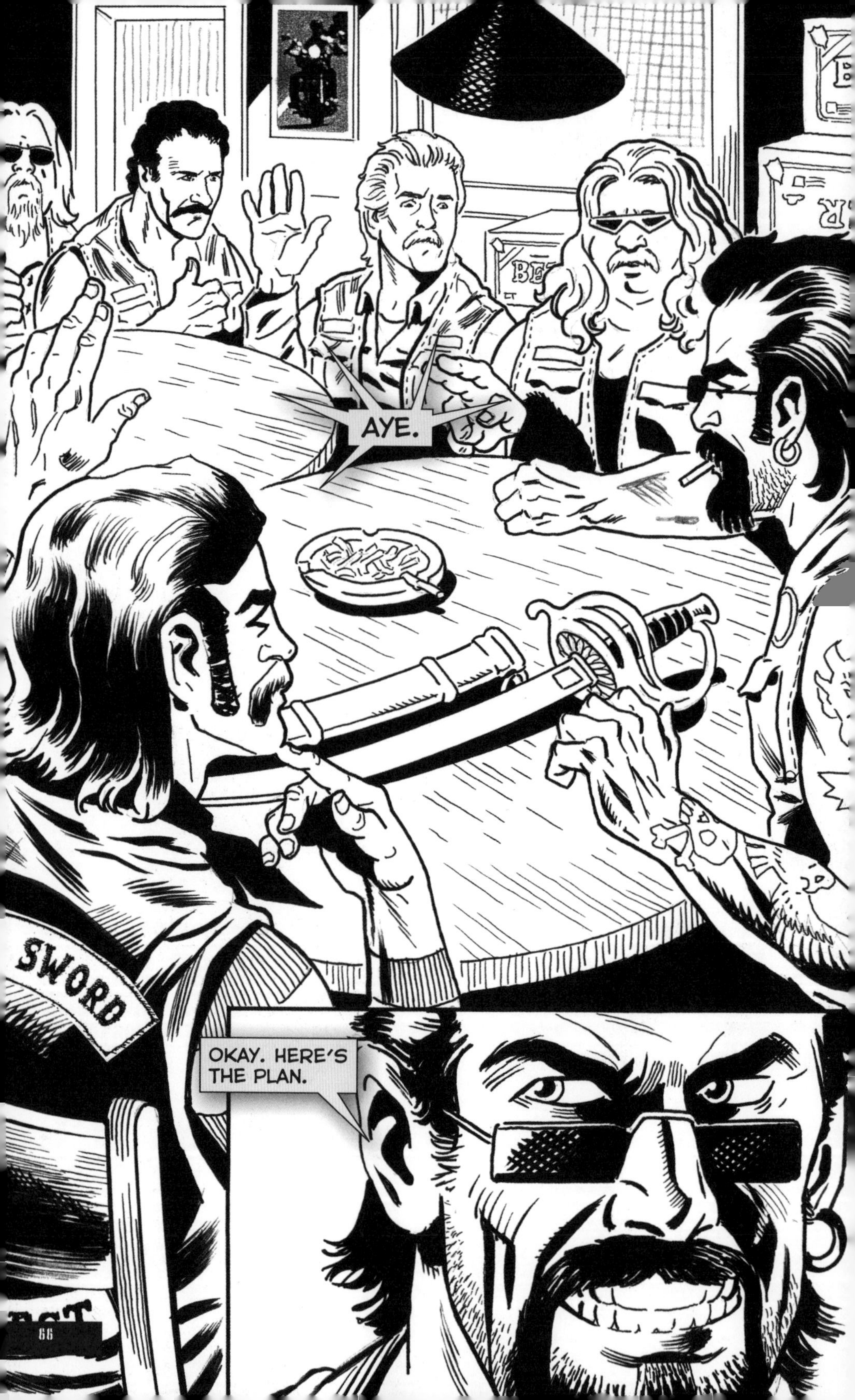
AYE.
SWORD
OKAY. HERE'S THE PLAN.

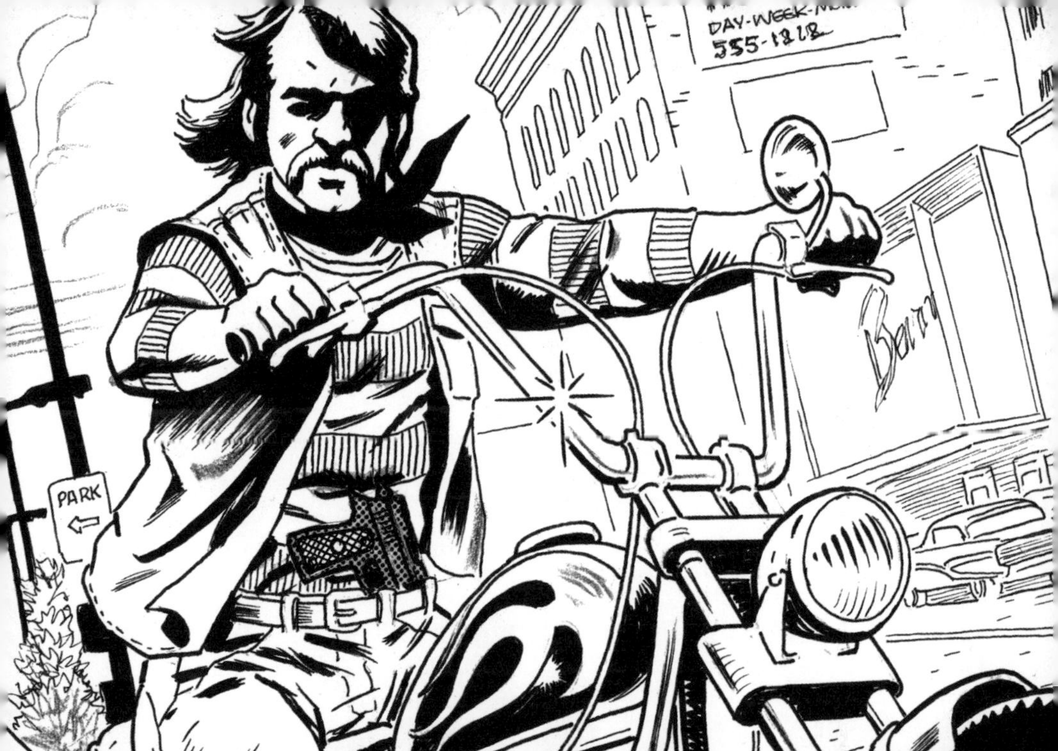

PARK

#8 BAIT

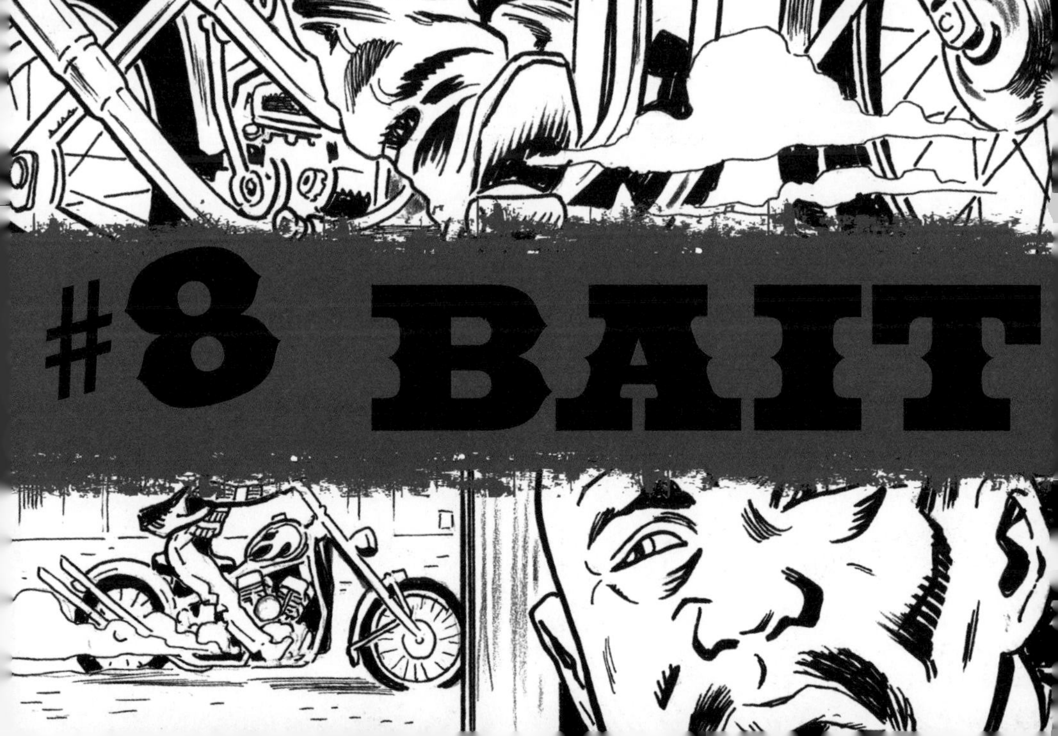

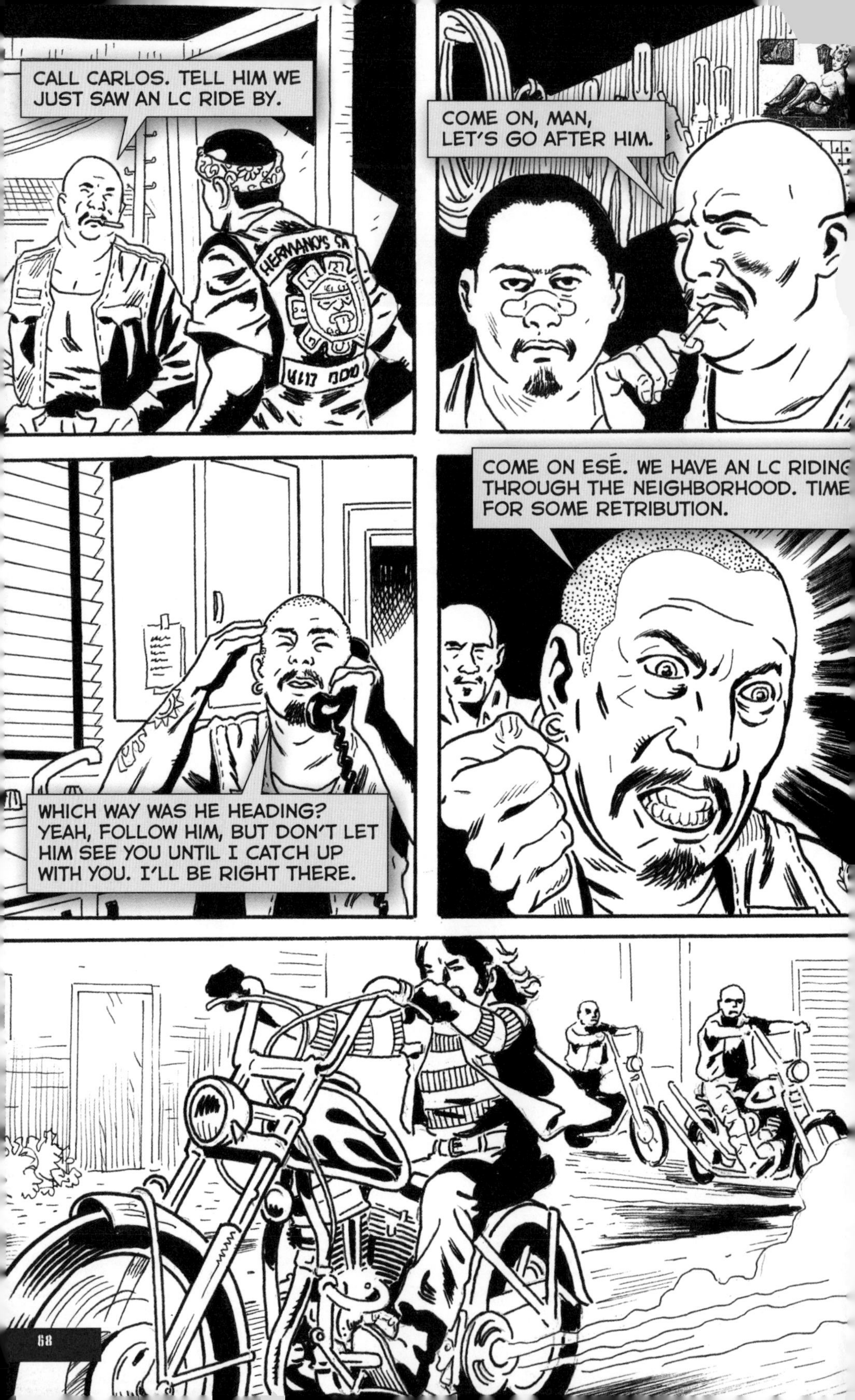
CALL CARLOS. TELL HIM WE JUST SAW AN LC RIDE BY.
HERMANOS SA
COME ON, MAN, LET'S GO AFTER HIM.
WHICH WAY WAS HE HEADING? YEAH, FOLLOW HIM, BUT DON'T LET HIM SEE YOU UNTIL I CATCH UP WITH YOU. I'LL BE RIGHT THERE.
COME ON ESÉ. WE HAVE AN LC RIDING THROUGH THE NEIGHBORHOOD. TIME FOR SOME RETRIBUTION.

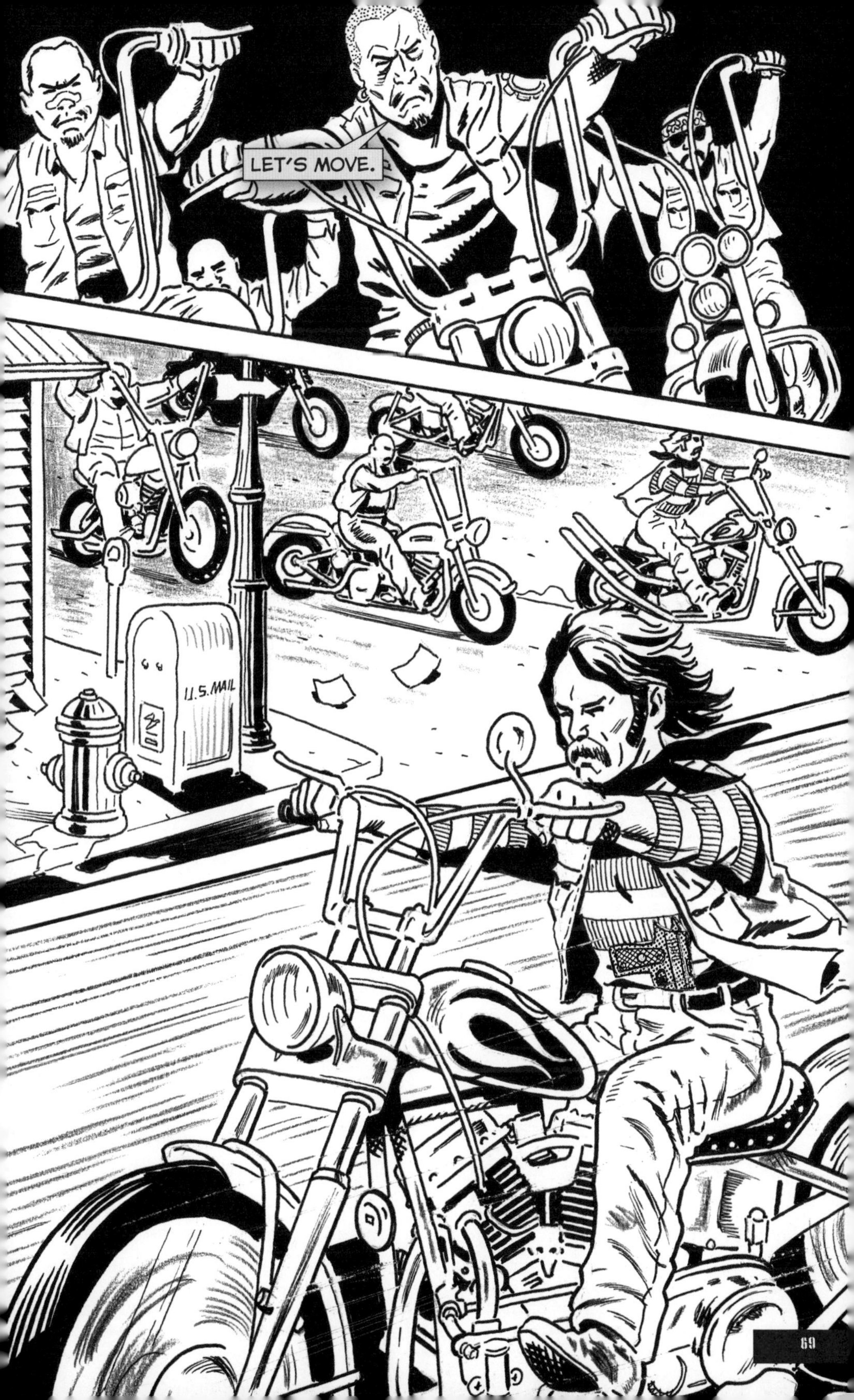
LET'S MOVE.
U.S. MAIL

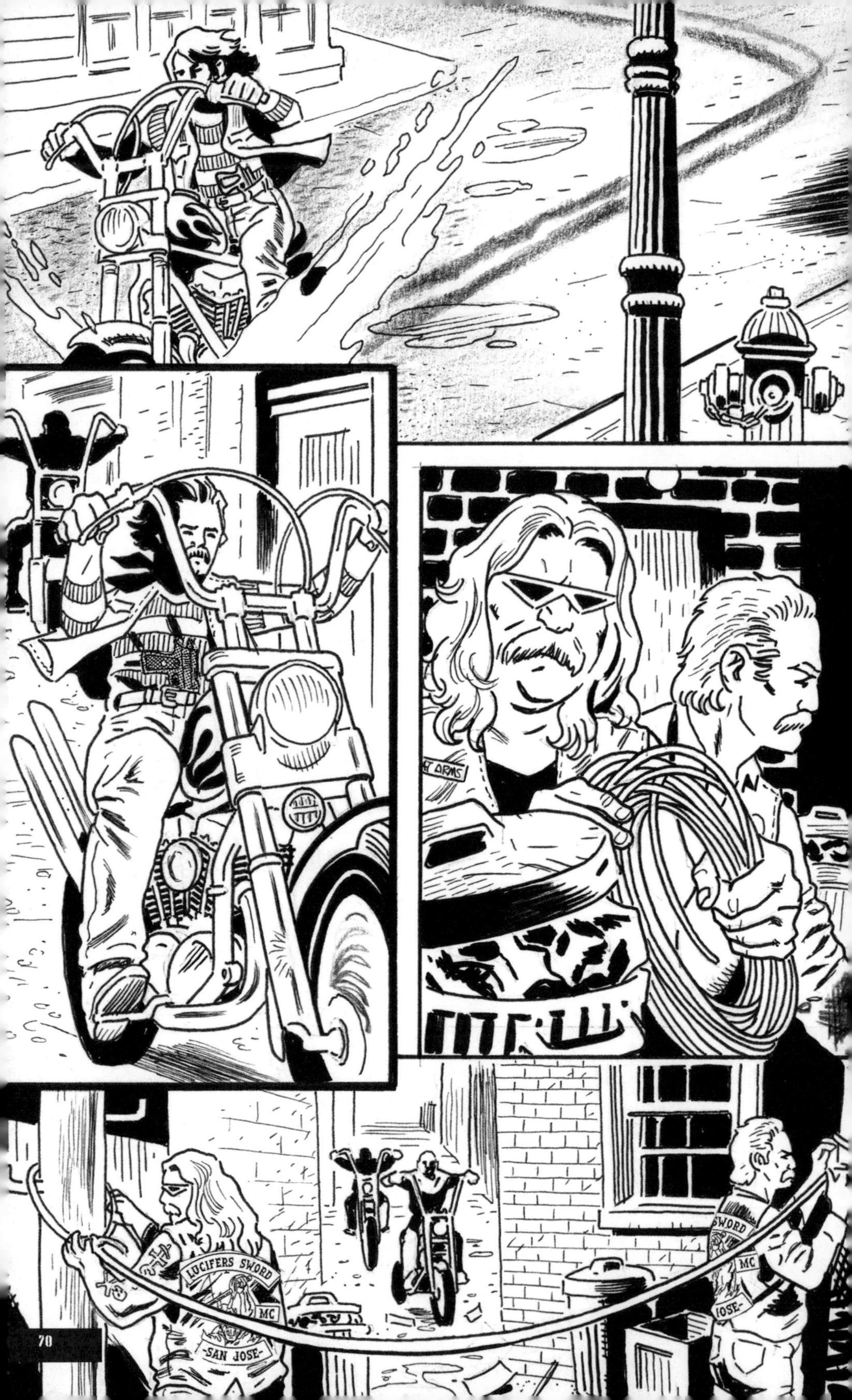
LUCIFERS SWORD
MC
-SAN JOSE-
SWORD
MC
JOSE-

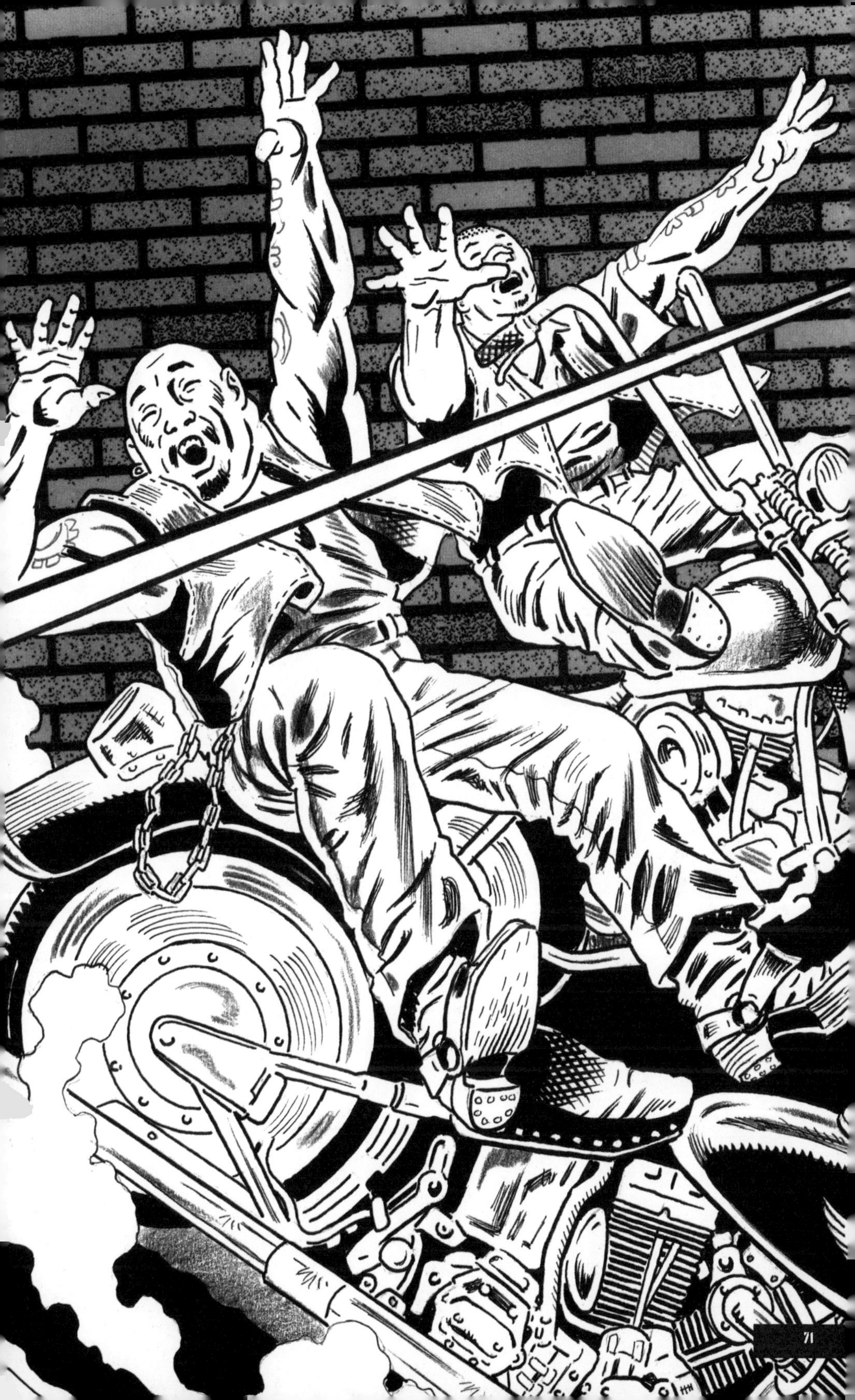

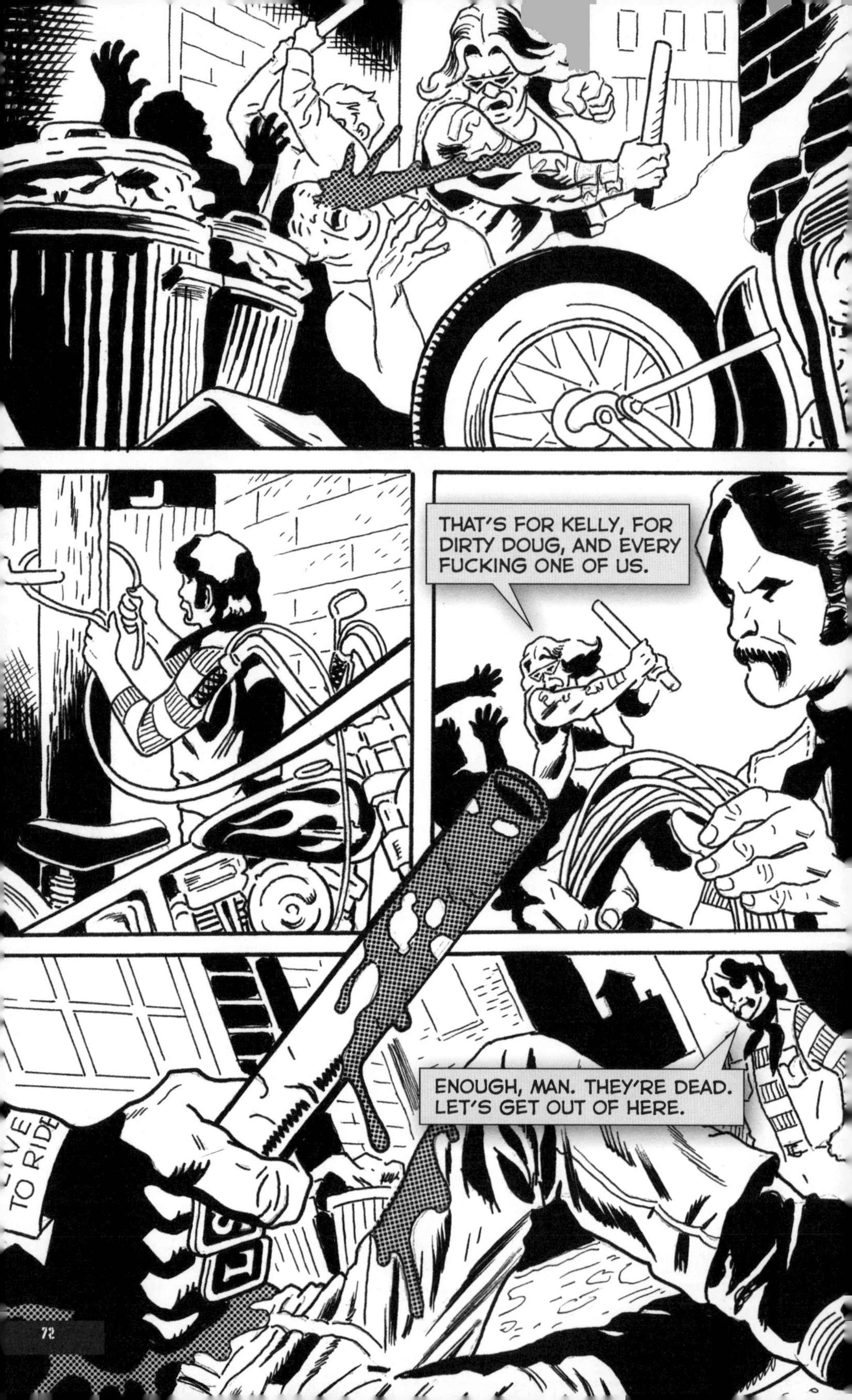
THAT'S FOR KELLY, FOR DIRTY DOUG, AND EVERY FUCKING ONE OF US.
ENOUGH, MAN. THEY'RE DEAD. LET'S GET OUT OF HERE.
TO RIDE

DECISION TIME #9

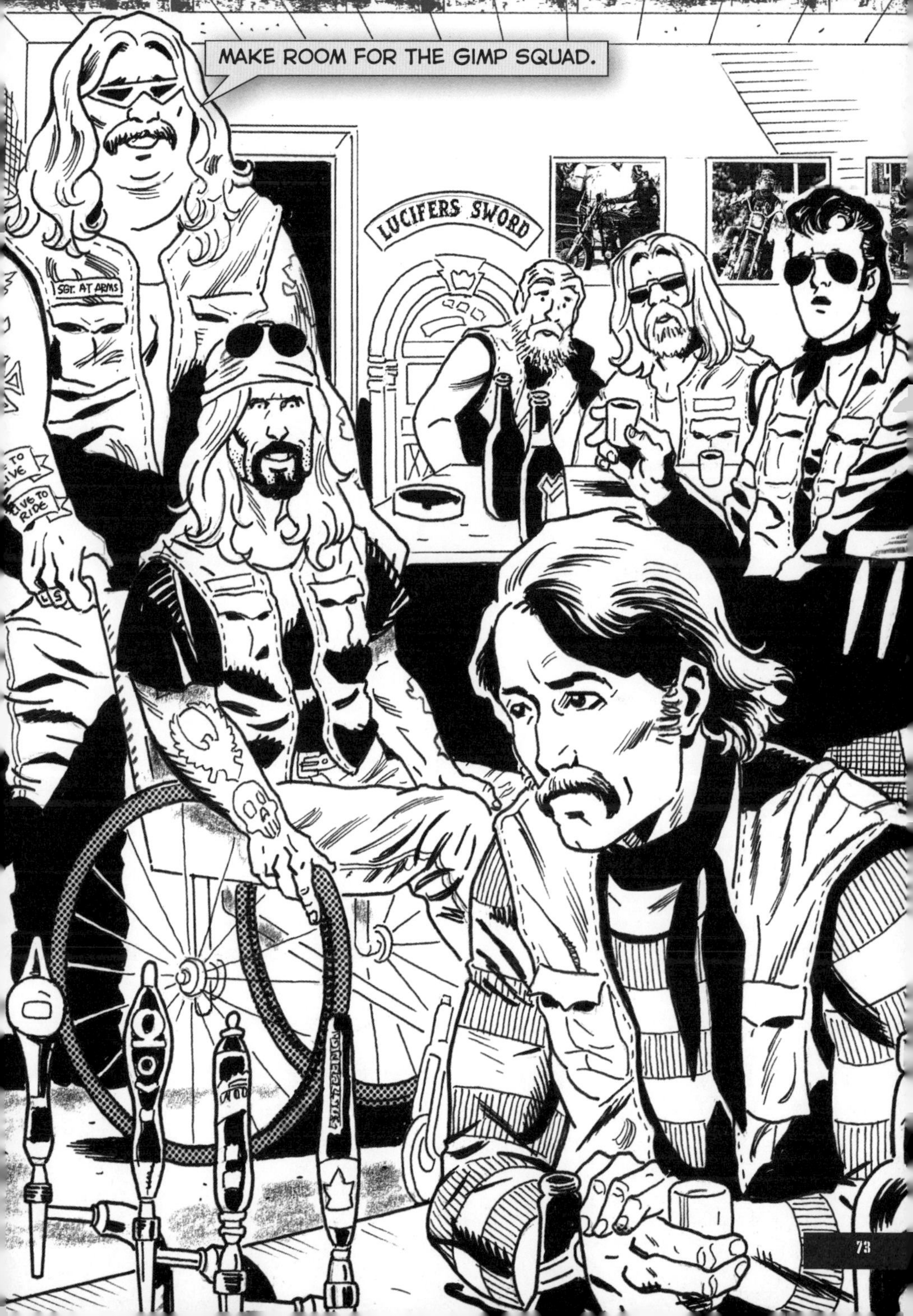
MAKE ROOM FOR THE GIMP SQUAD.
LUCIFERS SWORD
SGT. AT ARMS
LIVE TO RIDE

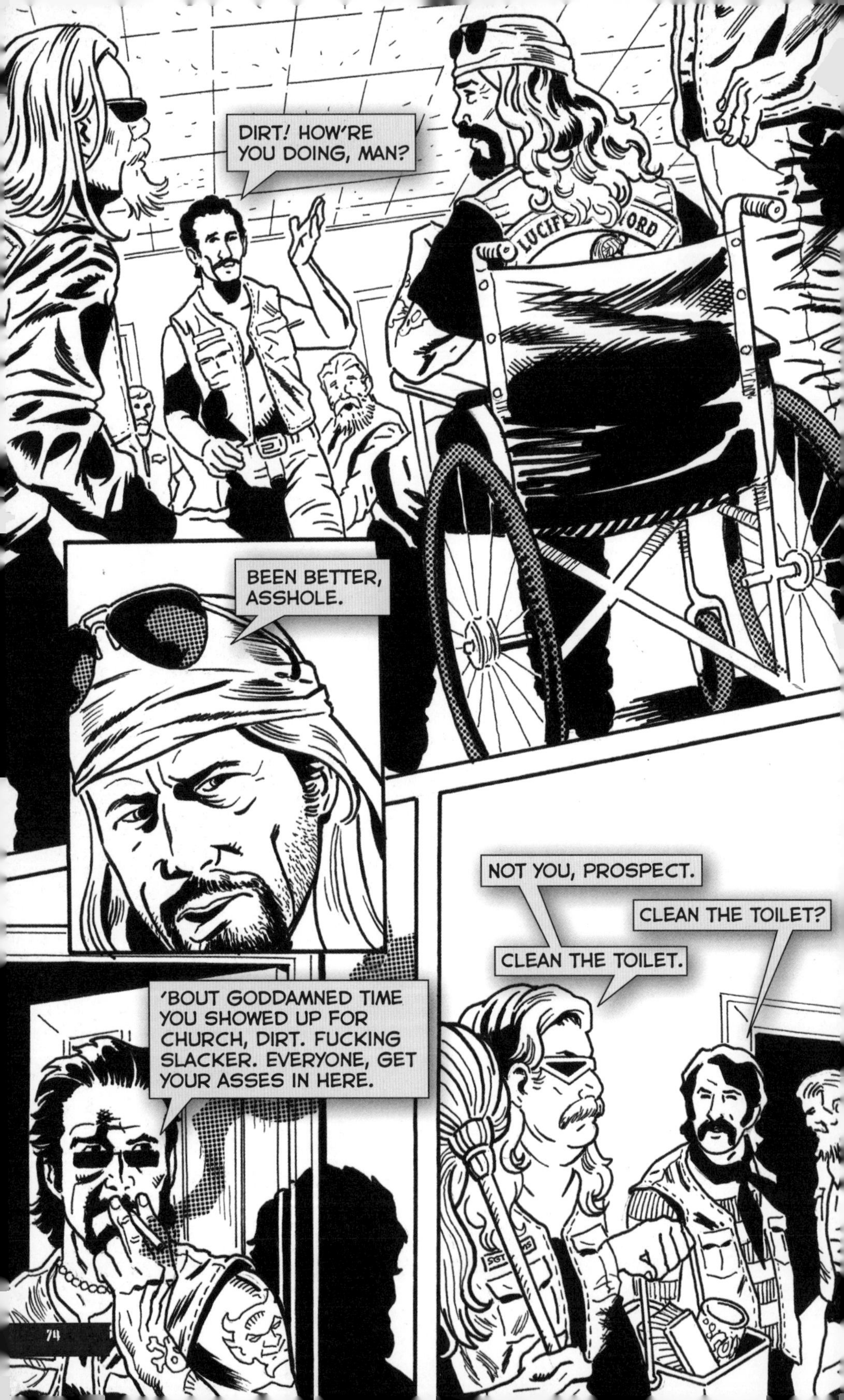
DIRT! HOW'RE YOU DOING, MAN?
BEEN BETTER, ASSHOLE.
'BOUT GODDAMNED TIME YOU SHOWED UP FOR CHURCH, DIRT. FUCKING SLACKER. EVERYONE, GET YOUR ASSES IN HERE.
NOT YOU, PROSPECT.
CLEAN THE TOILET.
CLEAN THE TOILET?
SGT

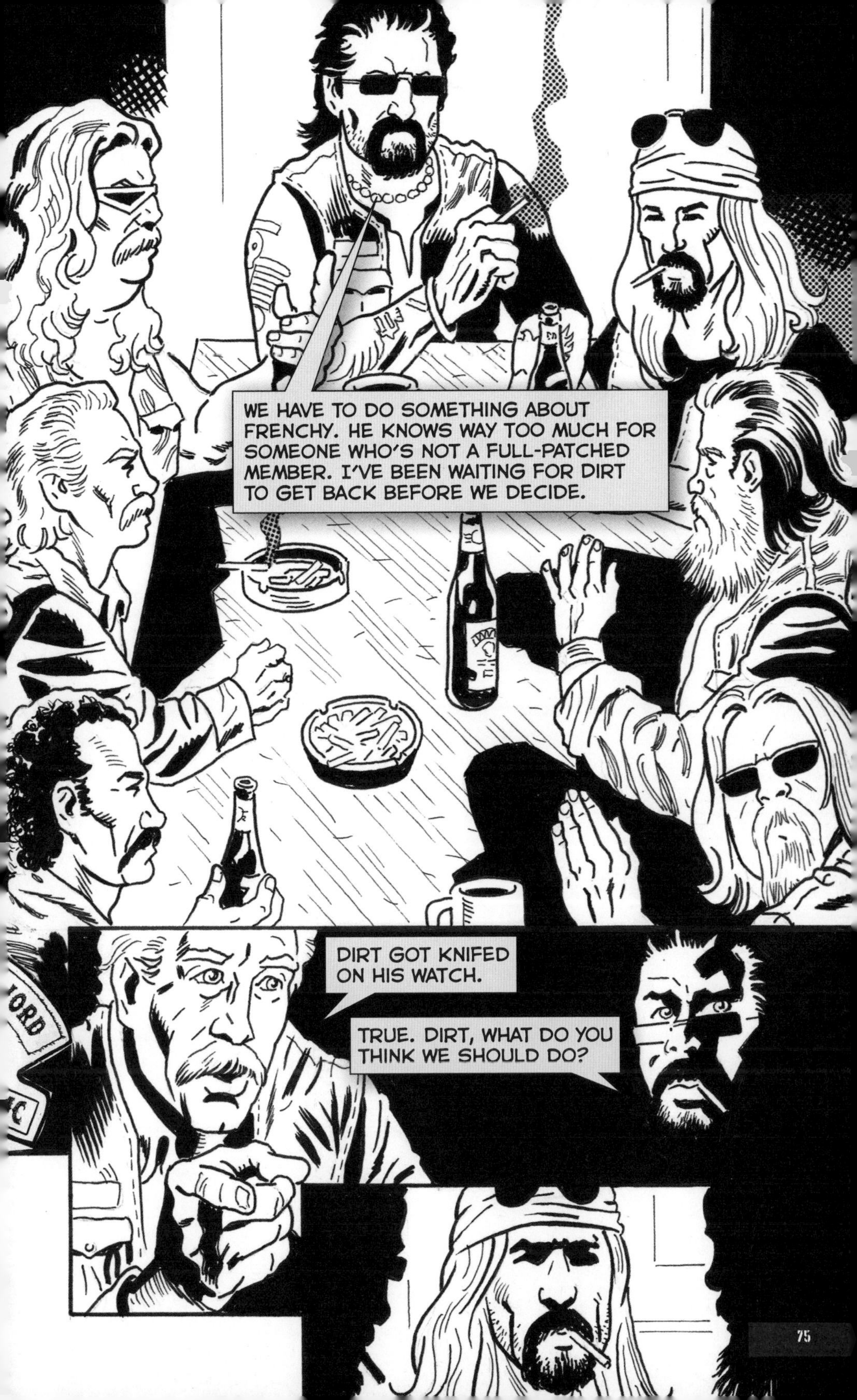

WE HAVE TO DO SOMETHING ABOUT FRENCHY. HE KNOWS WAY TOO MUCH FOR SOMEONE WHO'S NOT A FULL-PATCHED MEMBER. I'VE BEEN WAITING FOR DIRT TO GET BACK BEFORE WE DECIDE.
DIRT GOT KNIFED ON HIS WATCH.
TRUE. DIRT, WHAT DO YOU THINK WE SHOULD DO?

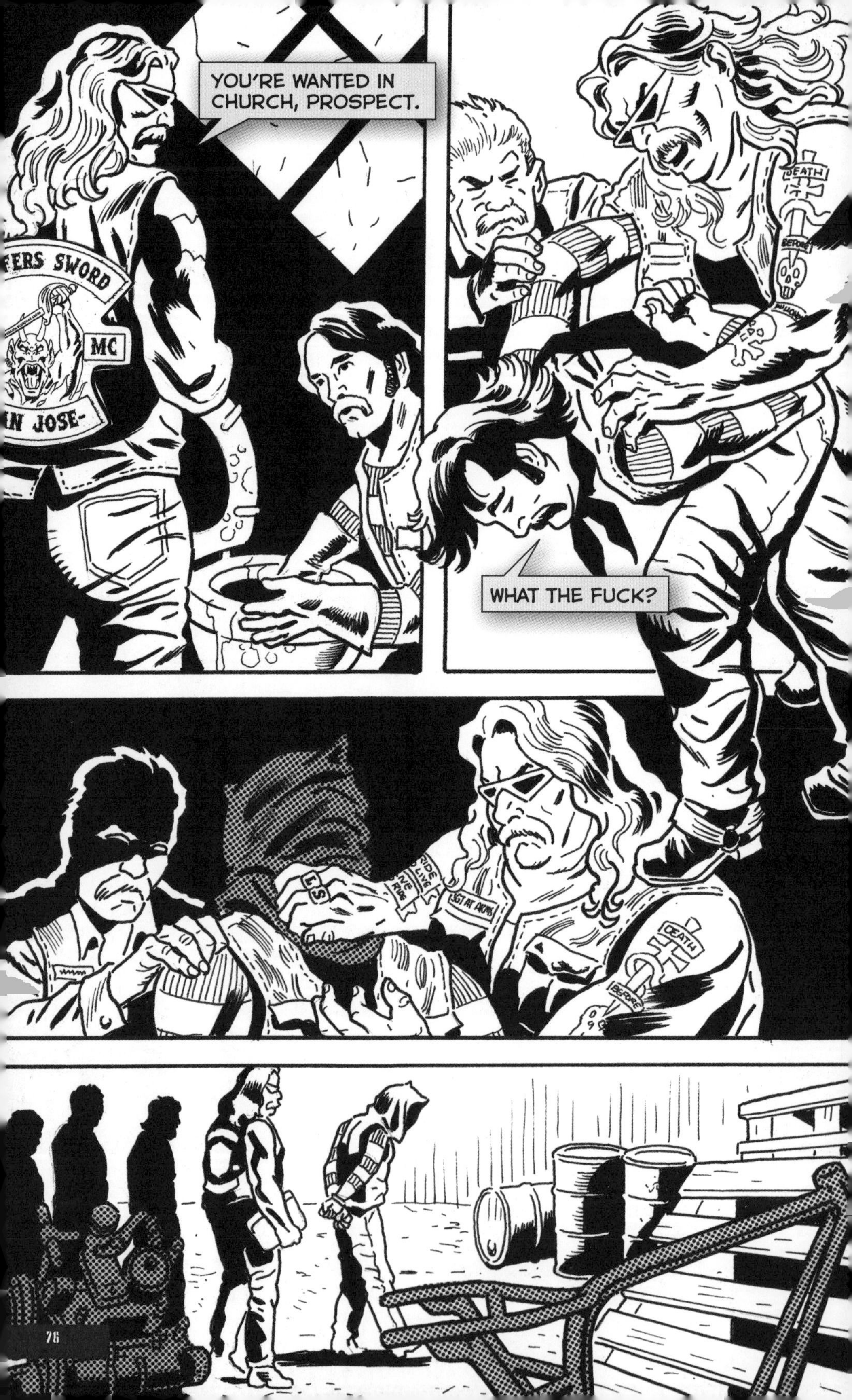
YOU'RE WANTED IN CHURCH, PROSPECT.
FERS SWORD
MC
AN JOSE-
DEATH
BEFORE
WHAT THE FUCK?
SGT AT ARMS
DEATH
BEFORE

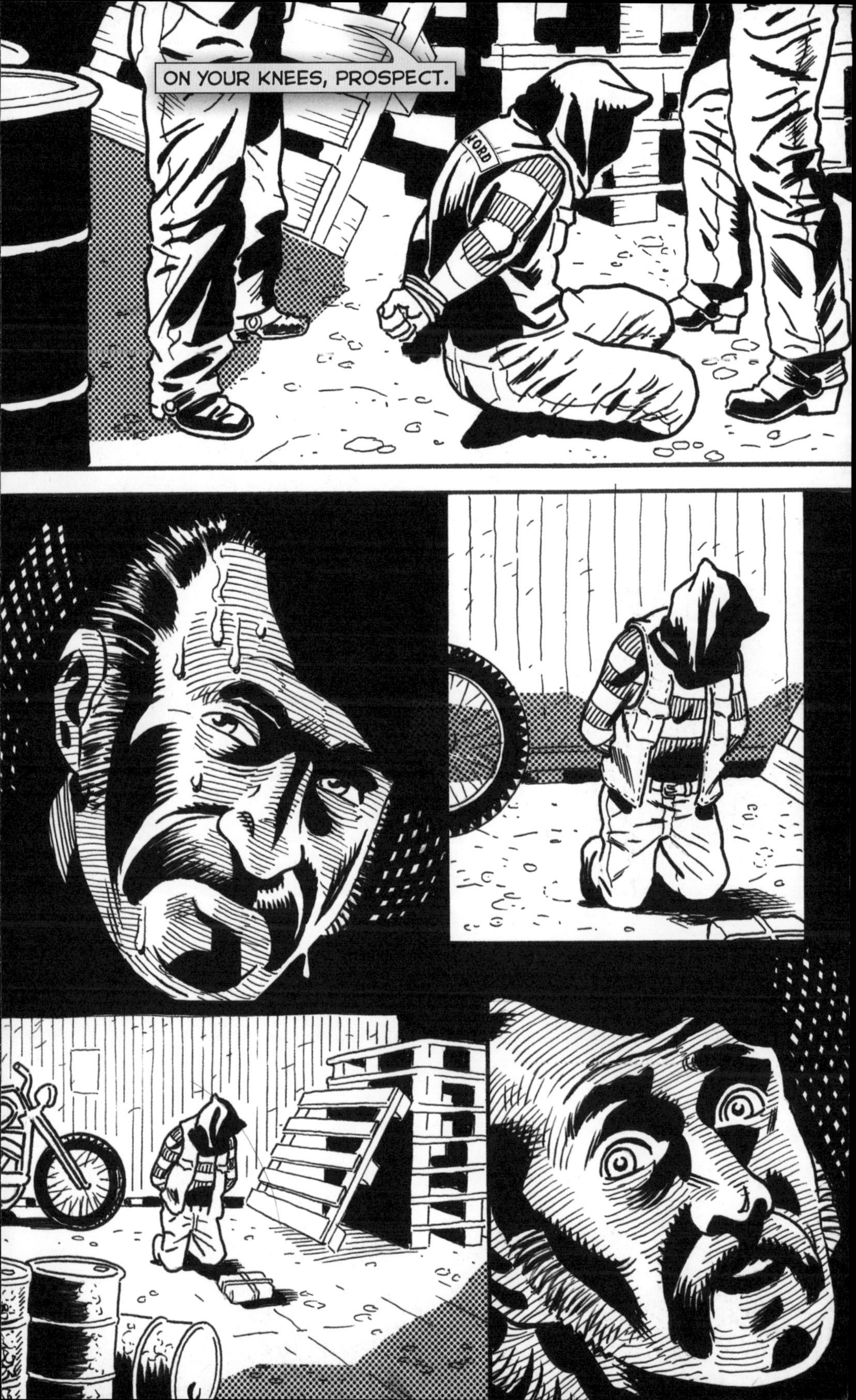
ON YOUR KNEES, PROSPECT.

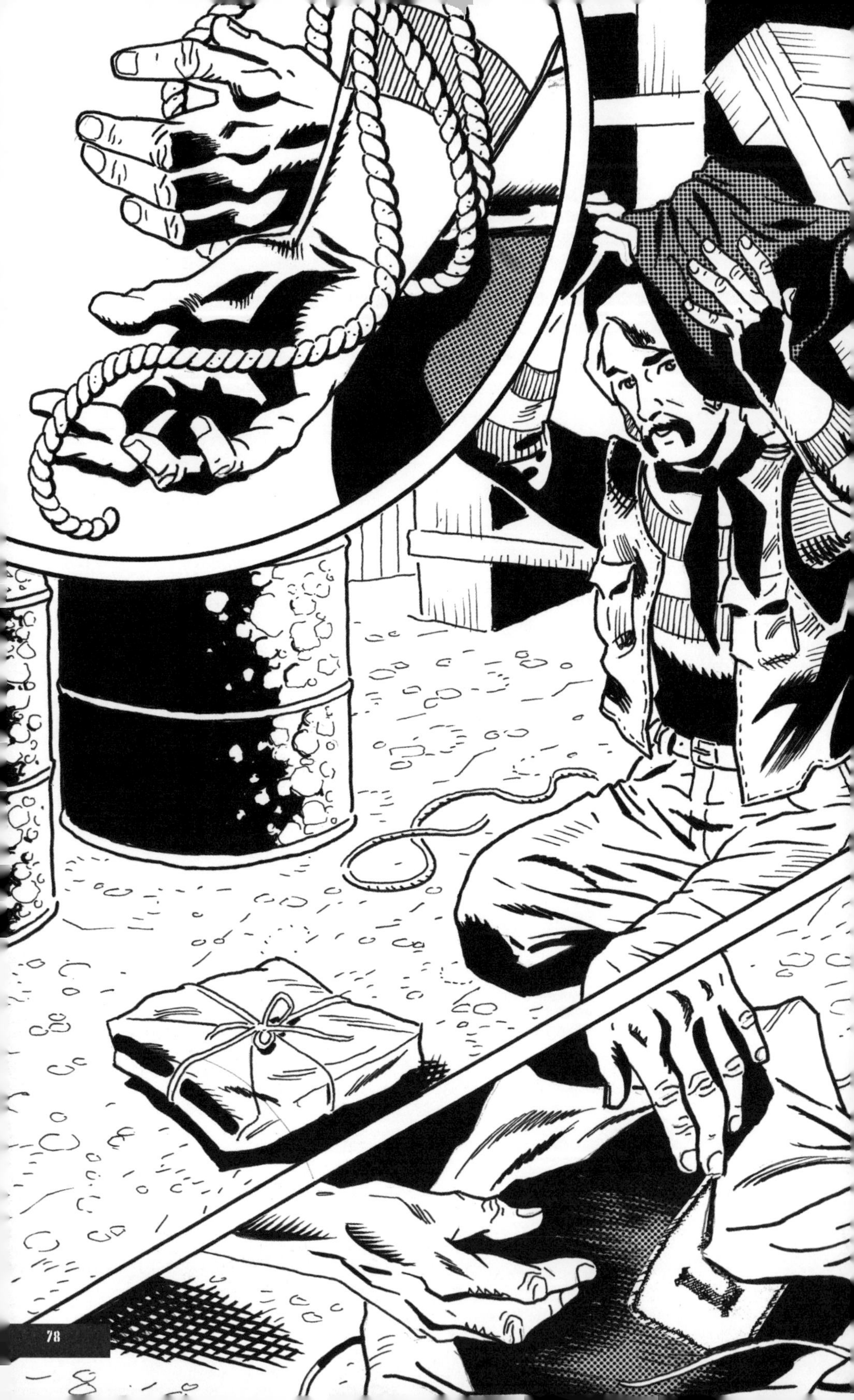

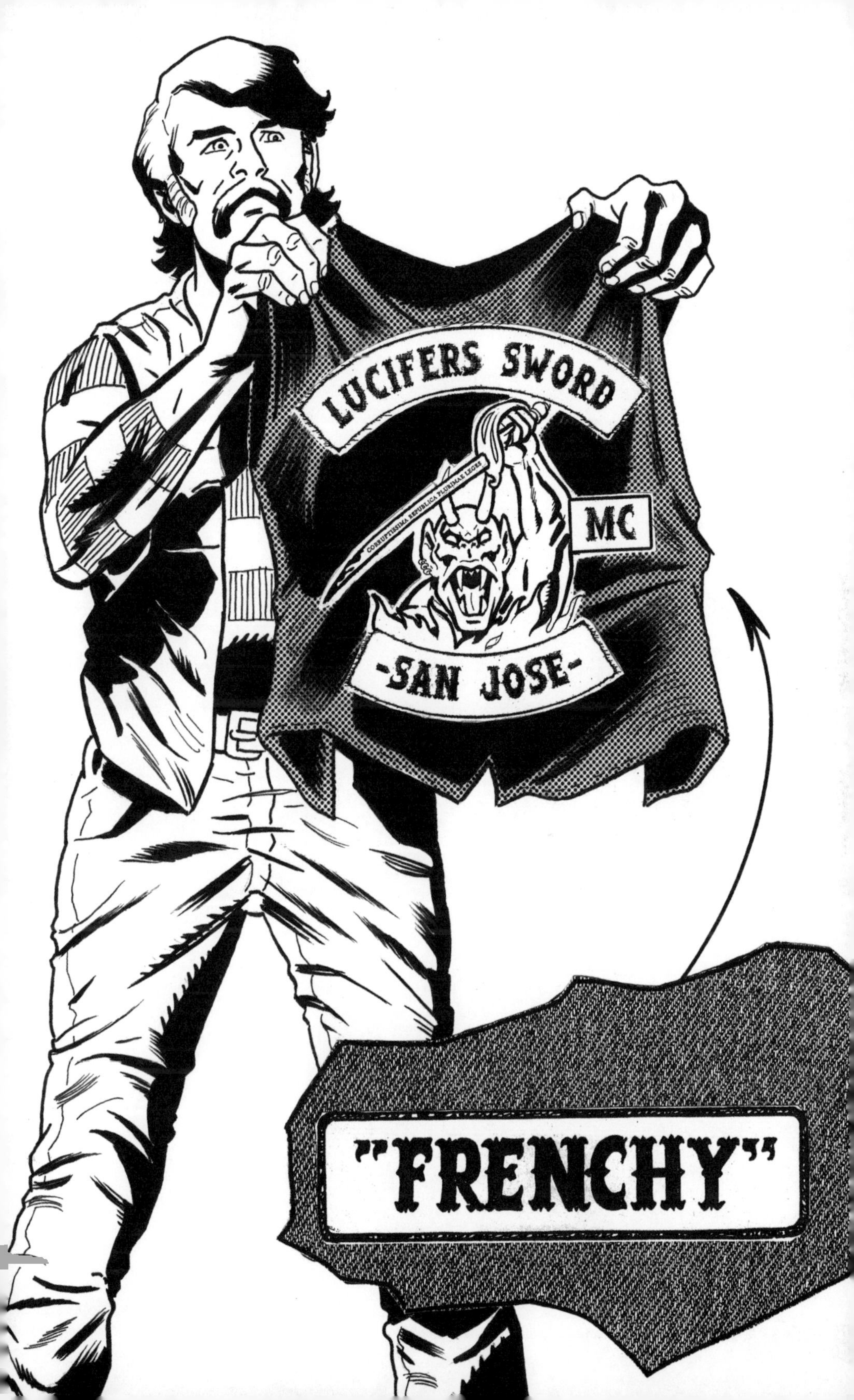
LUCIFERS SWORD
CORRUPTISSIMA REPUBLICA PLURIMAE LEGES
MC
-SAN JOSE-
"FRENCHY"

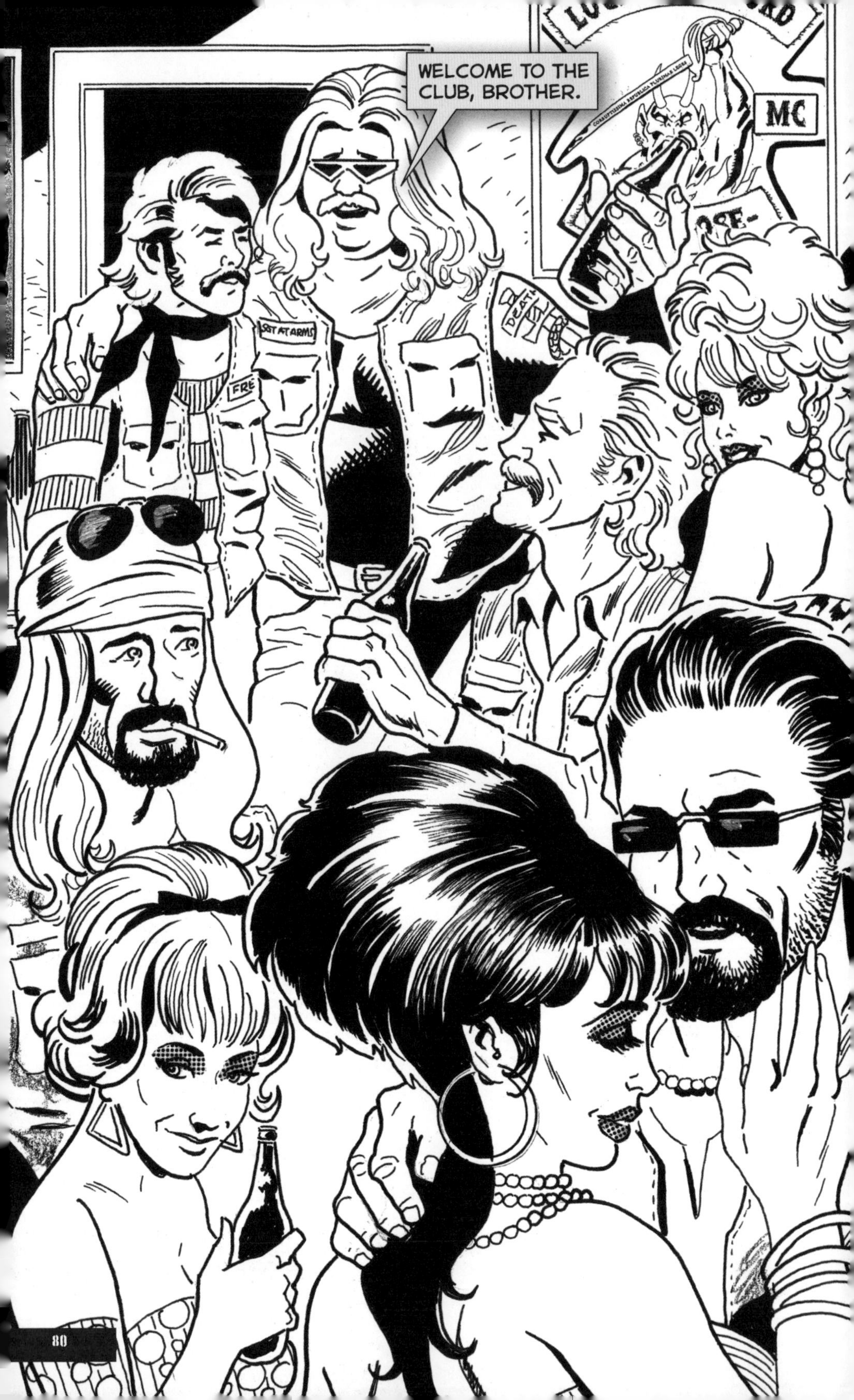
WELCOME TO THE CLUB, BROTHER.
MC
SGT AT ARMS
DEATH

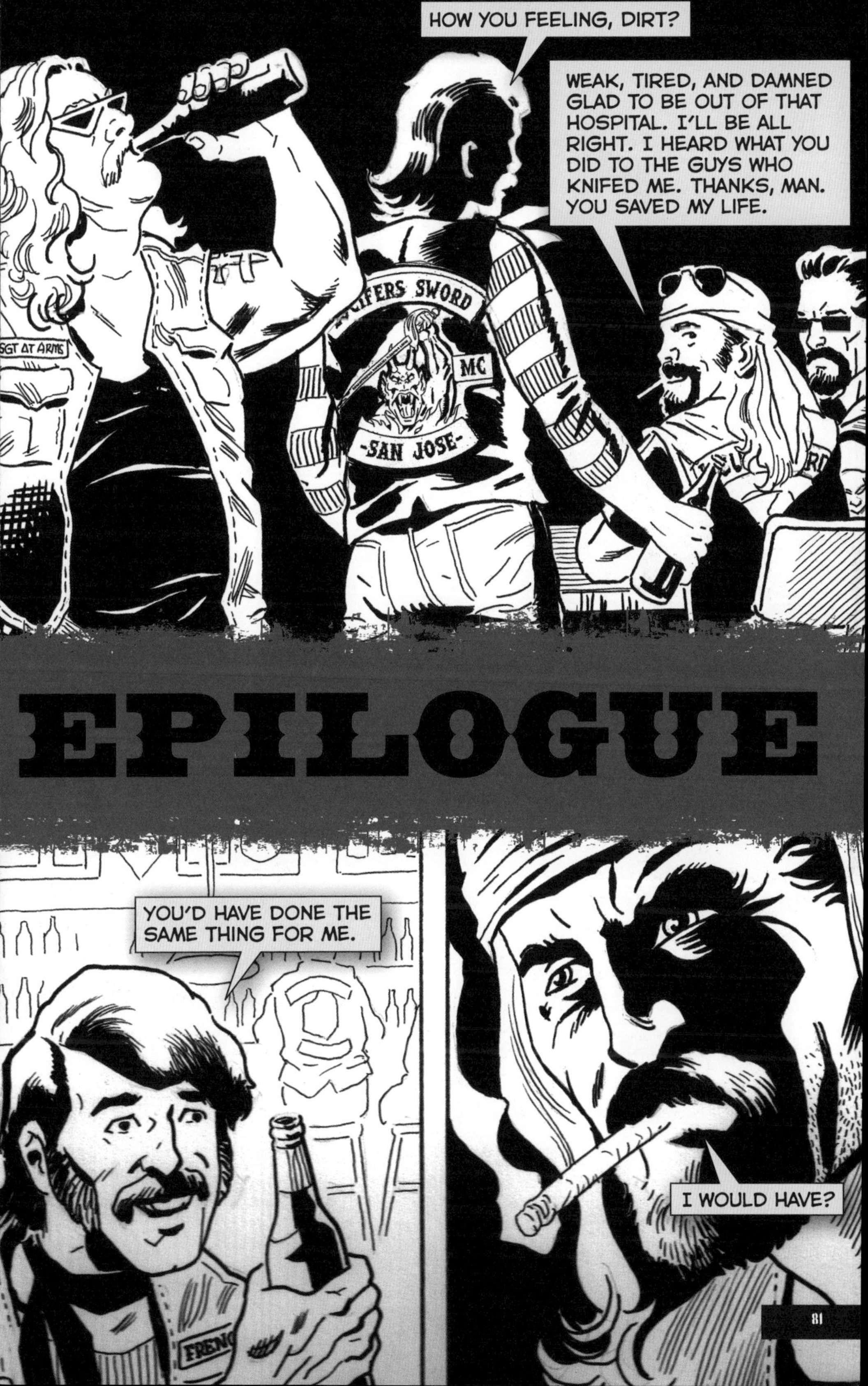
HOW YOU FEELING, DIRT?
WEAK, TIRED, AND DAMNED GLAD TO BE OUT OF THAT HOSPITAL. I'LL BE ALL RIGHT. I HEARD WHAT YOU DID TO THE GUYS WHO KNIFED ME. THANKS, MAN. YOU SAVED MY LIFE.
SGT AT ARMS
MC
-SAN JOSE-
EPILOGUE
YOU'D HAVE DONE THE SAME THING FOR ME.
I WOULD HAVE?

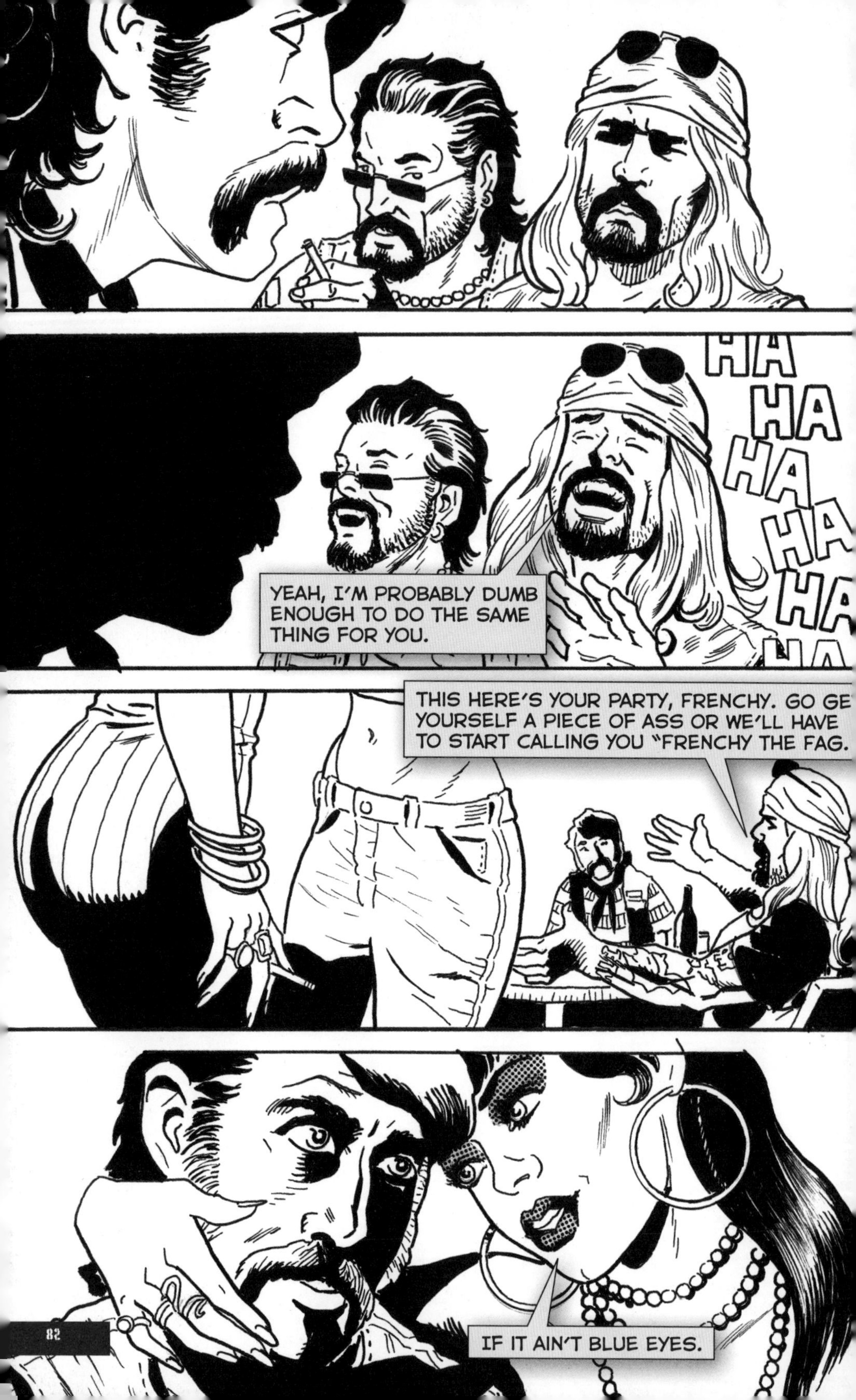
HA HA HA HA HA HA
YEAH, I'M PROBABLY DUMB ENOUGH TO DO THE SAME THING FOR YOU.
THIS HERE'S YOUR PARTY, FRENCHY. GO GE YOURSELF A PIECE OF ASS OR WE'LL HAVE TO START CALLING YOU "FRENCHY THE FAG.
IF IT AIN'T BLUE EYES.

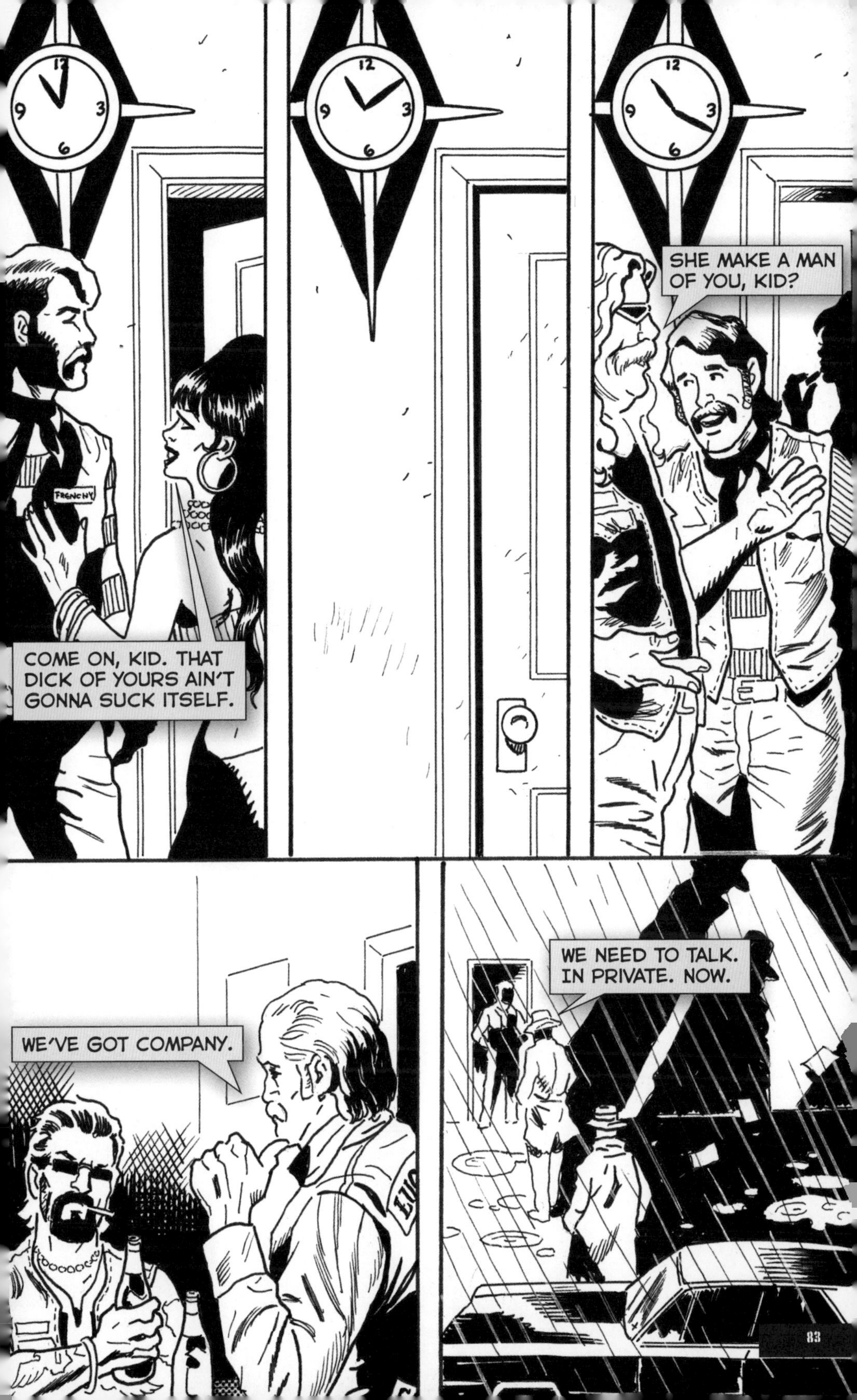
COME ON, KID. THAT DICK OF YOURS AIN'T GONNA SUCK ITSELF.
SHE MAKE A MAN OF YOU, KID?
WE'VE GOT COMPANY.
WE NEED TO TALK. IN PRIVATE. NOW.

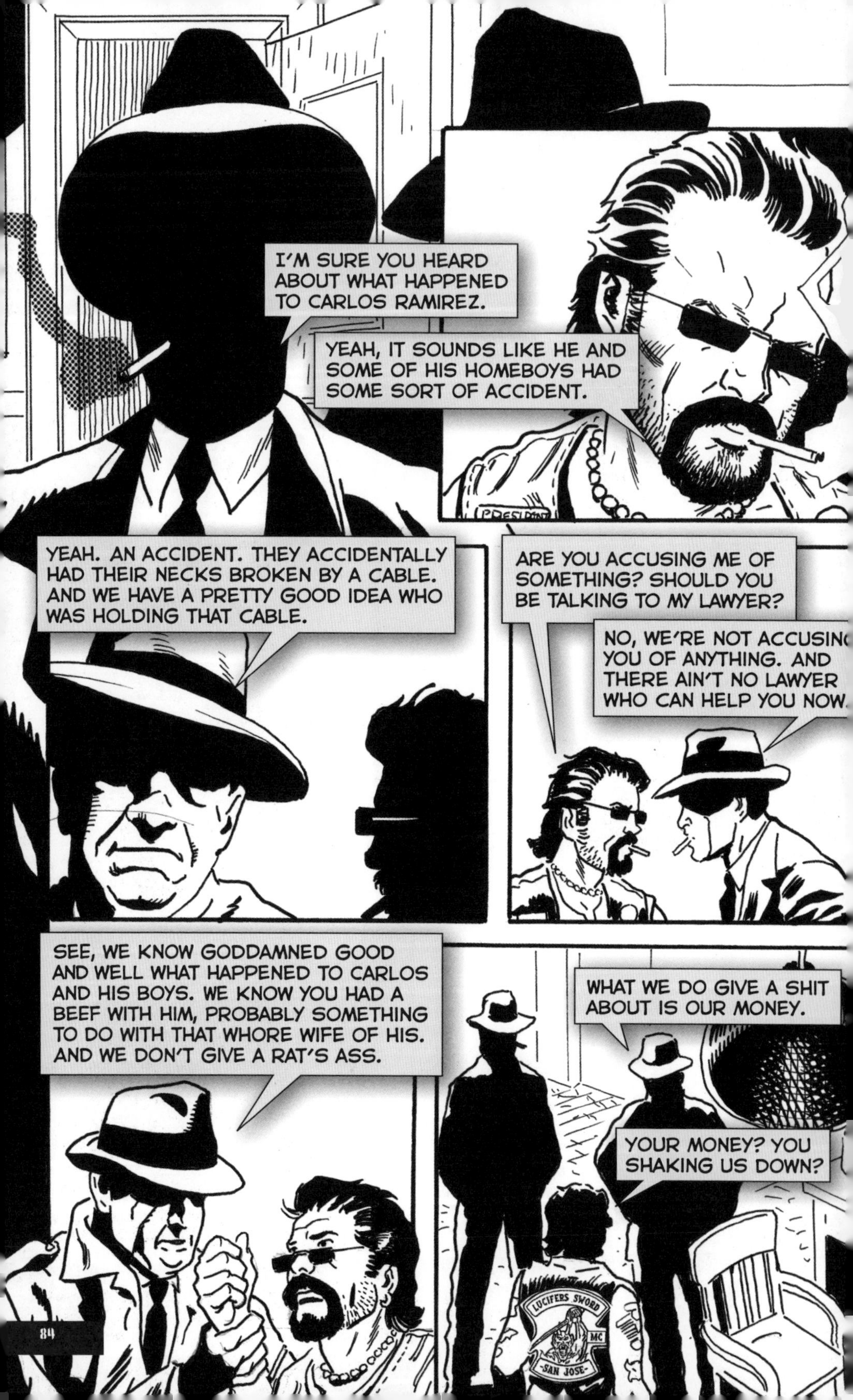
I'M SURE YOU HEARD ABOUT WHAT HAPPENED TO CARLOS RAMIREZ.
YEAH, IT SOUNDS LIKE HE AND SOME OF HIS HOMEBOYS HAD SOME SORT OF ACCIDENT.
PRESIDENT
YEAH. AN ACCIDENT. THEY ACCIDENTALLY HAD THEIR NECKS BROKEN BY A CABLE. AND WE HAVE A PRETTY GOOD IDEA WHO WAS HOLDING THAT CABLE.
ARE YOU ACCUSING ME OF SOMETHING? SHOULD YOU BE TALKING TO MY LAWYER?
NO, WE'RE NOT ACCUSIN YOU OF ANYTHING. AND THERE AIN'T NO LAWYER WHO CAN HELP YOU NOW.
SEE, WE KNOW GODDAMNED GOOD AND WELL WHAT HAPPENED TO CARLOS AND HIS BOYS. WE KNOW YOU HAD A BEEF WITH HIM, PROBABLY SOMETHING TO DO WITH THAT WHORE WIFE OF HIS. AND WE DON'T GIVE A RAT'S ASS.
WHAT WE DO GIVE A SHIT ABOUT IS OUR MONEY.
YOUR MONEY? YOU SHAKING US DOWN?
LUCIFERS SWORD
MC
SAN JOSE

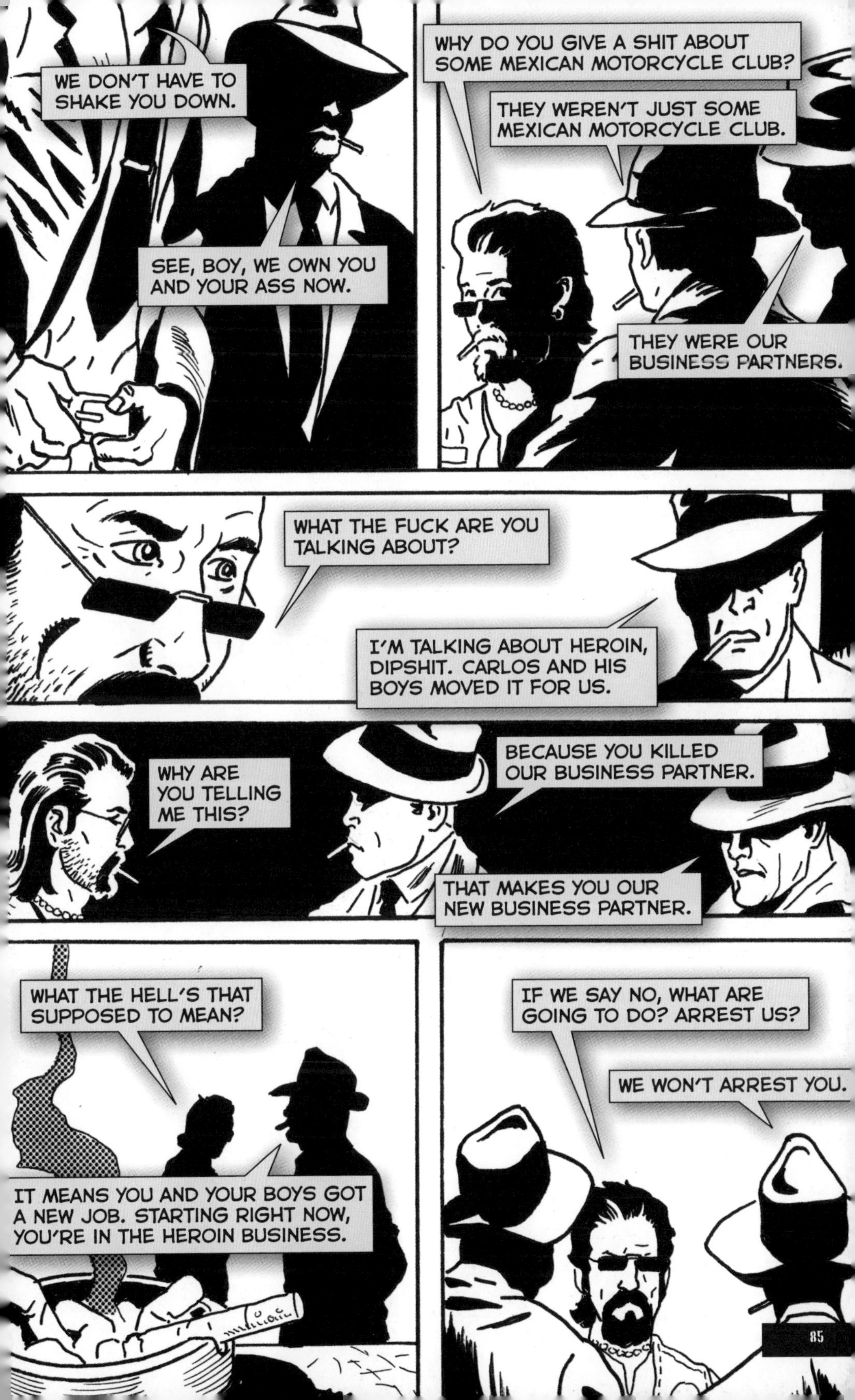
WE DON'T HAVE TO SHAKE YOU DOWN.
SEE, BOY, WE OWN YOU AND YOUR ASS NOW.
WHY DO YOU GIVE A SHIT ABOUT SOME MEXICAN MOTORCYCLE CLUB?
THEY WEREN'T JUST SOME MEXICAN MOTORCYCLE CLUB.
THEY WERE OUR BUSINESS PARTNERS.
WHAT THE FUCK ARE YOU TALKING ABOUT?
I'M TALKING ABOUT HEROIN, DIPSHIT. CARLOS AND HIS BOYS MOVED IT FOR US.
WHY ARE YOU TELLING ME THIS?
BECAUSE YOU KILLED OUR BUSINESS PARTNER.
THAT MAKES YOU OUR NEW BUSINESS PARTNER.
WHAT THE HELL'S THAT SUPPOSED TO MEAN?
IT MEANS YOU AND YOUR BOYS GOT A NEW JOB. STARTING RIGHT NOW, YOU'RE IN THE HEROIN BUSINESS.
IF WE SAY NO, WHAT ARE GOING TO DO? ARREST US?
WE WON'T ARREST YOU.

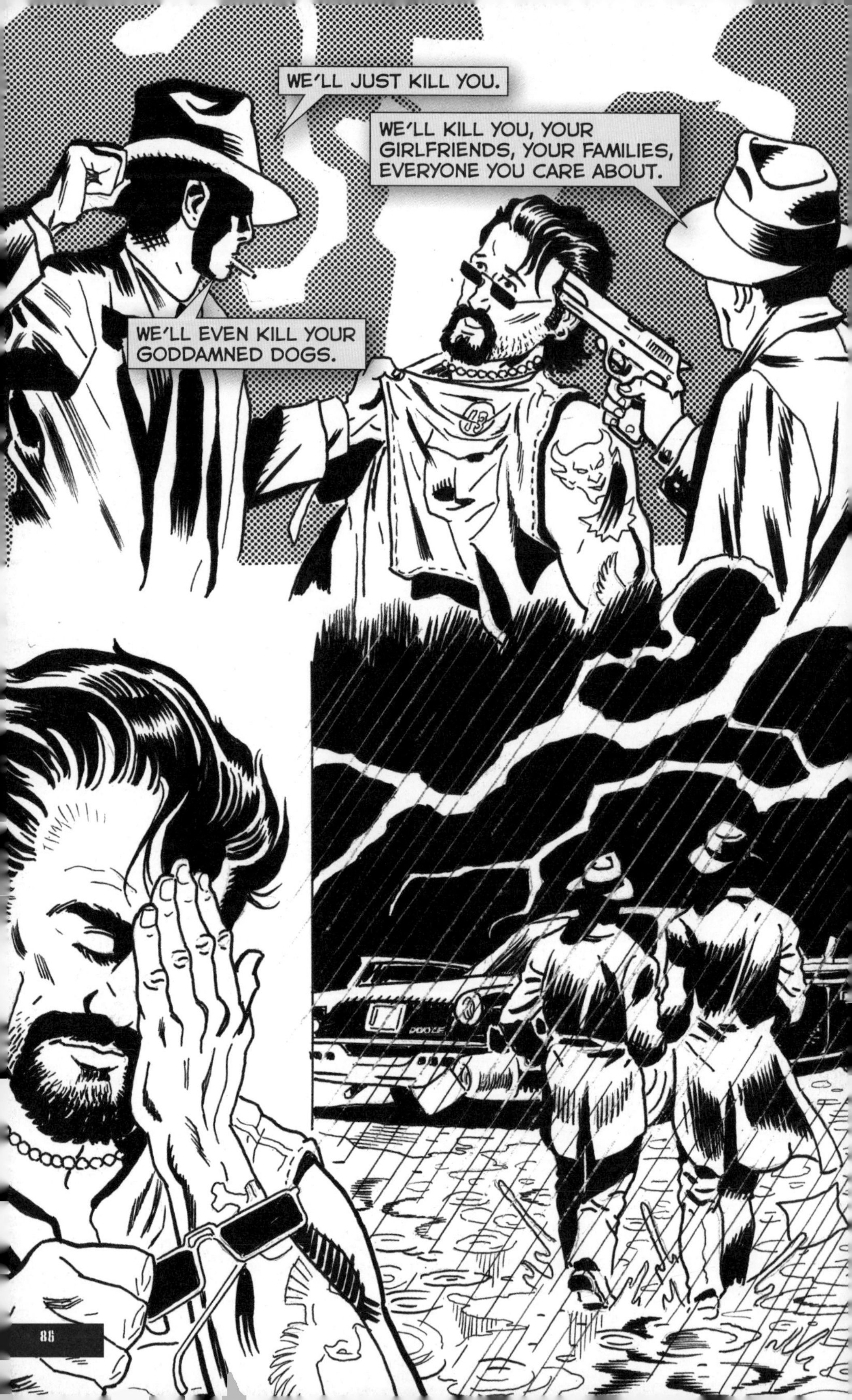
WE'LL JUST KILL YOU.
WE'LL KILL YOU, YOUR GIRLFRIENDS, YOUR FAMILIES, EVERYONE YOU CARE ABOUT.
WE'LL EVEN KILL YOUR GODDAMNED DOGS.

PHIL CROSS IS THE AUTHOR
OF *PHIL CROSS: GYPSY JOKER TO A
HELLS ANGEL*, THE BEST-SELLING BOOK
CHRONICLING HIS LIFE IN THE WORLD OF ONE-
PERCENTER MOTORCYCLE CLUBS. IN THE EARLY
1960S, CROSS, A YOUNG NAVY VET, JOINED THE
GYPSY JOKERS MOTORCYCLE CLUB AND EMBARKED
ON THE MOST ACTION-PACKED YEARS OF HIS
LIFE. THE JOKERS WERE IN THE MIDST OF AN
ALL-OUT WAR WITH THE HELLS ANGELS. THOUGH
PHIL WAS TOUGH—HE WAS A TRAINED MARTIAL
ARTS INSTRUCTOR—THE HELLS ANGELS PROVED
JUST AS TOUGH. AFTER A BEATING-INDUCED
EMERGENCY ROOM VISIT, MR. CROSS DECIDED
THAT IF YOU CAN'T BEAT 'EM, JOIN 'EM, SO HE AND
MOST OF HIS CLUB BROTHERS PATCHED OVER TO
BECOME THE SAN JOSE CHARTER OF THE HELLS
ANGELS. CROSS EVENTUALLY FOUNDED THE SANTA
CRUZ CHARTER OF THE HELLS ANGELS MC. HIS
FIRST BOOK, *PHIL CROSS: GYPSY JOKER TO A
HELLS ANGEL* TELLS THE STORY OF ONE MAN'S
FIFTY-PLUS-YEAR LIFE IN THE UNIQUE, OFTEN
DANGEROUS, AND ALWAYS EXCITING CULTURE OF
THE THREE-PATCH MOTORCYCLE CLUB.

RONN SUTTON HAS BEEN DRAWING COMICS FOR SEVERAL DECADES AND HAS ILLUSTRATED PROBABLY CLOSE TO 200 COMIC BOOK STORIES, WORKING FOR A VARIETY OF PUBLISHERS, INCLUDING A NINE YEAR STINT OF DRAWING ELVIRA, MISTRESS OF THE DARK FOR CLAYPOOL COMICS. MANY OF THESE WORKS WERE WRITTEN BY HIS LONG-TIME LOVE, JANET L. HETHERINGTON. SUTTON'S FIRST PUBLISHED COMICS GO BACK TO THE EARLY 1970S, AND HE HAS DRAWN HORROR, ROMANCE, MYSTERY, ADVENTURE, SCIENCE FICTION AND HUMOR COMICS (INCLUDING *FEAR AGENT, HONEY WEST, THE MAN FROM U.N.C.L.E., SHERLOCK HOLMES, THE PHANTOM, EDGAR ALLAN POE, VAMPIRA* AND OTHERS). FOR SEVEN YEARS HE ALSO DID FREELANCE COURTROOM SKETCHES FOR NEWSPAPERS AND TELEVISION. RONN HAS DONE EXTENSIVE MAGAZINE ILLUSTRATION AND WORKED PERIODICALLY IN ANIMATION (*SAVAGE DRAGON, RESCUE HEROES*). ASIDE FROM OTHER ONGOING COMIC ASSIGNMENTS, RONN IS CURRENTLY ADAPTING LEIGH BRACKETT'S *CITADEL OF LOST SHIPS* INTO A GRAPHIC NOVEL. SEE NEARLY 200 PIECES OF HIS ART AT WWW.RONNSUTTON.COM.

DARWIN HOLMSTROM HAS WRITTEN, CO-
WRITTEN, OR CONTRIBUTED TO OVER THIRTY BOOKS
ON SUBJECTS RANGING FROM GIBSON LES PAUL
GUITARS AND EXTRAORDINARY GOATS IN MYTHOLOGY
TO MOTORCYCLES AND MUSCLE CARS, INCLUDING THE
BEST-SELLING *LET'S RIDE: SONNY BARGER'S GUIDE
TO RIDING THE RIGHT WAY FOR LIFE, TOP MUSCLE: THE
RAREST CARS FROM AMERICA'S FASTEST DECADE,
CAMARO: FIVE GENERATIONS OF PERFORMANCE, BMW
MOTORCYCLES, THE HARLEY-DAVIDSON MOTOR CO.
ARCHIVE COLLECTION, GTO: PONTIAC'S GREAT ONE,
HEMI MUSCLE CARS, CAMARO: FORTY YEARS, MUSCLE:
AMERICA'S LEGENDARY PERFORMANCE CARS, BILLY
LANE CHOP FICTION, THE COMPLETE IDIOT'S GUIDE
TO MOTORCYCLES*, AND MANY OTHERS. HE HAS ALSO
WRITTEN SEVERAL NOVELS FOR GOLD EAGLE'S POPULAR
EXECUTIONER AND MACK BOLAN SERIES'. HE HAS
A MASTER'S DEGREE IN CREATIVE WRITING AND A
BACHELOR'S DEGREE IN PHOTOGRAPHY AND GRAPHIC
DESIGN, AND IS THE SENIOR EDITOR FOR MOTORBOOKS,
WHERE HE HAS WORKED FOR THE PAST FOURTEEN
YEARS. PRIOR TO THAT HE SERVED AS THE MIDWESTERN
EDITOR FOR *MOTORCYCLIST MAGAZINE*, WORKED AS A
REPORTER/PHOTOGRAPHER FOR A DAILY NEWSPAPER,
A FACTORY WORKER, A FARM HAND, AND WAS ONCE AN
ASSISTANT POTATO INSPECTOR, MAKING IT A CAPITAL
OFFENSE TO MURDER HIM ACCORDING TO THE OMNIBUS
CRIME BILL OF 1986, SO HE'S GOT THAT GOING FOR HIM.

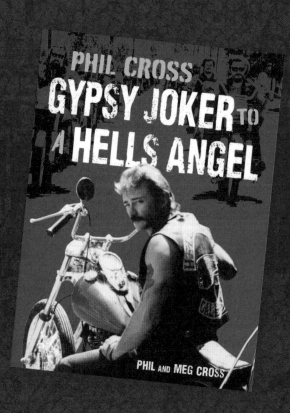

PHIL CROSS
GYPSY JOKER TO A HELLS ANGEL
PHIL AND MEG CROSS

Phil Cross: Gypsy Joker to a Hells Angel chronicles Cross' life and times in his own words and photos, from his early years with the Gypsy Jokers through his forty-plus-year career as a Hells Angel, a career that led to his being a fugitive on the FBI's most-wanted list (more than once) and a stint in prison. Chronicling both the bad times and the good—and in general he had one hell of a good time—*Phil Cross: Gypsy Joker to a Hells Angel* takes the reader on one of the wildest rides ever.

PRAISE FOR PHIL CROSS: GYPSY JOKER TO A HELLS ANGEL

"It's an entertaining, action-packed tome that's filled with all the chills and thrills one would expect from a biker's memoirs, and is well worth the read."

—*Thunder Press*

"He discusses dozens of his biker brothers and their experiences, with a matter-of-fact, surprisingly charming voice throughout the book. Yes, there's cursing, but there's also humor and pathos, and the reader comes away with a clear understanding of the unshakable bonds these men share from the time they join a club, to the end of their days. It's enviable and at times quite touching."

—*Bikernet.com*